INTO THE SOUNDS

A TAINE MCKENNA ADVENTURE

LEE MURRAY

SSP

ISBN:
978-1-0670332-0-0 ebook
978-1-0670158-9-3 print

Cover design by GetCovers

Squabbling Sparrows Press

INTO THE SOUNDS

A TAINE MCKENNA ADVENTURE

LEE MURRAY

SSP

ISBN:
978-1-0670332-0-0 ebook
978-1-0670158-9-3 print

Cover design by GetCovers

Squabbling Sparrows Press

1

Fiordland, 1973

David Summers put the Ruger Mini 14s to his shoulder and eased the barrel out the door.

"Any time, mate," the pilot, Wallace Makepeace, drawled.

David peered at the tangle of beech swaying in the rotor wash and waited for a flash of brown hide. A swathe of mist drifted past and the trees appeared again.

Wait, wait...there!

A wapiti stag bounded from the bush, startled by the whump of the chopper blades. The big deer ran across the valley floor, splashing through the stream bed and out the other side. Now in the clear, the animal took off, weaving, desperate to outrun the chopper.

David fired off a half-dozen shots, spent cartridges flying everywhere. But below them, the bullets glanced off the stony ground. The deer kept running.

"I meant today," Wallace said dryly.

David took his time, sighting the deer and squeezing off

another shot. This time, the deer dropped. David ducked his head back inside the chopper.

"That's a pretty good haul!" Wallace licked his lips.

"I reckon," David replied. "Maybe forty in the last hour." It had to be at least that: the barrel of his rifle was too hot to hold. "Some big fellas, too. Did you see the size of its antlers? I'm guessing that wapiti has to weigh around six hundred and fifty pounds. What do you reckon that is in kilograms?"

"Fucked if I know. Bloody metric. Six hundred and fifty dollars a beast will do nicely. Hey, I'm not greedy, I'll settle for an even five hundred dollars."

David grabbed on to his seat as Wallace banked steeply, circling the exposed stream bed to check out the carcass, making sure the animal stayed down.

Wallace shouted over the wind shear, "What do you say we give it another half hour before we call it quits? See if we can make it a round fifty?"

David wasn't keen. They weren't the only crew out here. A hike in venison prices had prompted a slew of illegal operators, everyone wanting a bite of the silly money on offer. There'd been more than just poaching going on, too. The papers were reporting hunters being shot at from the ground, choppers crashing, arson, even outright brawls. It seemed there was no honour amongst thieves.

"I dunno," David said, but his eyes were still on the bush in case they flushed out another animal. "Already we're up for ten trips to recover the meat."

"You still worried about those military Iroquois?"

"They could be anywhere. They say they're shooting real bullets." David propped the Ruger against his knee.

"Bah. I call bullshit. The government aren't actually going to have the air force shoot New Zealand citizens out of the sky for a bit of poaching. At best, they'll do a flyby and waggle their fingers at us. Maybe give us a stern look for being naughty boys." He laughed. "Where's the harm? We're not even really poaching. We're providing a valuable service, stopping the deer from trampling the precious native bush. It's not our fault that people have gotten a taste for venison."

David grinned. When Wallace put it like that, it didn't sound so bad.

"Anyway, it's the government's fault, only letting one outfit cull the deer," Wallace ranted.

David shouldn't have got him started.

"A licence to print money and only one company gets a look in? No wonder people have their backs up. We've got a right to make a living, same as anyone else."

David looked out over the valley as Wallace turned the helicopter away from the cliffs. It wasn't just a living; it was a bloody good one. Some days the pair of them pulled in more than a month's wages before breakfast, even after they split the debt on the chopper. But the risks were high, and they were growing. There was only so long you could beat the odds.

He glanced at his wife's photo taped to the windshield. Soft brown hair curling around her face, Gina smiled back at him. She was the reason he was doing this. Their future together. But last night in bed, this frenzied venison war had got them to talking.

"It's too dangerous, love," Gina had said, her chin resting on his chest, one leg slung over his. "All the money in the world isn't worth diddly-squat if you aren't alive to spend it."

She ran a finger across his chest. "You should get out before you get hurt. We could cash up, buy that little place up near Nelson."

David shifted slightly; Gina's weight was causing his shoulder to go to sleep. Even if it was time to cash up, a three-bedroom weatherboard in Nelson wasn't exactly what he'd had in mind. There had to be something more to life than just buying a house and settling down. It didn't have to be extraordinary, just something less...ordinary.

"What about Wallace?" he'd replied. "I can't just leave him."

Gina had looked at him from underneath her lashes. "You're not the only man in the universe who can fire a rifle."

"What do you say we split the difference?" Wallace's voice cut into David's thoughts. "Another quarter of an hour and we'll call it a day?"

"Works for me." David shouldered the gun again.

They bagged another two – both red deer – before Wallace circled them back to the stream bed where they'd downed the stag. There was enough space there to start recovering the meat.

They passed over the clearing and Wallace swore. "Will you look at that?"

David leaned out a fraction, cold wind stinging his face. He blinked. Two men wearing checked Swanndris were crouched beside the fallen stag. Already they'd hacked off the animal's head and lopped off the hooves.

"Who the fuck do they think they are?" Wallace snarled. "Bloody thieves!" David didn't like to remind him that they'd effectively stolen the animal in the first place. Wallace could be a handful when he had the wind up. Or if he had a half-dozen bottles of DB beer in him.

"Forget it, man," David urged. "It's not worth it."

But Wallace wasn't having a bar of it. He brought the chopper round again, like a shark circling its prey. If the pair on the ground gave a toss, they didn't show it. They just went on skinning the animal. Wallace waved his fist and cussed again.

"Let's just pick up the other deer," David said, a wave of unease gripping him.

Wallace shook his head. "I'm going to take us down. Lean out and fire a couple of warning shots at them, will ya? That should scare 'em off."

"What? No!" There was no way he was going to shoot at anyone.

Wallace wasn't listening. He brought the helicopter lower, the rotor wash whipping up sand and stones and hurling it at the raiders.

Blood up to his elbows, one of the men lifted his face to the wind. His eyes fixed on the chopper, he put down his knife. He stood up and lifted his rifle to his shoulder.

"Shit! Wallace! He's going to shoot—"

Bullets peppered the side of the chopper, the noise like a row of garbage cans hitting a pavement. The chopper lurched sideways.

"Shit!" Wallace pulled back on the collective to get them the hell out of there.

More bullets struck the back of the chopper.

Wallace twisted in his seat. "Fuck. I think they've hit the tail rotor."

"Is it bad?" It sounded bad. Maybe last night's talk of cashing up had jinxed their luck.

Wallace threw David a cheery grin. "I don't think it's too bad. If it had broken off we'd already be in a spin. Probably just dinged it. Better buckle up. I'm going to get our speed up and try to improve our stability. With a bit of luck, we can limp home."

For the next few miles, they grazed the treetops and lurched over ridges. They passed over one lake with the skids practically touching the water. David held his breath while his friend struggled to keep the chopper level. Wallace's hair was plastered to his forehead. His face was set like concrete. He clenched his teeth. For once, he didn't have much to say.

They were in a steep gully when a crunch sounded from the rear.

"Oh piss. Rotor's gone," Wallace croaked. He wrestled with the controls, but the helicopter spun wildly. David clung to his seat. Wind assaulted him. His body was thrown about. Left. Up. Down.

He saw sky, cliff, Gina's smile.

They were plummeting, the ground hurtling towards them. In a rush of grey, the forest swallowed them. David raised his arm to protect his face.

David opened his eyes. He was still strapped into his seat. He wasn't dead, but, fuck, his legs hurt so much he almost wished he were. A branch had shot through the windscreen of the chopper, missing him by inches. He pushed the foliage away from his face. One of his ribs must be broken, maybe more, because moving his arms was excruciating.

"Wallace? You okay, man?" David looked through the tangle of branches at the pilot seat. His partner wasn't there. Had he been thrown free, or had he climbed out under his own steam? For a second, David was seized with panic. Had Wallace left him here to die?

"Wallace!" he shouted, fingers scrabbling at the seatbelt. The strapping fell away. He tried to move, but a wall of pain engulfed him. His eyes blurred. He was pinned, his legs caught between the seat and the cockpit.

"Wallace!" He kept his breath shallow while he grappled with the undergrowth, his fingers bloodied and raw. "Wallace!" It was hard to scream.

At last, the window was clear.

David slumped in his seat. Wallace was outside on the ground. "Oh, you dumb fuck."

Wallace grinned back at him. He was wedged between two tree trunks, one arm lodged behind him. He must have been flung there during the crash because his leg was splayed to the side at the knee. His arm, the one David could see, was soaked in blood from a graze that ran from his shoulder to his elbow. Worse, it looked as if he'd slid face-first down the trunk, the skin lifting to reveal the ruined muscles underneath. His nose and lips were gone, leaving only his eyeballs staring out from a wall of raw mincemeat. His moustache and most of his beard would be somewhere under the flap of skin folded on top of his head. It was as if his face was a pair of sunglasses, pushed up there out of the way.

David's stomach roiled and he vomited, his broken torso heaving. The pain too much, he passed out.

When he woke the second time, he tried the radio, desperate to raise someone. Anyone. It was no use. The radio was a mangled wreck.

The Ruger!

He could fire off some shots. Maybe someone would hear him and investigate. Deep down, he knew it was unlikely – anyone hearing gunshots would think it was just another deer hunter, and they might even move away for better pickings – but he groped for the rifle anyway. The butt plate was within reach, but the barrel was pinned in the foot well. With some agonising pushing and pulling, he prised it out. His heart clenched. The barrel was crumpled, ruined like everything else. His legs. Wallace's face. David choked back a sob as the cold seeped into his bones and the shakes set in. He recognised the signs of shock.

That was it, then. He was stuck here. He wondered how long it would take him to die. Hours? Days. A week? A slow interminable death. Gina knew they were out here, but Fiordland was huge and, looking up, he could tell the helicopter was buried deep under the canopy. Search and Rescue could search for decades and never find him. The forest, the chopper, *this seat*, would be his tomb.

David shuddered.

Wallace, though, thought it was a great joke, the macabre grin fixed on his dial.

~

Manapōuri, 1973

Scrubbing at her face with her hands, Gina pulled herself out of the armchair where she'd spent the night. She checked her watch: 7:01. Too soon. They wouldn't have started searching yet. But perhaps David and Wallace had come in overnight? Quickly, she went to the window and parted the nets, hoping to see the chopper in the back paddock.

Wishful thinking.

There was only Wallace's Ford, parked up by the shed. She took a slow breath to contain her disappointment. She should've known they couldn't have snuck in last night without her hearing. Hard to miss the whump of the blades. Most days, it was enough to give you a headache, all their comings and goings. Today, though, Gina would give anything to hear those rotors. If God would just bring them back this one time, she'd never complain about the chopper's downdraft blowing her washing off the line again.

She went through to the kitchen and made herself a cup of coffee. The kitchen clock said ten past seven. Still too early. Taking a dog roll from the fridge, she opened the back door and cut a chunk into Duke's bowl, then turned on the outside tap to fill his water container. "Duke!" she called.

The sheep dog pushed open the gate of the kennel run and bounded over. Gina gave him a pat and left him to his breakfast.

Inside, she checked the clock again. 7:23.

She opened the oven and took out last night's casserole, scraping the dried remains into the bin. She'd cook something fresh for David when he got home.

When they found him.

She washed up the casserole dish and put it away, drying her hands on the tea towel before hanging it over the oven rail.

It was exactly 7:30am when she could finally dial the number on the pad beside the phone. She asked for Patrick Choat. The Southland search and rescue co-ordinator came on the line, his voice rough from years of cigarette smoke.

"Choat speaking."

"It's Gina Summers, Patrick. Has there been any news?"

"Not yet, love, but the crews are all out searching for them now."

"The weather forecast doesn't look hot."

"When did a little bit of rain ever stop us, aye? The boys'll stay out as long as they can. Try not to worry. David and Wallace are a couple of canny blokes. I'm certain they'll turn up."

Gina did her best to give her voice a cheery note. "Oh, I'm not worried. They'll have put down somewhere, I expect. I should probably count the beer crates out back. My luck, they decided to make a boozy weekend of it and forgot to let me know. By the end of today, David'll have his feet up front of the telly watching *It's in the Bag* and won't I be the one looking stupid?"

Patrick chuckled. "That's the spirit, love. Gotta stay positive, don't we? Have you got someone with you?"

"No, I'm fine. My neighbour'll be along later this morning," she lied. She wrapped a finger inside the curly telephone cord.

"Right, well, I'd better get on, Gina. I'll let you know the minute we hear anything."

"I'll be here," Gina replied, but Patrick had already hung up.

Sinking into the armchair, she put her head in her hands.

~

Fiordland, 1973

David lifted his head, the small movement making him wince.

He couldn't feel his legs. They were numb. His lips were cracked and dry. Right now he'd murder his mother for a drink.

Was that someone talking? Deer cullers, maybe? He strained to hear. *Someone* was nearby. David's heart leapt. He might not die after all.

"Hey, I'm here!" he called, his chest exploding in pain. "Over here!" They might not be able to see the chopper. He couldn't let them leave without him. He had to make more noise even if it killed him. He banged the mangled rifle against the side of the cockpit and rasped, "Help me!"

After a while, he ceased his banging, and listened. The talking had stopped. Were they coming? Was that rustling coming from behind the chopper? His rescuers trying to get through the undergrowth? Inhaling slowly against the pain in his chest, David did his best to calm himself. He needed to be patient. The bush about him was dense and the terrain was steep. He might not be easy to get to.

"Name's David Summers," he said, deciding to give his rescuers a voice to follow. "I don't mind admitting I'm bloody pleased to see you. Thought I was a goner, you know? Tail rotor was damaged, and we took a nosedive. I'm pinned in here. Been here overnight. Looks like my legs are a bit of a mess, so I hope you've got a fold-up stretcher with you. Heh, probably not. Maybe an aspirin. I wouldn't say no to one of those." He chuckled, the searing in his sides reminding him to think twice about laughing.

Murmuring reached him from behind the chopper.

With a jolt, David thought it might be Swanndri Man, come to finish him off. Unlikely; he and Wallace had travelled miles from the stream bed after the shots were fired. More likely the undergrowth was hard to navigate back there. If it was the shooter, David would just have to take his chances. It wasn't as if he had a lot of options.

"If you're coming from port side, be warned: my mate didn't make it. He isn't looking his best. A bit grisly."

David sensed movement. Seconds later, faces peered in at him through the chopper doors. Four men. Tall and fair. And apart from a scrap of white fabric tied around their hips, they were naked. Jeepers. Weren't they freezing? What was this? Some sort of hippie commune? Probably. They didn't call them the swinging 70s for nothing. There were plenty of alternative lifestyle sorts these days, although they tended to congregate in warmer spots, like Northland, right up at the top end of the country. David had never heard of any way down here.

"Hey," he said.

The men didn't answer.

"David Summers. Pleased to meet you." He felt a bit stupid introducing himself to a bunch of half-naked guys, but not so long ago he'd been convinced he was going to die.

As far as he was concerned, they could wear pink tutus and tiaras and he'd still be happy to see them.

At last, a broad-nosed man replied, spitting out a string of words at one of the others, who hissed back. That's weird. David didn't recognise the language. It might have been Māori – he'd never bothered to learn more than a few words – but it didn't *sound* like Māori.

While the pair argued, a third man offered David a drink from an old canteen. David took the canteen and gulped it down. It was bloody awful stuff, some kind of tea, but after a night stuck in the chopper, David was gasping.

Broadnose barked something, bringing the argument to a close. Then, using two wooden spears as levers to bend back the crushed metal, he and Canteen prised David out of the chopper.

David screamed, rocked by a wave of nausea and pain. He hit the ground. His left leg felt like it had been stabbed with a hot poker. He glanced down. His calf was misshapen: the skin intact, but his Achilles had been severed, the tendon popped off the bone, the useless muscle bunched behind his knee.

He wasn't going to be walking out of the forest any time soon.

They carried him; they carried Wallace, too, David drifting in and out of consciousness. The next time he became aware of his surroundings, they were on a beach, the rocky cliffs of the Sounds soaring above them. Oblivious to the cold, the pale men plunged into the water, taking Wallace with them. David caught a glimpse of his friend's face – the skin mask with its empty eye sockets – as he slipped beneath the surface.

Broadnose grappled with David, pulling him into the freezing water.

"What? No—"

They'd saved him so they could drown him?

Like hell.

Twisting out of Broadnose's grasp, David scrambled frantically for the beach, his useless leg trailing. His broken ribs screamed and his cuts stung as he crawled from the water. The man grabbed him, yanking him back. David barely had time to take an agonising breath before he was dragged under.

Broadnose got David in a bear hug, squeezing his ribs and immobilising him. Pain flared, making him dizzy. If he passed out now, he'd drown! Too weak to put up a fight, David stopped struggling and clung to his remaining breath.

Broadnose started swimming, zipping them smoothly through the dark water. He wasn't trying to drown him. He was *taking* him somewhere. And it was freezing, like swimming in an ice bucket.

Letting himself be carried along, David tried to get his bearings. Saltwater met freshwater in these Sounds where the sea carved great caverns into the land, some of them more than 500 yards deep. He could believe it: below him, the saltwater layer was dark as an All Black jersey. Broadnose was sticking to the murky freshwater layer and a shelf about three yards below the surface. The other men, still dragging Wallace, had entered a cave. David's pulse pounded as they followed them inside.

Not a cave, but a tunnel. *Does this go anywhere? Running out of air.*

Broadnose moved them swiftly through the silence. A

horizontal fissure as big as a truck gaped to their right. Through the murky gloom, David spied movement.

Something was in there. Something huge. Oh my God, it was coming out. David wanted to scream, to tell Broadnose to get them the hell out of Dodge, but the pale man just tightened his grip on David and continued on. Helpless, David could only watch in horror, his lungs bursting, as slowly, slowly, a monster emerged.

It was colossal. More than fifty yards from tip to tail. With a cone-shaped body the size of a whale, it glowed eerily. Squid tentacles, white and thicker than a tōtara trunk undulated in the swell. A gigantic pupil eyed David malevolently.

David's bowels loosened, warmth swirling about his legs.

Suddenly, Canteen peeled off from the group in front. He swam towards the monster, pulling Wallace's corpse with him. David's heart thudded. Canteen thrashed Wallace about in the water. Then he let go and glided away.

There was a swirl of suckered limbs, and two barbed tentacles reached out, stabbing the offering and drawing it in. A massive beak closed over Wallace and the sea monster slunk back into the shadows.

Broadnose pulled David away as Wallace's face floated free.

2

Fiordland, present day

Ka was sunning himself on a rock, his feet tucked beneath his haunches, when a change in air currents alerted him. The wind had picked up: the leaves rustling. He sniffed the air, sensing only the normal forest aromas of beech and decay. Still, something had alarmed him. A flash in the sky caught his eye. The silver birds were coming again. For the moment they were far away, but the low whump-whump of their wings was getting louder. He scuttled to the bottom of the boulder, and, cupping his hand, threw droplets at the children playing at the water's edge. They didn't scream. They knew better than that. They turned to look at him. He signalled that it was time to go. They didn't have to be told twice. Stealing away, they slipped soundlessly beneath the surface and out of sight.

~

Rotorua township

Rawiri Temera shifted in his bed and squeezed his eyes tight. The morepork hooted again, the owl's plaintive call sending shivers up his spine.

No. Not again. It was over. He'd been so sure.

But the morepork's keening continued, and Temera knew it would not stop until he'd ventured once more into the spirit world. He dragged his creaking body out of bed. He inhaled deeply, the dank smell of detritus and bracken thick in his nostrils and, in spite of his dread, his heart leapt.

He took a step forward into the dense undergrowth of the Urewera forest. He was nine years old again, his skin smooth and his limbs bounding with energy. It was a heady feeling, and bittersweet.

He lifted his eyes and scanned the canopy for the owl. She was hard to find, but the moon lent a hand, its silvery light revealing a sliver of yellow eye, her feathers camouflaging her against the gnarly grey bark of the beech.

"Hello, old friend," Temera said to the morepork.

The little owl's reply was shrill and urgent. In an instant, it had flitted from its branch, taking up a perch further along the narrow trail.

"You want me to follow you." After all these years, Temera knew what was expected.

The morepork hooted impatiently.

Temera clenched his jaw. The owl rarely called him without reason. Sometimes those reasons were good ones. Other times, not. But he had no time to contemplate her purpose because the bird-messenger was off, weaving a path through the branches. Temera-the-boy darted after her, careering through the forest, leaping logs and ducking under fern fronds, revelling in his youth as he chased his spirit guide through the tribal lands of his forefathers.

Temera ran for hours. At first, he barely noticed: his legs were fresh, and the forest was a wondrous place. Soon, though, the bird led him out of the Urewera ranges and into another forest, one that was unfamiliar and dark. He began to get weary. The mud sucked at his feet and the trees crowded in on him, their branches thick and menacing. The owl flew on, oblivious. Finally, when Temera felt he couldn't run another step, they emerged from the trees beside the ocean.

Temera sat on the cold sand, his lungs heaving with exertion. "This is it?" he said to the morepork. "You brought me to the ocean." It was only possible in his dreams. The ocean was too far from Rotorua for anyone, let alone a boy, to reach in a single night. For that, you needed a vehicle, a full tank of gas, and the motorway. Temera didn't question the impossibility. He'd never fully understood his gift, which was as fluid and elusive as the waves pounding before him.

"Who am I here to see, then?" he asked, but, her task completed, the spirit guide had disappeared. Temera stood up. Brushing the sand off his pants, he ambled to the water, dunking his toes in the foamy surf.

"Come on, why am I here?" he shouted at the waves.

A swell rose out beyond the breakers. Was this the message? He swallowed his fear and stepped closer, the waves breaking around his thighs. Beneath the water, the dark shape surged forward. It was brooding. Ominous. The theme from *Jaws* ran through Temera's head. His mouth went dry.

I'm not actually here, he reminded himself. *Only my*

wairua-spirit has made the journey through the forest. My body is back home in bed. Nothing can hurt me here.

Still, he took a step back. No point tempting fate.

Temera peered through the darkness. Fringed white, a wall of water thundered toward him, dark and full of threat. A wave swept him off his feet. The next thing he knew, he was under the breakers, cold stealing away his breath. He tumbled, helpless, churning waves tossing him this way and that. His eyes were full of salt and sand, blinding him. Where was the surface? His chest tightened. His lungs screamed.

I'm not here. I'm not here!

He woke, sweating, his pyjamas sticking to him as if it were summer. His old heart was pounding ninety-to-the-dozen. It was a wonder it didn't give up the ghost. Lying in bed, he forced himself to take a deep breath, then another, and another, until his pulse slowed.

Shit a brick! That was scary.

Wrestling himself upright, he put his ear to the wall. In the next room, his great-nephew Wayne's snoring was like the roar of a bull seal. The boy could wake the dead with that racket. It's a wonder Pania put up with it.

Except it hadn't been Wayne's snoring that had woken him.

Temera shuddered. His night terrors were back. For more than a year, he'd been getting his full quota of beauty sleep, but now his gift was intruding again. This was the second time the morepork had summoned him in a week. Temera sighed. The second time he'd been sent this message. But what message? And who was it for? Temera didn't know. He wished his old mātua were here to help him interpret what he'd seen. Who was he kidding? As much as he'd loved to see his old teacher again, he knew it wouldn't help. Telling the future was different for every matakite. Hell, his own visions varied, each message its own puzzle. Temera screwed his eyes up, enough to see the mosaic of colour behind his lids. It would help if things weren't so cryptic!

Blast it. He was awake now. He might as well get up and make himself a cuppa.

Swinging his legs out of bed, Temera put on his dressing gown and slippers and shuffled into the kitchen. Using only the dim light of the range-hood, he switched on the kettle and sat at the table, waiting for it to boil. While the water hummed quietly, Temera rubbed at the liver spots on the back of his hand. Old age had snuck up on him and she was a bitch. These days he had to pop a pill just to take a dump. On rainy days, it was all he could do to coax his muscles into taking him out to the potting shed behind the house. And the worst of it was he hadn't been home to the isolated farmhouse at Maungapōhatu for over a year – the bumpy ride in Wayne's truck was enough to rattle his teeth right out. He missed the place. By now, the porch would need repainting, and the gutters ought to be cleared of leaves. Sometimes, on the weekends, Wayne would drive him to the edge of the Ureweras as a kind of consolation. They'd put up their deck chairs, share a Thermos and a ciggie, and just sit there, inhaling the scent of the trees. It wasn't the same. So, when the morepork had come calling for him in the night, part of him had welcomed it, part of him had *wanted* to run barefoot through the forest, mud and ferns between his toes, mānuka branches scratching at his arms, his hair flying behind him like Superman's cape. It felt good to be back there.

Even if it meant facing a nightmare.

The kettle switch clicked off. Temera pushed back his chair and went to the cupboard. His favourite mug had been shunted to the back. He reached for it, moving the other cups out of the way with the back of his hand. One tumbled out. It bounced off the bench and smashed, shards going every which way.

Damn.

Temera was stooping to pick up the pieces when the kitchen flooded with light.

"Uncle Rawiri! Are you all right?" Wayne pulled a sweat-shirt over his head. Behind him, Pania was putting on her dressing gown.

"It's nothing. I couldn't sleep. Thought I'd make myself some tea. Dropped a cup." He waved at the floor. Not that there was any need. You didn't need special powers to see what had happened.

Pania got out the brush and pan. "Sit down, Uncle. Wayne will make the tea, won't you, Wayne?" she said, giving them both a look that said don't-even-think-about-arguing.

Temera sat while Wayne poured the boiling water into three cups.

"So, what's this about, Uncle Rawiri?" Pania said, tipping the broken crockery into the bin. She hung the brush and pan on the hook behind the laundry door. Then, putting a hand on Temera's shoulder, she slipped into the seat beside him. "Are you not feeling well?" Shall I make an appointment to see the doctor?"

"I'm fine. A bit of a headache, that's all. There's no need to fuss."

"But this is the second night you've been up this week," Wayne said, passing them both a cup of tea.

Pania wrapped both hands around her cup. "We're worried about you," she said softly.

Wayne was definitely punching above his weight with Pania. At least, Temera thought so. She was a good kid: pretty, smart, and a decent cook. She hadn't even flinched when Wayne had suggested Temera come and live with them. A lot of girls would have said no.

Her forehead crinkled in concern. "Uncle?"

Temera sighed. They may as well know. No one was going to get any sleep until this was resolved. "The nightmares," he said. "They're back."

Pania jumped up, the chair legs scraping on the wooden floors. "Your nightmares? I thought that was all over."

"It seems not."

"Quickly, Wayne, get dressed and bring the truck around."

Temera threw Wayne an amused look.

"Pania..." Wayne said gently.

She wasn't listening. "Is anyone hurt? How many? Do you know where they are?" She wasn't waiting for answers, either. Running to the cupboards, Pania yanked out the junk drawer, rummaging through it, pulling out matches, batteries, a stack of loyalty cards. "Where's the map gone?"

Temera suppressed a laugh. A year ago, Pania hadn't believed in his gift. She'd thought she believed, but she hadn't truly *believed*. Not deep down. It was different for Wayne. When he'd been a toddler, Temera had foreseen a squabble between the fire demons Te Hoata and Te Pūpū. Certain that Wayne was at risk from the ruckus, he'd gone to Wayne's parents, insisting they keep the child indoors. A few days later, a massive geyser had erupted immediately under Wayne's sandpit. The newspapers had liked that, printing a light-hearted article about fire demons and their pranks. Only, it hadn't been funny. The boy could have been playing in the sand when the boiling crater had exploded.

Perhaps that's why his great-nephew had invited him to live with him here in town. Maybe he felt he owed Temera. In any case, watching a geyser erupt in your back yard is the kind of thing that makes a believer. Seeing it. Living it. Pania hadn't known anything like that. For her, it was all ancient Māori hocus-pocus. She was Māori herself; she knew what a matakite was and she respected the culture, no doubt about that, but nowadays with science in schools, faith was hard to sell. People wanted proof. It wasn't until Temera had woken them up, demanding that they drive into the forest because people were dying, that Pania had seen his gift at work.

And she hadn't seen the half of it.

"Where's your pūrerehua?" Pania demanded. "On your bedside table? Wayne, you'll have to get Uncle's bullroarer for him. You know I can't touch it – it's sacred, tapu."

Wayne stood up, crossing the kitchen in two strides. He put a hand on his girlfriend's shoulder and drew her to him. "Babe," he said. "Slow down. It isn't like that."

She turned in his arms, facing him. "Not like what? What do you mean?"

"I mean, there's no disaster. We don't have to rush off. Sometimes Uncle Rawiri doesn't know what his dreams mean. At least, not at first. They're not always specific."

"But last time—"

"That was last time."

"Oh." Pania looked over Wayne's arm at Temera. "I'm jumping the gun, then?"

Temera gave her a smile. "A bit."

Wayne kissed the top of her head and let her go.

Sweeping the junk off the bench and back into the drawer, Pania returned to the table. The three of them sipped their tea. Outside, a pale blue smudge streaked the sky. Dawn was on the way.

Wayne broke the silence. "Do you want to talk about it, tell us what you know? We might be able to help."

Temera fiddled with the handle of his cup where the colour was wearing off. He shrugged. May as well. He wasn't making head nor tail of it on his own. "I was at the ocean," he said, then corrected himself. "My *wairua* was at the ocean, and there was something in the water just beyond the waves. Something big and dark."

"That's it?"

"Uh-huh."

"It's not much to go on," Pania said. Temera could hear her disappointment. "Are you sure it's a message?"

Temera nodded.

"Could it be a tsunami?" Wayne asked. "We've had a few quakes lately."

"I'm not sure. Maybe."

"What about a shark attack?" Pania suggested. "Or maybe a rip?"

"Every beach has rips and New Zealand has fourteen thousand kilometres of them. If the message is about a rip,

Uncle Rawiri would have to be able to pinpoint the exact spot. Otherwise, it'd be like finding a needle in a haystack."

Using both hands, Pania smoothed her hair over her shoulders. "Well, it doesn't always have to be bad, does it? What if the message is about something good?"

"Like what? Wayne asked.

"I don't know. Big and dark beyond the waves could be about finding an offshore oil reserve."

"You think that's good?"

"No, you're right," Pania said. "That'd only be good if you're the sort who thinks fossil fuels are the answer."

Good? The wave had felt full of menace.

"I know what's good," Wayne said, getting up and opening the pantry. "Hot toast. It's nearly breakfast time. Anyone else want a piece?"

"Trust you to think of your stomach. Go on then, why don't you make us all some? And put the jug back on too, please," Pania replied.

Soon the smell of toast permeated the kitchen. While Pania and Wayne went on with their guessing, Temera stared out the window at the morning sky. The dark water had swelled and hovered there beyond the breakers, controlled and waiting. Temera might've had a holiday from his night terrors over the last year, but before that they'd plagued him for more than seventy years, and the one thing he knew for sure was that the messages they showed him were never good.

3

Fiordland

The pilot eased the cyclic to the right and the helicopter dipped.

"Take a look at that," said their host, Department of Conservation Officer, Thomas 'Rocky' Stone, from the passenger seat.

Looking past Jules, Taine took in the terrain. It was breath-taking. According to his mother's people, the demi-god Tu-te-raki-whanoa had used his adze Te Hamo to carve these fiords from the rock. Admiring the graceful sweep of the snow-capped Darran Mountains as they plunged from the heavens into the turquoise waters of Lake Marian, Taine was inclined to believe it.

"What did I tell you? Best damn office in the country," Rocky said over his shoulder.

In the window seat, Jules flashed the ranger a smile, but her fingers, clamped on Taine's forearm, told him she was nervous. Jules wasn't thrilled about heights. Cliffs weren't on the top of her favourite things list either. Not since three years ago when, on a LandCare field trip for work, Jules and her friend, Sarah, had been swept up in an unexpected landslip. She'd spent a harrowing night clinging to a cliff face, coming away with her confidence in tatters. Sarah had been less fortunate, sustaining a head injury which had left her severely disabled.

Giving her hand a reassuring squeeze, Taine turned back to the landscape. Jules was right to be apprehensive. Covering 1.2 million hectares of soaring mountain ranges, carved valleys, and pounding waterfalls, the national park wasn't just achingly beautiful, it was deadly. Even showing it respect, the region could surprise you with its rugged terrain and blink-of-an-eye weather changes. You didn't have to venture off the trail to come to grief either. A couple of years back, two experienced trampers walking the Kepler Track had lost their lives when they were buried by a freak avalanche. Rescuers had dug them out of the snow like potatoes from the garden.

"Well, that's your tourist experience for today, folks," Rocky said, as the pilot pulled them out of the valley and headed south. "No extra charge."

Taine grinned. Jules was the one who was working. Moved to a policy role at the Department of Conservation fifteen months ago, she was here to witness first-hand deer culling operations in remoter regions of the Sounds, but Taine – Sergeant Taine McKenna, NZDF – was on his first real R&R in over a year. Taine hated taking leave. Army leave chafed more than a polyester shirt in summer. It wasn't his thing, sitting on his arse watching Netflix. And then, when Jules had announced she was heading into

Fiordland National Park, it wasn't just the days stretching out in front of him but the nights, too.

He jumped at the chance to join her.

A nudge from behind brought him back to reality. NZDF Private Matt Read nodded towards the window and gave him the thumbs up. Read beamed. Chuckling, Taine lifted a hand in acknowledgement.

A recent addition to Taine's section, Read was another one who couldn't face a couple of weeks R&R sprawled on the couch. He was a good guy. Gutsy. Resourceful. Handy with a rifle and sharp as a tack. Quick too. Taine had seen him formulate a plan and act on it while everyone else was still considering the options. Some people might call Read heroic, but he was also impetuous and, in Taine's experience, that sort of behaviour could get a man killed. Taine hoped it'd never happen, that he'd never have to make that call to Read's parents. Still, they weren't on duty today.

There was one other passenger in the cab, Rocky's colleague, a DoC officer named Leo Herewini. With his bronzed skin, bushy eyebrows, and slicked-back dark hair, Herewini looked more like a 30s gangster than an environment officer. Taine had shaken the man's hand and the two had rubbed noses, sharing breath, in a salutatory hongi before they embarked. Since then Herewini had been quiet, leaning back in his seat, chewing gum.

A few others were still to join them. Leaving from Invercargill, a second chopper would be dropping off some private deer stalkers who'd been issued free licences to join this DoC Search and Destroy Mission.

"ETA five minutes, folks," Rocky said, knocking his

helmet with his knuckles. "You might want to check those helmets."

"Finally!" said Read, adjusting the strap on his.

Taine caught Jules' grimace. Her face had gone pale. Taine tightened his helmet, then gave Jules' hand a last squeeze before pulling on his gloves. "It'll be all over in a few minutes," he said.

"That's what I'm worried about," she joked.

"Coming in close now," the pilot called. Taine glanced through the window. They were hovering thirty metres above ground, the chopper's skids almost grazing the treetops.

Herewini threw open the cabin door. Wind whipped into the chopper, the drone of the blades loud despite their headgear.

"Hold her steady, Phil," said Rocky, who had clambered through from the front. The equipment bags were lowered over the side. When the gear was down, Herewini clipped the rope to his harness.

Rocky, the safety man, checked the j-hook.

Out of habit, Taine ran through the steps in his head.

Get Ready.

Throw the rope.

Sit in the door.

The Conservation man had clearly done this before. Cool-headed and methodical, he snapped through the stages, stepping on to the skids, and pivoting 180° so he was facing Taine, his leading hand on the rope and his brake hand in the small of his back.

He turned his head to check the terrain below him.

"Clear," Rocky shouted, signalling to Herewini. "Go!"

Herewini jumped away from the chopper, descending in three controlled brakes before he disappeared beneath the trees. A classic Hollywood rappel.

"Read."

"Boss?"

"How about you go first, and we send Jules down to you?"

"Sure thing."

Within minutes, Read, too, had disappeared into a gap in the canopy.

"Jules. You're up," Taine said.

"Of course," she said. "Why wouldn't I want to leap out of a perfectly good aircraft? I mean, what's not to like?"

He gave her a wink. "You're going to be fine."

Gingerly, she flipped the seatbelt, got out of her chair, and made her way to the open door. Taine was sure he could see her shaking over the rattle of the aircraft. She was mumbling to herself. Running through the steps, perhaps? Whatever she was saying, it was too low to be heard over the roar of the turbine engines. Taine gave her a reassuring smile as Rocky ran through the safety checks.

Taine repeated the safety checks and took a good look at the j-hook. It wasn't a matter of trust. This was Jules. He needed to be certain.

Several minutes passed before Jules managed to get herself into the sit position, and a lot longer before she could coax herself to pivot the 180° to face Taine and Rocky inside the chopper.

Finally, she had her feet braced on the skids and her knees locked.

Her knees were locked all right! They were as rigid as girders.

She checked behind her to scan the terrain, then turned back. And Taine hadn't thought she could look any paler. The quicker they got her on the ground, the better. Rocky gave her the signal to go.

Jules hesitated.

Rocky signalled again.

Come on, Jules. You can do this.

Jules leapt.

You didn't have to be Einstein to know she hadn't jumped out far enough. She swung back again, her body weight pinning her against the chopper. Taine had seen scores of soldiers do the same thing.

Leaning out, Taine gave her a wide grin. Fortunately, she hadn't flipped backwards, but she was making hard work of freeing herself. Taine was going to have to do something.

Let's hope she doesn't kill me afterwards...

One hand on the door frame, Taine positioned his boot in the middle of her chest.

Jules' head snapped up. She scowled, her protest dragged away in the rotor wash as Taine gave a little flick of his foot and pushed her away from the chopper.

She swung backwards and down. Taine swore he could hear her screaming.

He waited for the tug on the rope.

"You go!" he shouted to Rocky when it came.

Rocky gave him the thumbs up, got into position, then leapt away.

Taine eyeballed the rope. It was potentially long enough to reach the ground, give or take a metre or two. He'd fast rope down. It was dangerous, but it was quick. There was no one left in the chopper to tell him otherwise. Taine adjusted his old Army issue Impact CT gloves, tightening them at his wrist. They weren't exactly heat resistant, but it wasn't far. He signalled to the pilot, grasped the rope and jumped.

~

Jules talked herself through the stages.

Right hand, brake hand…

Actually, now that she was clear of the chopper, this rappelling was kind of fun.

Despite the pilot's skill, they'd veered to one side of the tiny clearing, close to the trees. A branch tickled her shoulder. Quick look; since she was supposed to be studying how Conservation managed local pest species. No sign of possum damage…

She flipped backwards.

Whoops!

She hadn't been paying attention, and now she was dangling upside down in mid-air. She wasn't in any real danger, but she felt sick all the same, like taking a turn on an amusement park ride after eating too much candyfloss.

She fought to right herself, her arm twisted painfully backwards, her stomach muscles straining to curl her body upright.

"It's okay, Jules," Read shouted up at her. "You've only a couple of metres to go and you're hooked on so you're not going anywhere."

"Don't worry about trying to right yourself," Herewini called. "Just let the brake rope out slowly…"

Her arm felt like it would shatter, twisted up her back, but she did as she was told and, seconds later, she dropped to the ground, safe and sound. Read was helping her out of the harness when Rocky landed, Taine touching down just seconds after that.

∼

His adrenalin still pumping, and his palms as hot as hell, Taine clapped his hands together. Just metres away, Jules was handing Read her helmet. She lifted her ponytail free of the back of her jacket, laughing. Her fear had evaporated, now that she had her feet firmly back on the ground.

Rocky strode over to Taine, yanking off his helmet, his face red and his hair plastered to his head. "What the hell do you think you're playing at?"

"The rope was there, and I figured—"

"It was there. It was *there*? Well, who died and put you in charge? Free roping! You could have been killed or injured and this trip would have been over before it started!"

Read stepped away from Jules to jump into the conversation. "With all due respect, sir, McKenna's an NZDF sergeant and hardly a rookie. He's a highly trained—"

Rocky spun, his hands on his hips. "I don't care if he's Daniel bloody Craig! This isn't the army here."

Taine looked to where Jules stood open-mouthed. What had he been thinking? This wasn't his show. He and Read were here at Jules' invitation and the Department's sufferance.

Read was about to say something, but Taine raised his hand.

"Stand down, Matt. Rocky is absolutely right. I should have rappelled down the same as everyone else."

"But you've fast roped before—"

Taine cut across Read's protest. "Not with that rope. Or from that helicopter. Into this terrain. Anyway, the fact that I've trained for it isn't important. I put the operation at risk, and it wasn't my call to do that. This isn't our parade."

Taking a step forward, Taine held his hand out to the Conservation officer. "I hope you'll accept my apologies, Rocky. I was out of order. I wouldn't tolerate that kind of behaviour from my own men, and you certainly shouldn't have to put up with it from me. It won't happen again."

There was a pause before Rocky nodded and took the proffered hand. A grin spread across his face as they shook. "Still hot, huh?"

Letting go, Taine pulled off his gloves, smiling sheepishly. "Feels like I'm juggling a couple of hot potatoes." The gloves in one hand, he slapped them against his palm. "These old things weren't quite up to it. Another couple of metres and I might've had to jump for it."

"You were lucky."

"Yes sir, I was."

A small whirlwind enveloped them. The second helicopter had arrived.

Rocky called a start. "If you could all gather around, I'll make the introductions quickly and we'll get on the trail. Just to let you know, the weather forecast looks promising for the first couple of days: a clear day today for the most part. After that, well, this is Fiordland and anything can happen, so we'll need to be on our toes. Keep an eye on the rivers, that sort of thing. Any concerns, my rangers know their job, so don't hesitate to ask them. And if you're going to get lost, for God's sake, make sure one of them gets lost with you. I know you've all been in the bush before, but this place can be unforgiving.

"Right-o, so counting off we have Leo Herewini..." Herewini raised his eyebrows in the laid-back Kiwi gesture for hello. "...Marty Wong on my right, one of my most experienced officers when it comes to this neck of the woods, field officer Jessica 'Jess' Lye on the end there, and this here is Dr Jules Asher – she's a scientist and one of our top brass, come for a general look-see at our endangered species to determine how they're faring in these parts. She'll be taking notes, so if you happen to see a great spotted kiwi, maybe don't shoot it while she's watching."

Everyone laughed as Jules pulled an unconvincing frown.

"Okay, I don't like that look. Maybe don't shoot any Kiwis if you can avoid it. None of the greater spotted variety either."

When the tittering died away, Rocky consulted a tatty piece of paper. "Right-o. Our guests: we have Taine McKenna and Matt Read accompanying Dr Asher." He waved his paper at the pair of them. "These boys are from the NZDF, so I imagine they'll be handy with a rifle, although I'm told they've been on leave a few days already and might be a bit trigger-happy. I'd give them a wide berth if I were you."

There was more laughter.

Trigger-happy.

Taine would be a happy man if his friend, Trigger, were here. He couldn't imagine much hunting in his friend's future. Hard to fire a rifle with only one arm, although if anyone could manage it, it'd be Trevor Grierson. In the army, you don't get handed the nickname Trigger for nothing. As far as Taine was concerned, Trigger was a bigger man in every way, taking the loss of his arm in his stride, along with a new role in military intelligence at the NZDF head-shed, Freyberg House in Aitken Street in the nation's capital. Trigger: reinvented as a squirrel. It was hard to get your head around, like casting Dwayne Johnson as the Tooth Fairy.

The big guy had balked at the collar and tie, though.

"I'm grateful for the job and I don't mind sitting at a desk – I was going to have to hang up my boots sometime – but there's no need for me to look like a fucking penguin while I'm at it," Trigger had said.

Taine smiled in spite of himself.

Rocky was still on the introductions. "We have Barbara Reckwerdt—"

"Barb." The woman smiled, her curls bobbing.

"Sorry, *Barb*." He coughed. "Barb's done a lot of deer hunting Stateside; thought she'd come down for a taste of our Kiwi wapiti."

Taine noted the American had brought her own gun. It was a 7mm-08 Remington: lighter than a Winchester, yet with a low trajectory and limited recoil. Plus, the bolt action and short barrel made it a good choice for accuracy and manoeuvrability in the bush. Seemed Barb Reckwerdt was serious about her shooting.

"How do you rate my chances?" she asked Rocky. From his experience with American troops, Taine guessed her accent was from somewhere in the Midwest.

"Pretty good, actually," said Wong, replying on Rocky's behalf. "Wapiti tend to congregate in certain places."

Wong didn't have your average Asian build. In fact, he was a solid unit. Wide as an axe-handle, Taine's old man would have said.

"Wapiti elk are a nuisance species if they're uncontrolled," Wong went on. "They kill all the new growth, stop the forest from regenerating." He stripped a few tiny leaves off a nearby silver beech, letting them fall by way of explanation. "Our estimates have wapiti numbers up this year, which is why we've called for a cull."

"Well, that's bad news for the deer and good news for us," said one of the two remaining men. The pair stood side by side, their backs to the beech tree at the edge of the clearing.

"And you must be..." Rocky peered at his paper, pulling it away from his face and squinting at the words.

"John Loughlin," said the shorter of the two. Taine suspected he was bald under the orange hunter's beanie. "And this is me mate, Karl."

"Pringle," the other man finished.

"Where are you guys from, then?" Wong asked.

"Turangi," said Loughlin.

"So, what do you do for a crust up there? Trout fishing tours?"

"We work for DoC," said Pringle.

"You're joking," said Wong.

"He means the other DoC," said Loughlin. "Corrections.

We work at the prison. I'm a Corrections officer, and Karl here is an OEI."

"An OEI? What's that when it's at home?"

"An Offender Employment Instructor. Karl teaches carpentry to the inmates. Gives them a skill for when they come out."

"Yeah?" said Wong, looking at Pringle. "That's great. Good on you, mate."

Pringle blushed.

Taine had to agree. Education made all the difference. The NZDF had been running skills-based schemes for troubled young people for close to a decade and the results had been impressive.

Rocky took a mint tin out of his pants' pocket, jammed the crumpled paper in, and then slid the tin back. "Well, since we're all acquainted, let's go kill some deer, shall we? Wong's our guide. So, we'll follow him."

The group stooped to pick up their bags.

"The central plateau has plenty of good hunting," Wong said to Pringle as he adjusted the straps over his shoulders.

"Yep, plenty of hunting in the Kaimanawa. Sika deer. Pigs," said Pringle, adjusting his own pack.

"What made you come all the way down here, then? You could have saved yourselves the airfare."

"Fancied a change," said Pringle.

"Thought we'd break out from where we've been," said Loughlin, the Corrections officer guffawing at his own joke, Taine catching Pringle's frown at the unnecessary noise. Then Wong led off, the Corrections officers stepping into the woods after him, their voices fading.

Jules was on the other side of the clearing, adjusting her

pack. Taine grabbed his gear while he waited for her. Herewini went by, tilting his chin to acknowledge Taine. The man hadn't said much, but already Taine liked him. There was something solid about him; it was hard to put a finger on it, but he reminded Taine of finding a $20 note in an old coat pocket.

"Yeah, I'm afraid to say my folks are die-hard rednecks from the Big Cheese – Sun Prairie, Wisconsin, to be exact," Barb was telling Read. What was it about Americans and their voices? They were always so loud, as if they had a megaphone taped to their lips.

"Is that anywhere near Osh Kosh?" Read asked.

"Ah, so you've heard about our air show," said Barb, her blonde curls bouncing as she smiled. "Let me tell you a story about that show..." The pair stepped onto the trail, followed by Jessica Lye.

"Right, have we got everyone?" Rocky said.

"Coming." Jules hurried over, tucking a stray wisp of hair into her headband. Her face was slightly flushed. Was she nervous about setting off into the forest? Was that her ulterior motive for inviting Taine to come? She'd been in the forest on only two occasions in the past few years; neither had been a walk in the park.

"Jules, you okay?" Taine said.

"Of course," said Jules.

"Off we go, then," said Rocky and, pulling aside a ponga frond, he stepped into the bush.

4

Fiordland

The parrot screamed.

Tim Mahoe gritted his teeth as the cage bumped against his hip for the nth time. He shifted the strap on his shoulder only to have it slip and jab him again.

Fuck.

Carrying the cage was a pain. It was also monumentally brazen. Tim's companion – he wouldn't exactly call him a friend – didn't agree. Digby said the cage-trap was how they *avoided* interest.

"We hide in plain sight," he'd said. "Anyone asks, we tell them we're DoC rangers collecting specimens for study purposes." He'd laughed harshly when he said it. "You never know, that last part might even be true."

Tim went along with it because, in all the times he'd come into the park, running into someone hadn't been an issue. He'd googled it once: only eighteen inhabitants in a region the size of the Serengeti. There were visitors: the occasional hiker, hunters, and the odd helicopter overhead, but that was about it.

Perfect for their purposes.

The cage smashed against his hip again, but this time the parrot pushed its beak between the bars and sunk it into his leg.

"Shit!"

Digby turned back, elbowing his way through the scrub to join him. "What?"

Tim put the cage down and inspected the spot where the kea had stabbed him. A rent in the trouser fabric revealed a small puncture in his thigh, a bead of blood forming.

"The blasted bird stabbed me," he wailed.

Digby smirked. "Don't be a baby. That 'blasted bird' is going to sort your gambling debts."

Frowning, Tim rubbed at the wound to take out the sting. It was true that he had a bit of an appetite for online gambling – *that part* wasn't a secret – but he didn't recall ever mentioning his debts to Digby. It unnerved him the way the man knew so much about his business, although his information wasn't entirely accurate. Selling this bird wouldn't clear Tim's debts. An entire sack of kea wouldn't get him out of the hole he was in right now. They'd have to nab themselves something rare like a South Island kōkako for that. Or possibly a huia. He huffed. Huia had been extinct for more than half a century.

"It's the trees. They're too dense," Tim said, hating that he sounded like a moany teen. "I keep hitting the cage against the trunks." The least Digby could do was offer to carry it for a spell.

Digby didn't take the hint. "We need to get higher, anyway," he said, striding off.

Tim didn't go after him straight away. Instead, he thrust his hand into his pocket, fiddling about until he found a rubber band. Slipping it over his fingers, he opened the cage. It took a few minutes – the stupid bloody bird refused to cooperate – but eventually he got the elastic over the parrot's beak, twisting it twice to hold those vicious snappers closed. When it was done, he lifted the cage and hurried after Digby.

A half-hour later, Tim and Digby emerged from the bush. Heads lowered against the gusting wind, they made their way up the rugged incline towards the saddle. Tim hoped the climb to higher ground would be worth the effort. Digby had explained that kea nested in the forest but foraged higher up in the sub-alpine scrub and tussock. Sometimes, if you were lucky, you could find a whole group of them perched on a rocky outcrop having a natter, the kea equivalent of hanging out at the water cooler.

They were almost at the saddle when Digby ducked behind a large rock, yanking Tim down with him. "There's a group further down the gully."

Tim stuck his head out for a better look, then turned to lean his back against the rock. "It's a bunch of kids," he said

"Kids? On their own? Out here?" Digby poked his head out for a look. When he ducked back behind the rock, his eyes were wide. "They're all practically naked," he said.

"Weird. Must be some kind of primitive survival course. You know, making bivouacs, trapping, that sort of thing. They're carrying spears!"

"Why go so far to run around the park in the buff, though?"

Tim shrugged. That bit did seem weird, but then people were weird. "There's bound to be instructors around. Let's skirt the valley and keep out of their way."

Digby shook his head. "I'm going to follow them."

"Follow them? What the hell for?"

"They might have something we can confiscate."

"Like what? Anyway, we're not rangers."

Digby shrugged. "Stay here if you like. It's fine with me." He shot off after the kids. Tim grappled a moment with the cage, then scrambled after him. He didn't have any choice, really. Digby was the one who had the contacts. Tim needed him if he was going to see a cent.

The kids were moving quickly. To keep up, Tim and Digby stashed their gear where they could find it again later, picking up the chase without it. It seemed the kids were heading for a small lake, fed by one of the hundreds of streams criss-crossing the area. Bounded steeply by a sheer rock wall on one side, the slope down to the lake on the near side was gentler.

Tim and Digby took a wide angle to the shore, making sure they kept to the trees, so they weren't seen. The slope was soggy and their boots sucked in the mud, slowing them down. More than once, Tim thought the noise would alert the kids, but either the rush of the stream drowned out the slurps, or the kids were too far ahead, because they didn't turn around.

At the bottom of the slope, Tim and Digby hid in a thicket of ferns, barely a stone's throw from where the kids were standing waist-deep in the water. The children were chattering to one another. Tim spoke te reo, but it didn't seem to be Māori. He didn't recognise any of the words.

One of the children lifted an arm, causing droplets of water to tinkle on the lake surface. He waved at the others with an open palm.

Tim's mouth dropped open. The boy's hand! It was webbed, the splayed fingers each joined by a flap of translucent skin. The others returned the boy's gesture. Their hands were webbed too. They were...*mutants*!

The children dove under the water.

Tim sucked in his breath and clutched at a nearby ponga, his heart thumping. "Did you see that?" he whispered.

"The fingers? Yeah, I saw it."

"What the fuck are they?"

"I reckon they must be inbreeds," Digby replied. "Shush, they'll be coming up for air in a bit."

But five minutes passed with no sign of them.

"They must have got out somewhere else," Tim said. Digby hissed at him to shut up. The surface was rippling. A pale back appeared, then dived again.

They'd been submerged for ten minutes. Maybe more.

"We should so something," Tim said urgently.

"I *am* doing something," Digby said. "I'm timing them." He tapped his watch and threw Tim a smile that could curdle blood.

Finally, the surface broke again, and one of the children reappeared, a fish flapping on the end of his spear. The child deposited his silvery prize on the bank, then plunged a second time.

Tim's pulse thundered in his ears. "Did you see that?" he whispered. "He was down there for *ages* and he was fine! He wasn't even gasping."

Digby held up his watch to show fifteen minutes had passed. "Mer-people," he announced.

Tim nodded. That had to be it, although if he hadn't seen them with his own eyes, he wouldn't have believed it.

"This is amazing," Digby said.

"I know. Living Mer-people. Here in New Zealand. It's incredible."

They fell silent, their eyes on the water as, one by one, the kids plopped fish on the bank. When they'd disappeared beneath the water again, Digby signalled to Tim to move up the bank out of earshot. Lying in a hollow where they could keep an eye on the lake, Digby said, "We should catch ourselves one."

Something in his tone made Tim shiver. "And what then?"

"We sell it on, like we were going to do with the kea."

"I don't know," said Tim. "They look human."

"They're not, though, are they?"

"Well..."

"They have webbed fingers and they can breathe underwater. Anyone you know can do that?"

Tim shook his head.

"Exactly. Because they're not fucking human, that's why." Digby's eyes flashed darkly. He grabbed at Tim's elbow, gripping it tight. "Do you have any idea how much one of those Mer-kids are worth? A cool million."

Tim's eyes went wide. His heart quickened. "A million dollars? That's crazy! How can you possibly know what they'd be worth?"

Digby unsheathed a hunting knife from his belt. "Because," he said, the blade glinting wickedly in his hand, "we'll be the ones setting the price."

5
——————

On his way to re-join the children, Ka stopped a moment to relieve himself in a clump of flax. He should hurry. He said he would meet them at the lake.

Lately, he had allowed the children to spend more time on their own, forcing himself to stay away. This period in their training was always hard. Juggling their independence against the risk of discovery. But if they were going to feed and protect the People one day, it was the only course. Ka was confident that they would not encounter anyone. With the cooler weather, the number of strangers always dwindled, and the hunters with their guns rarely ventured this deep into the forest. They kept to the ridges and valleys where the wapiti grazed. Ka had heard the thunder of their guns earlier and knew they were a long way off. Still, he was nervous.

He shook off and started down the slope. Half way down, his heart skipped a beat. The muddy bank revealed a mess of footprints. Fresh ones.

Strangers' footprints.

Every sense zinging, Ka leaped into a stand of mānuka. The strange ones had been here before him. They had left behind their catch.

Seeing Ka, the bird struggled in the trap, but it did not make its usual raucous squawking. Checking that no one was about, Ka bent to look. Its beak was clamped shut with a strange piece of flax.

Why would they leave it here? he asked himself. Because the bird was heavy and clumsy and its captors wanted to flit quietly; he answered his own question. Out here in the forest, stealth meant they were either hiding or...hunting!

The children!

Ignoring the scratches to his arms and legs, Ka bounded out of the scrub and raced down the slope. His breath catching, he passed the holes where the strangers' feet had sunk deep into the sucking mud.

At the lake shore, there was no sign of his charges. Ka slipped into the water. The children glided out from beneath the murky banks. Ka felt a surge of relief, but too soon he realised that it was only Kahu and Pene who had emerged. Where were the others? Ka led the pair out of the water, and they ducked into the shadows. Their eyes wide with fear, the children clutched at Ka's arms as they told him their story.

"They were sneaky. We did not see them creep up on us," said Kahu. "We were under the water. They took Tau!"

"And Ro and Mere!" Kahu's sister exclaimed, her face pinched with anxiety. "The bad people had knives. When Ro surfaced, they grabbed her and cut her. I saw the blood swirling, and I stayed in the water."

"You did the right thing," said Ka. "If you had not, they would have captured you too."

Pene wasn't convinced. Biting her lip, she looked at him sadly from under pale lashes. "Will we all die now?"

Ka put a hand on each of their heads. "No, no. We will find them," he said gently, his eyes searching the other side of the lake. He spied a glimpse of the strangers' cloaks. Even from across the lake, they were as red as fresh spilled blood.

For an instant, Ka thought about pursuing them himself. It was his fault the children had been captured, his carelessness that had led to their discovery. If he were to swim across the lake, he might catch them. But just as quickly, he discarded the idea. He could not attempt it with Kahu and Pene. And nor could he leave the children and go on alone; there might be other strangers still lurking. These men were like hungry seagulls and the children were shellfish: too easy to grasp in their sharp beaks.

His decision made, Ka crouched to face Kahu and Pene. "This is too big for us to fix on our own. We must hide our tracks and return to the caves for help." While the children obscured signs of their presence, Ka pursed his lips and sang the song of the kōkako, ending on a long and pure note, so the captured children would know that the People were looking for them and be comforted. With three captive children, the thieves would be forced to travel slowly. There was time. The People could still be saved.

Ka gathered the two remaining children to him, and they ran.

∽

Aitken Street, Wellington

Trevor 'Trigger' Grierson unbuttoned his collar and loosened his tie. It was hot up here, as hot as his last tour in Afghanistan. The air-con must be on the fritz. He glanced through the glass partition separating his desk from the rest of the ninth floor of NZDF's Aitken Street offices. It was like peering out from inside a fish bowl. He'd been swimming around and around in circles in this aquarium for four months now, since completing the rehabilitation for his arm.

Half an arm.

A wave of resentment threatened to engulf him. He hadn't asked for anyone's fucking pity. Thrusting his chair backwards, he stood up and turned his back to the main office pool to claim a moment of privacy. Over the railway station rooftop, the wind whipped up the grey waters of the harbour. He wished he were out there in the wild. Afghanistan. Egypt. South Sudan. Hell, he'd settle for a cold barracks in bloody Waiouru. Instead, he was trussed up in this prissy suit, with a prissy tie and an even prissier title:

Senior Analyst – Foreign Military Forces.

It only *sounded* important. It was the army's way of putting him out to pasture now that his soldiering days were officially FUBAR.

He glanced backwards through the fishbowl partition into the open plan area. Michael, one of the computer analysts – the one who looked like he'd barely left school – grinned at Trigger, yanking at his own tie and pretending to choke. Trigger smiled. His new colleagues were a great bunch, some of New Zealand's smartest people: intelligence analysts, technicians, strategists. They were a mix of civilians and soldiers, including a few vets like him who'd seen active duty. Whatever their backgrounds, they'd been quick to welcome him to the team, inviting him for Friday night drinks at the Thistle Inn around the corner. A couple of times, Trigger had made an effort to join them for a brew before walking the two blocks up the hill to his new digs in Thorndon. That wasn't quite true. The first time, he'd walked home. The other time, he'd got himself well and truly wasted, and two of his office mates had had to give him a fireman's lift home. He was turning into an old soak. An angry cantankerous old soak. Trigger wondered what the brass said to them before he'd taken on the role. It didn't seem to matter how badly he behaved, they kept inviting him.

People are nice to cripples.

Clasping his stump with his good arm, Trigger spun on his heel and stepped closer to the window. It was all he could do not to throw a punch at his own reflection. This bitterness was crippling him. His NZDF counsellor had said it was normal to feel this way, that it would pass, but Trigger was angry at his mates, the army, the *entire world*, for taking his arm and his career. So far, he'd managed to keep a lid on it – keeping his anger hidden from his friends – but it was getting harder. He was born to be a soldier, not shift papers from left to right across a Melteca desk.

His breath fogged the window. Trigger wiped it away with his sleeve. At least he was getting paid; that was a kindness. But the army had its limits. Sooner or later, they'd realise he was a spent shell and move him on.

The hairs at his neck rose. Someone was behind him.

He spun, resisting his soldier's instinct to duck. Michael was hovering in the doorway.

"Um, sorry to bother you, Trevor, but—"

"Trigger."

"Right, Trigger. I was wondering if you had a minute."

The kid looked terrified. Trigger forced himself to smile. "Is this about the air conditioning?"

The schoolboy shoulders dropped. "It's a pain, isn't it?" Michael gave his tie another tug and stuck out his tongue. "Evan's already asked someone from maintenance to come up and have a look at it. It's been on the blink since—"

Trigger interrupted. "Michael, was there something you wanted to talk to me about?"

"Oh yes. Sorry." He waved a sheet of paper in front of him. "It's probably nothing. Actually, I'm sure it's nothing, only I was just checking the routine alerts, and I saw that the National Maritime Surveillance Centre sent through this satellite image..."

Trigger held out his hand for the print-out, but rather than passing it over, Michael stepped into the office and smoothed the document flat on the desk. The image showed the east coast of the country. Trigger couldn't see anything untoward. "What am I looking at?" he asked.

Michael's face lit up as he pointed to a spot on the image. It was as if someone had spilled their drink on an old Polaroid, leaving a blurry splotch. "That smudgy oblong in the middle of the ocean is a submarine, and it's hovering on the fringes of our territorial waters."

"On the fringes. Would that be inside the Territorial Sea Baseline or outside?"

"Outside."

"Right." Trigger picked up the image with his good arm, lifting it up to the light for a better look. It was too hazy to make out much, let alone an insignia. In fact, if Michael hadn't told him, Trigger wouldn't have recognised it as a sub. If it was, and Maritime seemed to think it was, it was still outside the TSB by twelve nautical miles.

"Maritime advised that it's likely to be a case of 'innocent passage'," Michael said.

"Do we know where it's heading?"

"Not yet. This image shows it as it's about to surface, or diving after having surfaced, which is how Maritime picked it up. Like I said, it's probably nothing. Could be it's just come up to recharge its batteries. It's pretty cool, though, isn't it? First time I've seen a sub caught on satellite."

Trigger lowered the image and looked at Michael. "Maritime didn't say who it belongs to?"

"I forwarded their report to you. They haven't speculated on who owns it. We already know it isn't ours." He paused. "That would be because we don't own any." He gave an exaggerated smile, as if the statement was part of a stand-up routine.

Trigger frowned. "And there's nothing set up with the Australians or the Americans at the moment? No naval exercises?"

"Not that I know of, but I can try to find out for you."

"No, that's fine. I'll look into it."

He would have to dig deep. If the Americans decided to bring a submarine into New Zealand waters, there was a good chance they could breeze right in without anyone suspecting a thing. Experts at stealth, they could park a submarine under your bed and you'd never know it. It was a good thing NZ-US relations were cordial.

"Thank Maritime for the intelligence and ask them to signal us if it moves into internal waters."

"Sure thing."

"No, scrub that. I want to know where it goes."

As Michael left, Trigger sat and examined the image. Like the boy said, it was probably nothing.

6

Fiordland

Digby kept them to the gullies and streams where the trees were dense and the water washed away signs of their passage. With the three kids in tow, it took a couple of hours to reach their evening accommodation. Tim gave a low whistle. Definitely not 5-star; you could barely call it a hut. The building was three metres square, its split timber walls crumbling in one corner and the corrugated iron roof sloping inwards. The whole thing might have been painted red once. It was hard to tell. It certainly hadn't been painted since. It was so ancient, DoC hadn't even bothered to maintain it, abandoning it to the bush.

Tim had no time to take off his boots; Digby sent him back to the lake to hide their tracks. He didn't argue. Taking those kids by force had turned the two of them into frickin' kidnappers. What kind of sentence does that carry? Ten years? Maybe twenty? He wasn't in a hurry to get caught.

Retracing their steps, he considered making a run for it – hoofing it back to civilisation – but he didn't have the guts, not without his gear. It was too risky. For one thing, he didn't know the way. He had a vague idea, but he wasn't certain. It was like deepest darkest Peru in here, too easy to take a wrong turn and get lost. He could die of hypothermia within hours. Digby was the real bushman. Tim was just here to carry the bags. Then there was the risk of the kids' people coming after them. He didn't have children, but his sister had a couple. She would kill for hers, no question. Why should these kids' parents be any different, even if they were mutants or Mer-people or whatever the heck they were? He'd already seen with his own eyes what the kids could do; who knew what the adults were capable of? Mostly, though, Tim didn't trust Digby. What was to stop him coming after Tim and slitting his throat while he slept? Clearly, it wasn't the first time the guy had wielded a knife. What did he really know about Digby anyway?

Digby was just some guy he'd met down the pub...

...he'd left the office, ambling over to the Sprig and Crown rather than going home. It wasn't his home anymore anyway. It belonged to the beneficiaries of SB and RW Johns Trust, or at least it would in another ten days. Selling the house would only slow the bleeding.

He waited at the curb for the traffic to pass before crossing the road. He couldn't believe the mess he'd got himself in. It started out as a few hundred dollars borrowed from his revolving credit mortgage. It was meant to be a one-off, the money intended to tide him over until payday, and then he'd put it back. Or grow it, if he played it right. But a few hundred had become a few thousand, and one month had become two months, and before he knew it, he'd lost all the equity he owned in the house. It wasn't his fault. There had been that hot tip that had turned out to be about as hot as yesterday's leftovers. And the economy hadn't helped. He just needed a couple of good trades and things would be fine. So, he'd dipped into the company trust account. Well, why the hell not? It was just sitting there, earning a measly three percent. A Queen Street prostitute could show more interest than that! He'd figured he'd invest it, pocket returns over and above three percent, and put the capital back.

At least, that had been the *plan*.

Lately, it was taking all his energy just to hide the losses. The partners would find out soon – it was inevitable – and when they did, he'd lose his job and any chance of working as an accountant again.

It was hypocritical bullshit anyway! The clients were happy enough for Tim to do what had to be done to maximise their revenue: moving money around to keep their tax low, shifting funds into trusts, teasing open fiscal loopholes. Anything that served to squeeze the maximum profit from their investments. He could steal the crown jewels on their behalf and it wouldn't worry them – so long as they didn't have to know how it was done. But get caught helping himself and that'd be another story. Even if the Charted Accountants didn't cut him loose, New Zealand was a small place. He'd be up shit creek without a paddle.

Unless I can get a stake.

A decent stake, a few good decisions, and he'd be back on his feet.

The Sprig and Crown was busy. It usually was on a Friday. Tim ordered a Boddington's, turning to survey the room while he waited for the bartender to pour it. He didn't want to run in to one of the partners. They'd expect him to bring his beer over and chew the fat. Tim wasn't having any of that. Tonight, he just wanted a drink.

The bartender put the beer on the counter. The creamy foam slid down the sides of the glass and disappeared into the towelling runner. "That'll be nine dollars, thanks, mate."

Tim pulled out his wallet. Opened it. Fuck. It was empty.

Feigning surprise, he scratched his head. "Ah, wouldn't you know it. Looks like the missus has cleaned me out." Actually, Tim's girlfriend had moved out six months ago, and hadn't spoken to him since.

The bartender rolled his eyes. He'd heard it all before. "Eftpos is fine."

Tim's cards were emptier than his wallet. He made a show of searching anyway. "Sorry. Looks like she took that too. I'm going to have to take a rain check on that beer."

The bartender frowned. "Sorry, mate, I've poured it, you pay for it."

Tim shrugged.

But, standing a couple of paces away, Digby held up a ten. "I'll get that," he'd said. "Can't let a man go without his beer, can we?"

"Hey, thanks."

"No worries."

They'd taken their drinks to a corner booth. Well, Tim could hardly drink on his own when another man had paid for his beer, could he? Digby got in another round. And another. Tim was well on the way to being pissed when Digby had suggested the jaunt to Fiordland.

Elbows on the table, he leaned in close. "Look, I'm not

one to interfere, but you were saying before that your girl-friend cleaned you out? I might be able to help you make a quick couple of thou. You wouldn't have to do much. Just help me carry the gear. That is, if you're interested."

"What gear?"

Digby checked over his shoulder for eavesdroppers, then lowered his voice. "Let's just say I've got a client with a line on exotic pets who'd like to get his hands on a couple of alpine parrots."

"Kea?" Tim spluttered, putting down his beer. "But they're endangered."

"Shhhh, not so loud, man. They're *protected*. It's not the same thing." Digby lifted his glass, emptying it in a single swallow, then wiped his mouth with the back of his hand. "It's all rubbish anyway. There are hundreds of them. No one's going to miss a few. And catching them is like catching Lemmings – they practically fall in your lap."

"Yeah." Tim crinkled his nose. "I don't know..."

"Well, think about this; they're worth a few thousand each," said Digby. He cocked an eyebrow, then, grabbing their empty glasses, headed back to the bar.

Tim watched him go. A few thousand. It wouldn't repay the trust money, but it'd sure as hell give him the stake he needed to trade his way out of the crapper.

Digby returned, a fresh beer in each hand.

"So, when are we going?" Tim said.

By the time Tim got back to the hut, Digby had the kids tied up in the corner, fabric stuffed in their mouths.

"You took your time."

Tim felt a flash of anger. Digby was calling all the shots,

but if they got caught he wouldn't be the only one going down for it. "Well, I assumed you wanted me to do a thorough job," he retorted.

To his surprise, Digby backtracked. "Yeah, yeah, okay. Fair dues."

Tim's eyes adjusted to the gloom. The hut was small and sparse, its only furniture a fire-pit, a stool, and a narrow bench. There was a window on one side. Cracked and covered in mildew, it wasn't much chop for looking out of, but at least it kept out the draught, unlike the collapsed back corner where a vicious wind whipped in. It was as miserable as a Scottish dungeon. Hopefully, they wouldn't have to stay long.

The elder of the two girls whimpered. As well as the slice in her side, Tim noted fresh bruises on her face.

"What did you do to her?" Tim demanded.

"Nothing. I had to get some proof, didn't I? Photographs of her webbed fingers and toes. Not my fault the bitch wouldn't cooperate." Crouching, Digby put his face close to the girl's, sticking his tongue out. "But that's okay. I like 'em feisty. I got us some nice pictures in the end." He prised open her mouth and stuffed the sock-gag in deeper. The girl gagged, cringing away from him, webbed feet scrabbling on the crude boards as she pulled herself deeper into the corner.

Digby laughed, the sound coarse in the small space.

Tim tried not to cringe. *Jesus. The guy's sick.*

"Keep an eye on them, will you? I'll be back in a bit."

"Where are you going?"

"I need to get to high ground, find some sky, so I can

make a sat call. I'm going to have a little chat with our buyer, tell him we've got a new product line."

"It's a big leap from a few exotic birds."

"They've handled bigger items."

Tim felt his bile rise. What had he gotten himself into? Keeping his voice even, he said, "It doesn't matter, they're not going to have that kind of money on them."

Digby's face dropped. Clearly, he hadn't thought that far. No doubt his was a strictly cash business.

"They can wire it," he said. "When I see it in my account, then I'll know."

"As will your friendly neighbourhood banker. I'm sure it won't look too suspicious. You probably get million-dollar payments every other day."

Digby's face darkened. "I've got money."

Tim raised his eyebrows.

Digby bared his teeth. "Yeah, well, what do you suggest, Timmy?"

"You could put it in my account."

"And why would I do that?"

Because I know how to hide it.

"Because I just sold my house. A couple of million dollars turning up in my account is going to look like a settlement payment."

"Is your house worth that much?"

"Not really."

"You'd better think of another way. I'm not putting *my* money in *your* account."

"Then your only option is to take whatever cash they've got and hope it's worth risking a couple of decades in prison."

"Fuck you, man."

Digby stormed out of the hut, only to return a few minutes later. "Give me your account number," he said.

Tim tried not to smile.

~

The Catfish

Ajax Meredith opened the photo he'd received by sat phone, his eyes widening.

He exhaled slowly. He mustn't get too excited. It could very easily be a scam. Any schoolkid could mock-up a convincing image on Photoshop these days. It didn't do to underestimate anyone. He might be small-time, but Digby was a shady piece of work. Meredith almost laughed. Who wasn't shady in this business? It was just one of the hazards of being a smuggler, knowing which of the shady characters were *reliable*. That was his skill: connecting the goods to the cash, customers with buyers.

Or thieves with bigger thieves.

Meredith didn't give a rat's arse who he dealt with, so long as the transaction made him money. That included screwing over dear old Uncle Sam. No love lost there. The fat old bastard had hung him out to dry long ago.

Meredith enlarged the image. Webbed toes. Digby had made other claims too. Outlandish claims. Meredith enlarged the photo further. The image blurred.

Fuck.

He'd have to wait until he had the goods in hand before he could verify Digby's claims, but if the species was as exotic as the man said, then Meredith had the perfect client, or, at least, he knew someone who could arrange it. In fact, if this was the real deal, it could be the most lucrative he'd ever make.

~

Aitken Street, Wellington

Trigger took the stairs. By the time he reached the ninth-floor landing, his business shirt was slick with sweat and he was gasping like he smoked a pack a day. He could smell the beer he'd had with lunch seeping through his pores. Leaning over, he hunched against the bannister. The missing hand throbbed, but he ignored it. It felt good to have raised his heart-rate, even if it was just a bunch of stairs.

It was pathetic how quickly he'd gone to fat, though, now that his buddy Taine wasn't riding his arse to stay under the NZDF 125kg weight restriction. The army wasn't entirely heartless. They let you go a kilo or two over that, but only if it were solid muscle. Straightening up, he squeezed the softening bulge at his midsection. He really was going to the pack. Hopefully, there was still muscle underneath. He resolved to do the stairs more often, then, smoothing his shirt, he passed his card through the scanner and opened the door.

Michael intercepted him on the way to his office, his schoolboy face bursting with excitement.

Trigger didn't break step. "What is it?"

"Another report from Maritime," Michael said, struggling to keep up. "You asked me to let you know."

Trigger's head snapped up. "My office, now."

Back at his desk, Trigger used his back as a shield while he tapped out his password, then he stood back and signalled to Michael to take a seat. "Okay, show me what you've got."

Michael's fingers whizzed over the keys. "Maritime sent this through to us at military intelligence twenty minutes ago, while you were at lunch," he said. "They've spotted that sub again this morning." He typed some more.

"In internal waters?"

Michael swivelled the screen towards Trigger. "Not yet, but here are the coordinates. Now, if we extrapolate, the submarine appears to be on course for the South Island. The Sounds area."

"Marlborough?"

"Fiordland."

"Nothing much of interest there."

"The conspiracy theorists say otherwise."

Trigger knew the stories. A handful of conspiracy groups claimed the Americans regularly used Fiordland as a haven for their submarines. If you were looking for free garaging for your submersible, the Southland Sounds were a good choice. They were deep enough, plummeting 450 metres in places, with the steep-sided mountains providing the clandestine cloaking. And there was no one down there looking over the back fence to notice you coming and going.

Michael twisted to look up at Trigger. "I wonder if it's an American vessel heading for Antarctica."

"Possibly." Trigger doubted it. He'd checked the shared intelligence databases when the submarine first surfaced and not seen anything from the Americans. Still, it wouldn't hurt to check again. More likely, it was an Australian military exercise they'd overlooked. Or a Greenpeace vessel, perhaps. The environmental group were becoming more and more militant in their attempts to get their concerns in front of the government.

"Here's the interesting thing," Michael said. He was like a kid with a new video game. "Our sub is moving fast. Estimating the time to reach the second plot point puts their speed at around twenty knots. I think that's what you call a great rate of knots," he said, giving Trigger a cheesy stand-up grin.

A submarine heading for New Zealand waters and at speed? For the first time in ages, Trigger's pulse hiked, and it had nothing to do with climbing the stairs.

7
____

Fiordland

Jules admired the view as Taine crawled into the sleeping bag beside her, his white t-shirt showing every muscle. Honestly, it was like dating the poster boy for an action movie.

"What?"

"Nothing. I'm glad you came, that's all. We haven't had a chance to spend much time together."

"There was France." He grinned.

Jules rolled her eyes. Their trip to France hadn't exactly been a holiday.

Taine lifted his arm and she wiggled closer, resting her head on his shoulder. He closed his arm about her. The wind whistled outside, singing as it funnelled through the rocks and caught in the crannies. Wong had had them set up camp in the lee of a ridge, ready for an early start in the morning.

"Hear that?" Taine said.

"The wind?"

"Not the wind," he replied. "It's the patu-paiarehe, the fairy people, playing their flutes. Some people call them the Tūrehu."

Jules smiled. "I thought the Tūrehu lived in the Urewera forest?"

"My grandmother used to say the fairy people were everywhere. They make their homes anywhere the forest is isolated and misty. They're shy – hiding themselves away in the daytime – but at night, we can hear them speaking to one another through their music."

Jules concentrated on the sound. It did resemble the notes of a flute. Soft and mournful, with occasional trills like a piccolo. She shivered and snuggled closer to Taine. "Whatever they're saying, it sounds sad," she said.

As Jules drifted off to sleep, a morepork hooted in the distance.

The sky was just lightening. Ahead of Taine, Wong tracked the deer herd through the lowlands, following the characteristic scratches the animals' teeth left in the bark. The wapiti had passed through here, moving out of the bush and up onto the ridge to graze between the tussock. Wong signalled to the party to remain hidden at the edge of the treeline, downwind from the elk. Wapiti had incredible hearing and a keen sense of smell, but so far, the herd appeared unalarmed. There were six of them, a stag and his cows, just a little short of three hundred metres away.

Wong motioned to Barb, the paying customer, to take her pick.

Standing slightly behind her, Taine watched as the American lifted the Remington to her shoulder – she held it like an old friend whose stories she'd heard a thousand times – and tracked the movements of the herd, searching for a preferred target.

In military situations, a sniper's objective is to select the target that would best destabilise the enemy. It's why soldiers don't salute officers in the field, the gesture an instant giveaway to any sniper in the vicinity. You may as well put a target on the officer and shout, 'shoot me!'. Out here, the size of the stag's antlers were the equivalent of that salute, so Taine wasn't surprised when Barb adjusted the barrel toward the stag, took three deep breaths, then exhaled slowly, squeezing on the pause.

The gun's roar echoed through the valley.

Taine didn't watch the stag fall, although he was certain it had. Instead, he kept his eyes fixed on Barb's finger as she followed through, squeezing the trigger to its full position, then releasing it slowly. She was ready for the recoil: the gun came back to her, positioned for a second shot.

Impressive.

The deer scattered, and two further shots rang out. More deer fell. Taine heard a whoop. Loughlin. Seems the guys from Corrections had picked off two of the spooked deer. The remaining animals bounded over the ridge into the next valley.

Beside Taine, Jules gave a little gasp.

Taine looked up the ridge to where Barb's stag lay, its neck twisted at a bizarre angle. Even at this distance he could make out the patch of blood that had blossomed at its shoulder.

"That was a double shoulder shot, Jules. It took the animal through both shoulder blades. When that happens, the animal's spine twists and snaps. It's the most humane approach. The animal dies instantly, and with less chance of injuring them first. It wouldn't have felt a thing," he said.

Jules nodded. "That's good."

Lowering her rifle, Barb wasn't as easily impressed. "It was slightly low, I think, but there was more wind up on that ridge than I expected," she said, matter of fact. "Let's take a look."

Taine caught Jules' shudder as they trudged up the hill to check out the trophies.

Fiordland, abandoned hut

"What time are they coming?" Tim asked.

Digby was slouched on the bench, his foot resting on the wall of the hut. "They're not coming here." He picked at his fingernail with the tip of his knife.

"Well, where's the drop off?"

Digby smiled lazily. "Somewhere else."

The bastard was driving him mad. Tim stood up and sat down again. There was nowhere to go in the tiny room. "How long will it take us get there? Don't forget we have to drag the kids with us. They'll slow us down."

Actually, Tim was pretty sure they wouldn't. Yesterday, he'd seen how the kids' webbed feet had acted like snow-shoes, allowing them to move quickly where he and Digby had sunk to their knees in the mud. And the wind and cold didn't seem to bother them either. Last night had been so bitter, Tim had thrown the kids a blanket, but they'd only looked at it, which didn't make sense. Did they mistrust him so much, they'd rather die of hypothermia? Or could it be that mutants didn't feel the cold? They were wearing only a strip of hessian around their hips, and yet he hadn't seen them shiver.

Digby laughed. "Relax, Timmy. We'll make the drop. In the meantime, we're staying put. I don't want to risk the rest of the people from Atlantis finding us, you know?"

"Get your arse out here, Digby!" a voice boomed from outside the hut.

Tim froze.

That was not a voice you wanted to fuck with.

"What the fuck?" Digby whispered. He dropped his feet with a clunk. "How'd he find us?"

"Triangulated the GPS on your sat phone, maybe?" Tim hissed.

"Bugger," said Digby, under his breath. Out loud, he said, "That you, Meredith? You guys are early. I can't see any money in my account yet."

"Yeah, about that. I changed my mind. Don't think I can fence that product for you. Bit too rich for me. I'm just here for the parrots."

Digby's face dropped, creases appearing in his forehead. "The fuck." Before Tim could stop him, he threw open the door and marched out onto the stoop. "What do you think you're playing at, Meredith?"

Tim stepped across the hut to peep through a gap in the

boards. Out front were four men. They were dressed in black and armed to the teeth, like a bunch of Ninjas.

"We had a deal," Digby protested. He stepped closer to the men.

It was a mistake. Tim knew it, could feel it in his bones. You didn't argue with guys with guns. Not when they had them pointed at you. Tim should call out, warn Digby. Instead, he clamped his lips shut. Squinting, he peeked through the slit in the boards.

"Actually no, I don't agree," Meredith said coolly. He tilted his head, the movement so slight it was almost imperceptible. The Ninjas saw it and responded. The clearing exploded in a burst of semi-automatic fire.

Digby's body jerked like a ragdoll, his head whiplashing cruelly. He fell backwards, but not before Tim saw his back peppered with holes. It was like watching one of those slow-mo clips of raindrops hitting a lake, only instead of tiny water droplets, shredded skin and muscle erupted from the craters. Tim ground his jaw, forcing himself not to scream.

"Like I said, I changed my mind," Meredith drawled.

Digby didn't argue.

Meredith nodded again to one of the men, who kicked at the body. Digby's tongue lolled sideways. "I don't think he's going to be talking to anyone, boss."

Meredith nodded. "Let's get the merchandise and move out."

Realisation hit Tim like a Kenworth truck: they were coming inside the hut. In seconds, he could be as dead as Digby.

Fuck the kids, and fuck the bloody money!

He had to get out. Get away.

Frantic, Tim glanced around. There was only one possible escape. Through the collapsed corner at the back. They might see him, but if he were quick, they might not. It didn't matter. There was no other choice.

With barely a glance at the kids, Tim dropped to his hands and knees and squeezed himself under the crooked timber, the noise of his anorak brushing against the wood like thunder in his ears. It was a tight fit. Tim held his breath and pushed up with his shoulder, forcing the timber to give.

The wood groaned and Tim nearly wet himself in fright, but, miraculously, the porch step creaked at the same time, masking the sound. Tim gave it everything, grasping the board on either side and hauling himself through the gap. Once his shoulders were through, he slipped out of the hut onto the ground like a new-born babe.

"Hey!"

There was a burst of fire.

Deafening.

Splinters flew. Scrambling, Tim waited for the bullets to hit him. He took a breath, quick and sharp. Still alive. No smell of gunfire. He'd expected cordite. Isn't that what the trashy thrillers said? There was just the damp smell of rotting wood. He staggered to his feet as another staccato punctured the air. Louder than a Times Square concert.

"The hut's too small. You'll hit the merchandise, you fool!" Meredith's scream sounded blunt and far away. "He went out the back. Go round."

The gunfire paused.

It was the break he needed. Tim ran, diving into forest behind the hut. He threw himself forward, using his arms to propel him through the mānuka, ignoring the branches that bit at his face and hands. He was an animal, hunted.

Bullets pinged, hitting the tree trunks.

Tim swerved.

Suddenly, his back felt oddly wet. Still on the move, Tim reached back and fingered the wound. Weirdly, it didn't throb until he touched it, then it exploded with pain.

8

Fiordland

Taine ambled up the hill to join Jules. It was late morning and Wong had them back at the camp on the ridge. The guests were gathered around the pile of beasts, four eight pointers and several cows. Mostly wapiti-red hybrids, the deer weren't the purebred trophies the guests had been hoping for, but that didn't stop the bragging.

"So, have you heard the one about the best place to shoot a deer?" Loughlin said, nudging a stag with his boot.

"Better than here? Where's that, then?" Herewini asked.

"Anywhere in the eye is fine," Loughlin said.

There was a roll of laughter, Barb's hoot carrying over the others.

Jules was sitting on her pack, sipping tea from an enamel mug. Taine dropped to his haunches beside her.

"They seem happy over there," Jules said, nodding to where Loughlin was holding court.

"They do," Taine agreed.

Jules snorted.

"You okay?"

"Taine, it's awful," Jules whispered. She wrapped her hands around the steaming cup and brought it to her cheek. "I didn't think it would be this bad. I know we have to do it. I just wish it didn't have to be so brutal. That last one, the male that Loughlin shot, did you see its eye?" Taine nodded. Loughlin's shot had taken the animal below the heart, hitting vital organs, but not killing it immediately. Wild with pain and fear, the buck had run several metres before collapsing, Read finishing it off with a shot to the head.

"It's too easy," Jules said, careful not to be overheard. "The poor deer don't stand a chance. What makes it worse is that we're on the end of the roar, so the animals are distracted. And most of them have never encountered humans before, so they don't know to be afraid. It doesn't seem fair."

"It never is, Jules." Taine reached forward and picked the pot off the Primus. "More water?"

"Thank you." She held out her mug and he topped it up.

She was quiet for a moment. They looked out over the Sounds, the valleys still swathed in shadow. Curling her wrist, she tucked the mug under her chin. "How do you justify it? As a soldier?"

Trust Jules to ask the sixty-four-million-dollar question.

Laying down his rifle, Taine sat on the tussock grass beside her. "There's no easy answer to that. Plenty of soldiers never come to terms with taking a life."

She turned to look at him, shading her eyes with her hand. "What about you? How do you justify it?" Her voice was softer than the wind across the tussock.

Taine plucked at the grass. "Me?" he said, as he stripped

a stem of its seeds. "For me, it's about protecting people's right to life and to freedom. When someone threatens the lives of New Zealanders, it's my job to protect them, even if that sometimes requires me to take a life. Sometimes it's necessary for the greater good," Taine said. "Like the way the deer have to be culled for the native species to survive. It's a balance."

"If someone attacks one of our citizens, they automatically forfeit the right to live, is that it?"

"That's simplistic, but yes."

Putting her mug on the ground, Jules hugged her knees. "Do all soldiers believe that?"

"In a nutshell."

"So, in a war, to the other side, you could be the threat."

Taine smiled. "It's in the job description. When a soldier signs up, he knows that sooner or later he's going to be putting his life on the line. I guess in a war you hope that your commanders are making informed decisions."

Further down the valley, Barb hooted at something Loughlin said.

The stillness was obliterated by the rat-tat-tat of a firearm.

A semi-automatic!

Taine leapt to his feet, snatching up his rifle. Down the hillside, Read did the same. They waited, ears pricked for the direction.

There was more gunfire, closer this time, the sound echoing through the gorge. Startled birds flew out of the forest canopy. The shooting ceased. Read obviously thought he had a handle on the direction, because he took off, leaping rocks and clumps of tussock as he descended the slope. Taine sprinted down the valley after him. They were just about to head into the treeline when an injured man stumbled out. He ran towards them, screaming.

Fiordland, abandoned hut

Jackson put his head around the door. "He got away from us, boss. Kilgour clipped him below the shoulder blade. The red jacket made him an easy target, but he must have taken it off because we lost him in the trees. Still, Kilgour swears it was a solid hit. Doesn't reckon he'll last long."

Meredith barely nodded. He'd seen the Mer-folk Digby had put up for sale. Their hands and feet were tied, and their mouths had been stuffed with gags to keep them from calling out. Cowered in the corner of the hut, they eyed him warily. One of them, a male, gave a muffled moan.

Was he trying to communicate with the others?

Meredith lunged and grabbed at it. The creature's wrists were tied, but still it fought back, twisting and writhing. Meredith immobilised it, clamping its skinny torso between his legs, then prised open its hand. Splayed open the fingers. They were webbed, the flap of skin reaching out to the tips of the appendages and ending in an elongated nail.

"Well, will you look at that?" He felt his grin spread. Digby hadn't made it up. What about his other claims? The one about them being able to stay submerged for a quarter of an hour or more? Or the fact that they didn't feel the cold. Pity they didn't have fish tails. But even if half of what Digby had said were true, the contents of this little hut were a trafficker's nirvana. Meredith smirked. He might even be able to retire.

Suddenly, the kid bucked, raking his nails down Meredith's face. Drawing blood.

Fuck!

Meredith backhanded the thing, hurling it to the floor, turning to grind his boot into the boy's wrist. He straightened up, panting. Wiped his face with the back of his hand. It came away bloody.

The creature groaned. Good. He hadn't killed it. Meredith rubbed his hands on his pants. That shouldn't have happened. He'd allowed himself to get distracted and let down his guard. They might look like kids, but who knows what these things could do? Now he'd hurt the male, they'd show him some respect.

Silhouetted in the doorframe, Jackson coughed. "Do you want us to go after the runner, boss?"

Meredith smoothed his jacket. The runner. Every moment the runner was on the loose, there was a chance of discovery. Meredith didn't want anyone talking about what they'd seen here, at least not until the commission had been deposited in his account.

Better to be safe than sorry.

He opened his mouth to instruct Jackson and Kilgour to hunt the bastard down and kill him, when he spied the sat phone perched on a crude bench running the length of the hut. Did Digby and his mate each have one? Meredith was willing to bet the chances were slim to nothing. This had to be the one Digby had used to contact him.

"Boss?"

Slipping the sat phone into his pocket, Meredith shook

his head. "No," he said. "Let him go. It's a two-day walk out of the forest. With luck, he'll die before he gets there."

It was possible the man might find someone to help him, a hunter or a tramper, and make it back to town, but even then, what could he say? Some tall tale about mermaids and mercenaries? They'd think he was off his head, delirious from loss of blood and pain. He laughed aloud. They might think the man was mental and lock him up.

Jackson nodded. "Shall we burn the hut?"

Meredith shook his head. "Nah. A fire will only bring the locals running. They don't like forest fires threatening their precious forests. Just have the men pick up any obvious shells. And bring the dead scammer. We'll dispose of him elsewhere," Meredith barked as Jackson turned to go. "Make it snappy. I want us out of here in five."

Meredith sniffed, his nostrils flaring. He wiped his face on his sleeve. With no body, no mermaids, and no mercenaries here at the hut, even if the runner made it back to civilisation, there'd be precious little to corroborate his story.

Ka stopped at the roar of the guns.

He lifted his face to the sky. Those were not normal guns, the ones the hunters used to hunt the wapiti. Even from far off, this thunder was faster and louder. It was as if, in the heavens, the demon-gods were raging war. The noise was so loud it bruised his eardrums.

Surely, this thunder had to be a sign?

Yesterday, when Ka had returned to the cave without the

children, the chief formed a hunting party. He had led the ten of them, all warriors, out of their cave-home and into the forest. They had been hunting the children's captors all night. They had not slept. Nor had they eaten. The moon had departed and the sun had risen and still they had found nothing, not even a misplaced footprint. Ka worried that they might never see the children again.

Once again, the sky crackled with noise, like demons stomping on the ceiling. Ka trembled. He looked to where the clouds were clustered at the tips of the trees.

The tracker, Māpura, tasted the air. "They are that way," he said, pointing out the direction. At his neck, a small flute bounced as he gestured.

The chief nodded. "We must hurry."

His people picked up their spears and disappeared into the bush. Together, Ka and Hine shouldered the silver trunk of the big gun and followed them.

The sun was high in the sky when they came to the little dwelling. The People were nervous, stealing silently out of the trees into the tiny clearing. Built by strangers, the hut had not been used for many years, but someone had been here recently: the ground was trampled, the grasses and ferns bruised.

The chief ducked his head inside the hut. "They are not here," he said.

Ka and Hine rested the silver trunk on the ground. Hine drew in her breath and sank to her knees. "There is blood here on the grass. A lot of blood. I think one of the children may be dead."

"Perhaps it was a wapiti," someone whispered.

They all knew this was not the blood of a deer.

Ka touched Hine on her shoulder. "Why would the strangers capture the children, only to kill them? They want them for the secrets of our People. And they cannot do that if the children are dead."

Hine lifted her hand to Ka's and smiled. "That Ro can be annoying."

"We will find your niece. Do not give up yet."

The chief crouched beside the pool of dark blood, touching the grass with his fingers. They came away wet. "This is recent," he said.

Māpura called to them under his breath. "Look here, the trees are injured." He stood at the edge of the trees, his fingers tracing the gouges in the bark.

"It could be the wapiti." It was the same idiot from before.

"Not everything is caused by the wapiti," another grumbled. This time, Ka didn't agree. Scratches in the bark *could* be made by the wapiti.

Pushing forward, Ka examined the tree trunk. "No," he said. "It is not a wapiti. This scraping was not created by a blunt tooth. See how the dents are clean and sharp as if they were sliced there with a pipi shell? It was a gun."

"Over here," said Māpura, who had moved deeper into the bush. He held up his fingers. They were flecked with blood.

"And here is one of their cloaks," said Hine. She handed the cloak to Māpura, whose nose was keener than a shark's. If the owner of the cloak had been in contact with the children, Māpura would know.

Māpura sniffed the garment. He breathed deeply, burying his nose in the soft insides, then turning the cloak and smelling the outside. It was a cloak fit for a chief. As glossy as a new leaf, it was the vibrant red of the kaka beak flower.

Māpura handed the cloak to the chief and nodded.

Hine and Ka picked up the silver trunk.

They had a trail.

Aitken Street, Wellington

Michael plonked the carton of Chinese food on Trigger's desk along with a ten dollar note and change. "I got you Mongolian Beef. I hope that's okay?"

"That's great, thanks."

"I figured you for a beef man."

Trigger looked for a utensil.

"Hang on." Michael, juggling his hot carton and a stack of serviettes, eventually dropped a fork on the desk. "I got you a fork..."

Trigger felt his anger rise. Just because he had no hand, didn't mean—

"...and a pair of chopsticks." The cheap chopsticks slipped out from between the serviettes and landed on the desk. "Wasn't sure if you knew how to use them."

The annoyance faded. "I know how to use them," Trigger said, holding the packaging with his teeth while he removed the chopsticks. He spat out the paper and it fluttered to the desk. "One of my best mates was Chinese. He taught me."

Scooping noodles into his mouth, Michael stopped mid-shovel. "Was?"

"Yeah, we lost him. A rescue mission. Classified."

"That's really rough. I'm sorry."

"Me too."

They didn't say anything much for a while, focused on eating. Apart from the whirring of the server in the room next door, and their chopsticks in their cartons, the office was quiet. A fluorescent light over by the elevators flickered intermittently.

"How long were you on active duty?" Michael asked. He took a swig from his can of Fanta.

Trigger put a piece of broccoli in his mouth. "Long enough. A few tours."

"Iraq?"

"Maybe."

"You're a bit of a legend here, you know."

Trigger almost choked. "Me? What for?"

Laying down his chopsticks, Michael wiped grease off his chin. He nodded at Trigger's arm. "They say you're a hero. That you lost your arm saving another soldier and a civilian."

Trigger snorted. "You shouldn't listen to rumours."

"This is military intelligence. Rumour and conjecture are our business."

"Or could be I'm just clumsy and shot my own arm off."

Michael tipped his chair back and put a foot on the wall. He shook his head. "I'm not buying it. You wouldn't be working here otherwise."

"So I'm a wiz at calculus."

"Yeah, right."

"You ever think rehabilitating crippled soldiers is just good marketing for the army?"

Michael shrugged. "Well, if that were the case, then you'd be working in stock control, wouldn't you?"

Grunting, Trigger hiffed both their empty cartons into the rubbish bin. "Well, how about you do your sleuthing on something useful and get back to work?"

"Classic evasion technique," Michael said, as he took himself back to his desk.

The submarine had surfaced again, still en route for Southland, and this time they'd gotten a lucky break. From the satellite image, they were able to determine the vessel's length, at around ninety metres, and a beam of nearly ten metres. And there was a partial mark, including two digits, painted on the sub's hull. Submarines were military hardware; there couldn't have been more than a thousand of them built worldwide in the modern era, most of them accounted for. Maritime checked Jane's military database and narrowed it down, then Michael hopped to, adapting recognition software to the purpose, and they'd started trawling through images. Even so, it was a half hour before Trigger whooped. "Get in here, Miss Marple. I think this is it."

They compared the markings on the sub with markings on Trigger's entry.

Michael whistled. "Close. Reckon that could be it."

"Soviet," Trigger said.

"Makes sense."

"Tango class."

Trigger did more one-handed typing and located the ownership history. "It was purchased by a private buyer at the break-up of the Soviet Union."

"A private buyer?" Michael said. "Who buys a submarine?"

"Someone with lots of money. These days you can probably get one on eBay. Where do you think terrorists and gangsters get their equipment?"

Michael looked sceptical. "Buying demilitarised equipment requires licences. They don't just sell them to anyone."

Trigger rolled his eyes. "Not everyone's a hero, kid. Right, let's do some digging. Find out who owns that submarine now."

When Michael left, Trigger picked up the phone. It was time to call James Arnold, his former commander, and talk about readying a section at Christchurch's Burnham Army Base.

9

Fiordland

The noise attracted her, the vibrations penetrating and insidious, like the fine sand that would get up under her mantle. She slunk across the sea bed, then rose through the water to settle on the rocky shelf. She'd already seen the big silver fish steal into the bay several tides ago, sidling in slowly, then hovering close to the surface as if dead. It wasn't dead. It made too much noise for that, creaking and moaning like the driftwood that floated in with the tide. Eventually it had gone quiet.

Now a new noise summoned her. She slithered over to investigate. Quietly undulating in the current, she'd watched as, above her, the silver fish had birthed its dark spawn. The brood had made for the surface and been gone some time. Back now, this time there were more of them, their vibrations stabbing at her brain. On another day, she would kill the spawn and quieten that thrum. Not today. She turned, intending to slither back beneath the overhanging rocks in search of easier prey.

Wait!

She tasted the water, walking her tentacles away from her body, the current lifting them...*blood?* It was too faint.

Her massive eye caught a movement at the surface. Dark against the blinding sunlight, a silhouette dropped through water. It tumbled clumsily through the depths and bounced gently on the shelf, disrupting a wave of debris.

The smell drew her.

She reached out to sample the water, creeping a tentacle closer and closer until she discovered the source. Blood. She wormed a sucker deep into the fleshy hollow.

A bubble escaped and her prize bobbed, threatening to drift away. She thrust a tentacle forward, plunging its barb deep into the bloodied flesh. Then, one eye turned to the spawn thrumming across the surface, she pulled the morsel close.

10

Fiordland, Conservation campsite

Taine scanned the edge of the trees, swathes of wiry mānuka spilling out from under the beech. The man on the ground had been shot. Was the shooter still in the area, watching them from the trees? If it were his call, Taine would send out scouts to sweep the area.

Except it's not my call.

Rocky made it to the foot of the slope. He gaped at the bloodied torso of the newcomer, his face turning as pale as doughnut frosting.

It wasn't a pretty sight. It'd been a miracle the man had still been on his feet when he stumbled into their campsite. He'd taken a bullet to his upper back and a glancing wound to his shoulder. There was an exit hole, which was lucky. It meant no hardware rattling around inside him to cause additional infection or injury. That didn't mean it wasn't dangerous. Or that it wouldn't hurt like all hell.

"How's he doing?" Rocky nodded to where Jules and Read were crouched over the injured man.

"Not fantastic," said Taine, keeping his voice low so the injured man wouldn't overhear. "A gunshot wound to the torso. The bleeding's slowed, but we can't know what's going on inside. A mess, most likely. We need to get him to a hospital."

"Do we know who he is?"

"Says his name is Tim Mahoe," Taine said. "From Invercargill."

"He's conscious?"

"For the moment." Conscious didn't mean out of danger. Taine had seen soldiers with bullet wounds. They could be talking one minute and dead the next. Sometimes, they'd hang on for hours. It was harrowing, and not only for the victim.

"Poor bugger," Rocky said, his eyes fixed on Mahoe.

Herewini arrived with the first aid kit. He pulled open the canvas kit, yanking out gauze bandages and adhesive tape. When he'd opened a dressing to slap over the wound, Read shuffled back to let him in.

"Anything we can do to help?" Barb called from where she and Jess were standing with Loughlin and Pringle a little back from the action.

"Could you see if anyone's got any painkillers? Paracetamol. Ibuprofen. Anything like that," Jules replied. "And something to keep him warm if you can. He's going into shock."

He wasn't the only one. Rocky looked like he might pass out.

"I'll come with you. I've got some painkillers in my pack," Jess said to Barb, peeling off from the others and heading up the hill with her. Their movement roused Rocky from his daydream.

"I better go, too, get the sat phone out and call the air ambulance," Rocky said. "If we're going to winch Mahoe into a chopper, we'll need to move him uphill away from the trees. It isn't going to be a pleasant wait for him. Best case scenario, the air ambulance is going to take a few hours to get here."

He turned to go, but Taine held his arm, stopping him. "Rocky, it isn't only the air ambulance we need. This isn't a hunting accident."

Rocky glanced down at Taine's hand.

Taine let go.

Rocky hitched his pants up over his belly and nodded. "You're probably right."

"Definitely right, I'd say," Read countered. "It's not like he was fiddling with his rifle and accidently shot himself in the foot. That was automatic fire we heard. Someone tried to kill this guy." His hands on his hips, he exhaled hard.

"It could have been an argument between mates that got out of hand," Rocky suggested. "Maybe they'd had a few."

Read threw up his hands. "That was rapid fire we heard!"

Taine stepped in before his private blew a gasket. "Mahoe claims he doesn't know who shot him. The only thing we know for certain is someone's running around the forest with an automatic rifle they're prepared to use."

Barb and Jess were coming down the hill with Wong, their arms laden with sleeping bags. Barb's eyes widened, and she sucked in a breath. Had Mahoe died? Taine turned to look.

A group of pale-skinned warriors stepped silently out of

the bush. Wearing only flimsy scraps of fabric, there was nothing flimsy about the spears they were brandishing.

"What the hell—" Rocky said.

Up until now, Jess hadn't seen the warriors. Startled, she panicked, dropping the sleeping bag she was carrying. With a shriek, she scrabbled backwards up the hill.

"Jess, don't—" Taine warned.

Too late.

She turned and ran. A spear whistled through the air.

Jules screamed.

The shaft sank deep into Jess' neck. It held her in space for an instant, held her hovering between life and death, before she crumpled to her knees, her blood fountaining from her severed carotid artery. The spear skewered her to the earth and she shuddered.

"Jess!" Rocky shouted, about to race up the hill to her, but screeching and howling, the warriors lunged for Rocky, their muscles bunched, spears at the ready.

"Rocky, don't move," Taine called. 'Not unless you want a spear in you, too."

Rocky pulled up.

"But Taine," Jules gasped. "Jess is hurt…"

"I know," Taine spoke softly. "We can't do anything for her now."

Loughlin raised his rifle. "Well, fucked if I'm standing here to be slaughtered. We're the ones with the guns."

Pringle was bringing the barrel of his rifle up when the warriors parted.

Herewini swore.

They had a cannon, the barrel resting on the shoulder of a woman every inch the warrior. An Amazon.

Another warrior, with an ugly burn on his forearm, leapt forward for a moment, thrusting his spear at Loughlin's face, then jumped back behind the barrel of the cannon. He let loose a stream of words. It wasn't English, it wasn't any language Taine could put his finger on, but his meaning was clear enough. He jabbed again in Loughlin's direction.

"Loughlin," Taine said quietly. "I think you might want to put your gun down. Slowly."

Loughlin didn't move. "What *is* that thing? A cannon? It's an antique if I ever saw one. What's the bet it won't fire? I bet they don't even have any shot."

"No way of knowing," Taine said, crouching to place his own weapon on the ground. "I think it could be a punt gun. They were used for hunting water birds in the 1800s, only they were banned for being too effective."

"Banned? These guys don't seem to have got the message," Barb said.

"If I'm right and it is a punt gun, a squeeze of the trigger could spew a half kilo of shot," said Taine. "And across a pretty big area."

"How big?"

"Tennis court."

"Bloody hell," said Read.

Spitting words, the burned warrior waved his spear angrily.

"Um... you guys," Herewini said. "All the chit-chat is pissing off this bloke, big time."

"Loughlin," Taine said.

To Taine's relief, Loughlin lowered his rifle and placed it on the ground. He raised his hands above his head. Beside him, Pringle did the same.

The burned warrior gave a satisfied grunt, then flicked both rifles down the hill with the tip of his spear. That done, he retreated up the ridge.

Smart move. Taine would have done the same. Higher ground gave the warrior psychological and tactical advantages.

Rocky dragged his eyes from Jess' corpse. "Who are you?" he said to the newcomers. "What do you want?"

What they wanted was for no one to escape. Jess' death was proof of that. Who were these people anyway? Plenty of tribes claimed this region as home, but Taine didn't believe these people were Ngāti Mamoe or Ngāi Tahu or any other hapu-subtribe. Nor were they a cult who'd decided to live off the grid, choosing to return to the ancient ways of living off the land. In that case, there'd be some vestige of their former lives still visible on them, things they could not bear to give up, like a cherished pendant or a watch. Instead, the only ornaments Taine could see were simple bone earrings and shell pendants. One of them wore a pūtōrino-flute on a flaxen string.

The warriors were babbling unintelligibly.

Still behind the barrel of the punt gun, the wide-nosed warrior with the flute hanging about his neck jabbed his spear, first at Herewini's chest and then at Jules, steering them out of the way. Out of instinct, Taine took a step forward.

The wide-nosed warrior's spear came within centimetres of his eye.

"I think he wants you all to move away from Mahoe," Rocky said.

"No kidding," said Herewini, who was giving the

dressing a final tug, securing it around Mahoe's chest. Mahoe groaned, then went quiet.

"You, too, Barb," Taine said softly, edging away. "This guy means business."

"I'm not moving," Jules addressed the warrior. She pointed to Mahoe's bandaged chest where already a blossom of red seeped through the gauze. "This man needs our help."

The warrior got louder, shaking his spear and stomping his feet. The wooden flute jangled wildly.

Taine clenched his fists. "Jules."

Please. He willed her to move. One thrust from the warrior and she'd be as dead as Jess.

"Jules," said Rocky. "You can't help him if you're injured. And that over there is a very big gun."

Jules hesitated, then, frowning, she eased away downhill. Taine breathed again.

"Okay, okay, take it easy," Herewini said as the spear poked at his stomach. Still mid-crouch, he moved towards Jules.

At his nine o'clock, Taine spied movement.

It was Wong. He'd inched his way back up the slope. The guide's gun had been slung over his shoulder while he carried the sleeping bags down to Jules, but now it was in his hands. Taine hoped he wouldn't do anything stupid. He turned his eyes to the warrior with the punt gun, praying he wasn't the nervous sort.

"Nobody move!" Wong screamed.

Taine's stomach sank. The gnarly warrior with the gun twitched...

Too far from Jules, Taine threw himself at Rocky and

Barb, arms outstretched, tackling them to the ground as the punt gun exploded.

Wait! Those fingers...

There was a blast.

Debris rained around them.

Jules was thrown to the ground, Herewini taking her with him. Shot and debris kicked up dirt like hailstones in a storm. All around her there was shouting. It was like an alien encounter, everyone screaming and no one understanding anything.

The stench of gunfire assaulted her. Her eardrums ached.

Jules raised her eyes and glimpsed the warrior with the gun propelled backwards a half a metre, a look of surprise on his face. To his credit, the man had kept his balance, and his feet. By some miracle, the barrel of the punt gun remained propped on the woman's shoulder. Her head had to be ringing, her eardrum burst.

Already Taine was on his feet. Knowing Taine, his plan would be to disarm the gunner in the commotion. Jules wanted to shout, to warn him, except she could barely get a breath: Herewini's weight had her pinned.

Before Taine could move, four spears turned in his direction.

"Is everyone all right?" Rocky called, still on the ground.

"I'm okay," Barb replied.

"Read. I'm safe."

"I'm fine," Loughlin said. "Pringle took a hit to his hip."

"It's just a bruise," Pringle said. "I'll live."

"Jules?" Taine said, without turning.

"A bit squished. Herewini isn't exactly a flyweight."

"Sorry." Herewini rolled away.

On her stomach, Jules flashed him a smile. The man's quick thinking had saved her from injury.

"Wong?" Rocky called.

Heart sinking, Jules looked around for their guide. The barrel of the punt gun, resting on the woman's shoulder throughout the mêlée, had been pointing up the ridge. Wong had taken the brunt of its fire. He wasn't moving.

The warrior with the burn, the one who'd flicked away Pringle and Loughlin's guns, was sprawled on the ground. He wasn't moving either. The warriors mustn't have known how far the shot would spread.

Taine knocked aside the spears with the back of his hand and pushed past the warriors if they were a bunch of pesky paparazzi. Jules shuddered. She clenched her jaw shut. Did the man have a death wish? Luckily, their captors, still startled by the power of the explosion, let him pass. He ran up the slope, pausing briefly to look at Wong before dashing to the fallen warrior.

Jules scrambled to her feet, glancing at Herewini as she rose.

"You go. I've got Mahoe," he said. Jules dashed up the hill to Wong.

Rocky reached him first. "No! No, no, no. He can't be dead."

Riddled with shot, Wong's right eye was missing, leaving only the bloodied socket. His jaw was slack, part of it blown away, and his skin, what remained of it, appeared plastic. It was as if he were wearing a ghoulish Halloween mask.

Jules fought back bile. He had to have died the instant the shot penetrated his skull.

Had to have...

Dragging her eyes away, she left Rocky with Wong, diving to her knees alongside Taine. He was up to his elbows in blood, trying desperately to cover the hole in the warrior's chest with his hands. Pink froth foamed between Taine's fingers.

"What can I do?"

"It's a sucking chest wound," Taine replied. "We have to seal off the cavity quickly or this guy will suffocate." Already, the man's pale skin had taken on a blue tinge. "There's a bag of scroggin in my trouser pocket. I need the plastic bag."

Jules went for a pocket at his hip, but Taine shook his head.

"Not that one. Right leg, on the side. Hurry."

She dug inside the pocket, found the bag, and flung the contents on the ground.

"Here."

Taine lifted his hands, then slapped the plastic dressing down over the wound, but not before Jules caught a glimpse of the man's lungs. She gasped. She'd never seen lung tissue that damaged before. Rather than pink and smooth, the lobes were stained dark red and frilled. The shot must have perforated the tissue, leaving the edges ragged and threadbare, like an old flag flapping too long in the wind. She swallowed. Out here in the wild, the man's chances were slimmer than a wafer.

"Jules, I need you to get me the adhesive tape and a wound dressing."

"On it." Jules raced back to Herewini, calling for the kit as she ran. "How's Mahoe doing?" she asked as Herewini passed her the kit.

Herewini rubbed the back of his arm across his face. "He's still alive. Gotta be hurting. We need to get him moved to a hospital pronto," he said.

Jules felt a surge of relief. She'd forgotten all about the ambulance, the police. As soon as the proper authorities got here, they'd get to the bottom of this, sort it out.

She was scooping up one of the sleeping bags when a thought hit her. "Did Rocky have time to call it in before…?"

Herewini shook his head.

Damn.

They couldn't worry about it now. Their first priority was stabilising these two. Saving their lives would come later.

Jules sprinted back to Taine with the gear. He'd done a good job creating a seal with the plastic bag. She'd only been gone a minute and already the dreadful sucking sound had improved. Still holding the bag in place, Taine shuffled back on his knees, allowing Jules to slip the bandage under the small of their patient's back. She was lifting the warrior's arm to bring the dressing over his chest when she noticed his fingers.

Syndactyly.

It was a common enough malformation. Affected something like one in every couple of thousand births. Here the syndactyly was near-complete, the man's digits connected near their tips, and instead of the fingers being fused tightly together in a club, they were separated by a wide flap of vascularised tissue. They were *webbed*. Jules' eyes flicked to the man's feet. Webbed.

And the others?

Jules cast her eyes around at the warriors holding them. She gave a start. Every one of them had webbed appendages.

Taine's steel grey gaze met her own. He'd seen it too.

11

———

The Catfish, Fiordland

After his shower, Meredith strode aft along the passageway to what had once been the sub's torpedo room, now used to store contraband. The rubber of his boots struck metal, the high-pitched squeak punctuating his steps. Meredith revelled in the sound. It was time to find out exactly what his new acquisitions were capable of.

He swooped into the room. "What have we got?" he asked Bones, his scientific director. Formerly a senior lecturer at a prestigious US university, Meredith had acquired Bones' services after the idiot had lost his tenure, and his wife, for an ill-advised fling with one of his students to whom he had awarded an 'A'. Although the grade had stuck, the undergrad hadn't. Meredith hoped for Bones' sake that the sex had been good. His name wasn't actually Bones. Meredith had thought it funny to reference the old Star Trek franchise, and since no one dared challenge him, the name had stuck.

"Nothing yet. We were waiting for you," Bones replied.

Earlier, Meredith had dismissed the others and appointed Jackson to guard detail. Jackson knew how to keep his mouth shut, and the fewer people who knew about these Mer-people, the better. Of the men aboard the Tango, fifty of them were paid grunts – Russians, Cambodians, and Filipinos mostly – while the rest were the submarine crew. It was the crew who concerned Meredith. Seamen were notoriously superstitious, and submarine crews had their own brand of weirdness. Probably something to do with being stuck for long periods under the ocean in a glorified baked bean tin. For a mariner, mermaids were symbols of doom. If word got out there were *mermaids* on board, who knew what might happen? They might jump ship or demand a sacrifice or something. The grunts didn't matter – they were disposable – but Meredith needed the salts to drive the boat.

"Right, let's get on with it," Meredith said impatiently.

"I thought we'd use the boy," said the scientist, waving a hand at the row of primate cages where their captives were being held.

Meredith swept his eyes over the mutants. The boy flinched under his gaze. He cradled his puffed-up wrist, the one that Meredith had stomped on this morning. Meredith raised his hand to his face, tracing his fingers along the scratch the boy had made.

"No," he said. "Not the boy. Use the female. The little one."

"With all due respect," Bones said, "it wouldn't be a particularly good test. Juvenile forms aren't likely to have the same resilience as adults, making it difficult to extrapolate results."

"Yes, except if anything happens, we'd still have a breeding pair."

"They're barely adolescent. I hardly think—"

"You hardly think what?"

Bones swallowed. He looked at the floor. "Nothing."

Meredith sat on a wooden crate to observe the proceedings. "Go ahead, Jackson."

Jackson dragged the smallest mutant out of her cage. Lifting her bodily, he dropped her into a large glass tank, pushing her head under the water before he sealed it. The Mer-girl hovered listlessly in the tank, staring out.

Come to think of it, there might've been a Star Trek episode a bit like this.

The creature drifted quietly, her hair swaying like seaweed.

Five minutes passed. Meredith had an egg sandwich brought to him from the galley while he waited. When he'd eaten it, he brushed a piece of yolk off his trousers.

"How long has it been now?" he demanded.

Bones checked his stopwatch. "Sixteen minutes, fifteen seconds." He blinked. "Sixteen minutes. And the water isn't even frozen, which would have served to slow down her metabolism. She ought to be dead. Oh wow. Just wow. I'm not sure you realise what we have here, Meredith. The ramifications are beyond imagining. The health applications alone—"

Meredith cut off the scientist's prattle with a wave of his hand. He doubted his eventual client would be too interested in the *health* applications.

"A find like this. I really think we should get her out. She might be getting to her limit, sir," Bones said. "We wouldn't want to lose her."

"She looks okay to me," Meredith said.

She looked fine, but she was agitated. Instead of drifting quietly in the tank, she was circling now, checking the corners, her eyes darting about. She wanted to get out. Needed to.

So, they could stay underwater, only not forever.

"Boss." Jackson tilted his head, indicating that Meredith should look at the other two. Their webbed hands gripped at the wire of the cages. Their lips were pursed, their brows creased as they watched their companion in the tank. The female raised her hands to her throat. They could have been any concerned bystanders at the scene of an accident.

He smiled. *They're capable of empathy.*

Jackson called from over by the tank. "Boss, want me to pull her out?"

Meredith kept his sights on the pair in the cages. "No need."

The Mer-girl's head whipped up. She narrowed her eyes.

"Meredith, I don't think you realise what you're risking," Bones intervened. "Each of these beings has a scientific value that is—"

"Shut up."

Meredith slid off the crate, his boots making a pleasing squeak as he landed. He sauntered over to the tank and put his fingers on the glass.

The girl in the water did not stop to look at him. She was too busy pushing at the walls, straining to break the water-proof adhesive. Meredith almost laughed as she banged on the glass and tried to force her mutant fingers between the panes. It was pitiful. A burst of bubbles erupted from her mouth.

Suddenly, a cage clanged behind him, the rattle urgent and demanding.

Meredith turned. The girl was throttling the bars, dark eyes flashing. In the adjacent cage, the boy didn't move. Meredith smiled.

Learned his lesson back at the hut, that one.

"Boss," Jackson said.

Meredith didn't glance back. "Our little mermaid looking a bit green around the gills, is she?"

"She's looked better. I think she might be dying."

"Let's just leave her in there a bit longer," he crooned. "See what happens."

Meredith watched the pair in the cages.

Bones' voice came at his back. "Commander Meredith, I really think—"

"I believe I told you to shut up, Bones."

The scientist scuttled away, and, judging by the sound of turning pages, suddenly discovered a keen interest in his paperwork.

Crouching, Meredith brought his face close to the girl in the cage, not close enough for her to scratch him with her nails – he wouldn't make that mistake a second time – but so she could feel his breath on her face.

She averted her eyes, refusing to look at him.

"You know," he whispered, "we don't need that little one. I think I'm going to let her die."

The girl in the cage let out a low moan.

"We're losing her," Jackson said. "Her eyes are rolling back!"

"Well, what do you expect?" Bones railed. "Of course she'll die. It's been twenty-one minutes. Twenty-one! No one can survive that."

The cage shook, and the girl screamed. "No! Out! Mere out!"

Startled, Bones dropped his clipboard.

Meredith smiled lazily. "Get her out, Jackson," he said.

Fiordland

Ka's heart pounded. He'd squeezed the belly of the gun.

Thunder had boomed. The gun belched flames. It was alive, its own living, breathing thing, and it did not favour the People. Bellowing with anger, it had punched Ka in the shoulder, throwing him backwards in disgust. Ka had battled to stay on his feet. It was faster than a tuatara's tongue, faster than a star shooting across the sky, the weapon's reach as good as any spear.

People fell.

Standing firm, Ka had held the silver trunk still while his cousin, Oma, pushed the little stick into the hole.

One of the strangers, skin like polished rimu and a pūrerehua about his neck, darted forward. It did not take him long to realise his companion was dead, killed by the gun's thunder. The dark one rushed to take out his vengeance on Māpura's brother, who lay on the ground nearby, his body laid open. If Wai was not already dead, he would be soon.

The weapon fed, Ka braced it against his shoulder.

But the chief had not given up hope of saving the children. While the strangers were scattered like gulls on the beach, he had sent his warriors to gather up their guns.

The Catfish, Fiordland

"You understand me," Meredith said.

The Mer-girl touched her webbed palm to the wires. The younger one in the crate beside her did the same, their palms joined. They spoke softly to each other in a language Meredith didn't understand. Ignoring him. Deliberately.

"Answer me!" he roared.

Both girls jumped.

Meredith did not like to be ignored. Not at all. He'd been ignored all his life. It'd started with his old man, who'd shot through the week before Meredith turned six. Meredith had never had so much as a birthday card from him since, not that he cared. These days, he could barely remember what the man looked like. Then there was his mother. She didn't leave, although perhaps things might have been better if she had. Instead, she'd married the man who owned the local picture theatre.

Meredith's new stepfather was a great guy. Everyone said so. A generous, attentive sort. Great with kids. Several nights a week, Uncle Gary used to look after little Meredith at the theatre while his mother worked her shift at the rest home, cleaning up old people's vomit. Meredith and Uncle Gary would sit up the back in the projectionist's booth where Uncle Gary had a game he liked to play to pass the time. Meredith hadn't liked the game, and he'd told his mother as much.

She'd turned on him then, her eyes tired and her hair limp after her shift at the rest home. "Well, let me ask you this, son," she'd said quietly. "Do you like to eat, because it's your Uncle Gary's job that's putting the food on the table." After that she had gone into the bathroom and closed the door. Meredith had heard the shower start up.

Unfortunately, Uncle Gary had found out about Meredith's betrayal and he hadn't been pleased. Nobody liked tattle-tales. Uncle Gary said there would need to be consequences, so Meredith became well acquainted with Uncle Gary's belt.

Among other things.

Meredith was smart: he'd learned to play the game, eating the food Uncle Gary so generously put on the table, and biding his time. When Meredith was fifteen, he was a foot taller than Gary and thirty pounds heavier. Uncle Gary decided the game didn't have the same appeal. Meredith stuck it out another year, got his GED, and joined the army the day he turned seventeen, signing his mother's consent on the enlistment forms.

He'd found his own way to screw Uncle Gary.

To start with, the army had just been a means of escape, but Meredith found he had an aptitude for certain precision skills. He'd worked hard on improving those skills. And since it was the army, where people are paid to kill, he should have got some recognition for his abilities. Several years passed, and Meredith couldn't get a break. Every promotion he'd applied for got knocked back.

In the end, he'd discovered the army's perfidy by chance. He'd been seeing a girl in the medical corps, nothing serious on his side, although she seemed to have a thing for him, and, on a dare, she'd got him a look at his personal records. Where was the harm, right? It was information about him, so why shouldn't he know it? The contents of that file had been revelatory. Turns out the army psychologists hadn't liked what they'd seen, claiming Meredith was too aggressive and lacked empathy. They said he was a borderline sociopath and was best kept to the rank and file. He'd been pissed as hell. Smarmy two-faced gits. Meredith had been in this situation before, so he knew the drill. He bided his time, honing his skills, while he served out his tour.

Now he ran his own business, using the same special skills Uncle Sam had trained him in. Now, nobody ignored Ajax Meredith. People listened when he spoke – and that included mutant Mer-kids plucked from a backwater at the arse end of the world...

Meredith ripped open the cage and dragged the older one into the room by her hair, slamming the cage shut after her. He yanked her head backwards. "You answer me, or I'll have Jackson put both your friends back in that tank and, if I do, they won't be getting out. Ever. Do you understand?"

The girl blinked quickly. Nodded.

Meredith let her go. She slumped to the floor.

"Right, what's your name?" he said, squatting close.

She blinked again.

He pushed his face into hers. "Your name!"

"I am Ro," she said.

"And what...what are you?"

"I am of the People."

"What fucking people?"

She shrugged. "The People."

"How many of you are there?"

She shook her head.

"How many!?" he roared, watching her flinch.

"I suspect she has no concept of numbers, sir," Bones interrupted. "It's very common amongst primitive peoples, the lost tribes in the rain forests of Peru and Brazil, for example. Typically, they're incapable of counting above ten and they only manage ten because they have fingers – or spaces between their fingers – and since these creatures don't even have that..."

A bag of animal pellets was leaning against one of the crates. Meredith tore open the bag, spreading pellets on the floor with a sweep of his hand.

"How many people?"

The girl shook her head.

Meredith grabbed her webbed hands and held them out. He took one pellet, held it before her, then put in her palm.

"Ro," he said. He took another pellet and pointed to the Mer-boy.

"Tau," she said.

"Tau." Meredith put a second pellet in her hand. Then, he added a third pellet. "Mere."

He pushed a pile of pellets towards her. "How many people?"

She pursed her lips.

Meredith jerked her around by her hair and pressed her face against the bars. "Want me to put your little friends in the tank?"

She inhaled deeply, then she pushed him away, got on her hands and knees and dragged a bunch of the pellets towards her. She made a pile. When she was done, she sat back on her haunches, her pale face even paler.

"Bones, count them."

Bones sifted through the pellets. "Forty-three," he said.

Forty-three. Meredith smiled. Captured or killed, they were all billable.

Jackson was leaning on his rifle near the door. "Think she's telling the truth?" he asked.

"Well, if she's not, we'll be down two passengers," Meredith said.

Meredith went back to his quarters to contact his client with the information. The client wanted the product, no question about that. They offered him a deal, one which would allow Meredith to pay out his men and buy a small island somewhere. Possibly two islands if he played his cards right. Only, they wanted more than the three specimens that Meredith had in hand, which meant another trip ashore.

"A minimum of fifteen specimens," the translator said. "Can you secure them?"

There were forty-three of them somewhere, according to the girl, Ro. A small enough community to have remained hidden in the deep grooves hacked out in the land. No doubt his little charge could be persuaded to reveal their whereabouts.

"Yes, I can get them."

There was a delay before the translator came back on the line. Her voice was sharp, like chalk on a blackboard.

"Excellent. But our mutual friends would like assurances that our competitors will not see the product."

"I've given you my word."

"Hmmm. It's not enough. Our friends would like exclusive access to the...blueprint, and for that..."

Meredith realised what the woman intended. "You want me to *eradicate* the possibility of anyone else obtaining the surplus material."

She gave a small cough. "You understand us."

Meredith nodded. Slightly messy, but it made good business sense. "Exclusive will cost you extra."

"Of course."

"Give me twenty-four hours," he said.

"Twelve."

"Eighteen."

"I'll expect your call."

Meredith checked his watch. He had until dawn.

He ordered the pilot to ready the sub for surfacing, while Jackson gathered eight men to go ashore. They were congregating in the passageway when Bones appeared, dragging the smallest Mer-kid by the arm. Meredith was counting on her natural instinct to run home to Mummy. Already, she looked beaten, her eyes downcast and her hair hanging limp down her back. She was wearing a long-sleeved t-shirt, cinched in at the waist with a piece of thin rope. As a precaution, Bones had ensured the sleeves dangled over her hands, hiding her deformity. The sight of those sleeves made Meredith think of his grade school history lessons, and of Anne Boleyn, Henry the Eighth's second queen, one of the ones who'd been beheaded. The unfortunate queen had worn long sleeves, supposedly to cover a mutant sixth finger, but when they'd dug her up, it turned out her fingers were like everyone else's.

Well, that wasn't the case here. There'd be no need to exhume Meredith's specimens. Not unless they failed to cooperate.

The radio operator stepped into the passageway. "Boss."

Meredith turned. "What is it?" he snapped. "We're a little busy here."

"I'm picking up encrypted radio traffic out of Burnham."

"What of it?"

"Burnham's a military base. Just out of Christchurch, it's the country's largest army installation this far south."

Meredith grunted. "There's always traffic. New Zealand's part of the Five Eyes intelligence alliance. Its partners continually send out signals to cover their activity." Impatient, he pulled the heel of his boot across the floor, the rubber emitting a delightful squeal.

The radio operator swallowed. "What I'm picking up are *bursts* of encrypted traffic, typical of hand-held P25s. It's probably nothing, but it could be the New Zealand army's got wind of us."

"The runner must have made it," Jackson said.

"Hmm." Meredith fingered the scratch on his cheek.

So what if the army knew they were here? It didn't matter. Burnham was a long way off and New Zealand had a ridiculous tin-pot army anyway – made up of reservists and unemployable riff-raff by all accounts. By the time that lot had hiked their sorry arses into the bush, Meredith and his men would have picked up the merchandise, deleted any chance of competition, and hauled anchor out of there.

"Tell the pilot to bring us up," he barked.

12

"What's going on?" Behind Taine, Barb's voice was shrill.

They were being bustled along at spear-point, herded downhill towards the bush, away from the campsite, from Wong and Jess' bodies and any chance of calling for help. Taine had placed himself between the group and the tips of the spears.

"They're taking us somewhere," Pringle said, keeping his voice low. "They must want something from us."

"What, though?"

"My money's on the Sankara Stones," Loughlin quipped.

"Can we please not talk about the *Temple of Doom*?" said Barb.

One of the warriors picked up Mahoe and slung him over his back. Mahoe shrieked in agony.

"Stop! No! You'll kill him!" Jules moved to step out of line. Taine grabbed her by the arm and held her back. He turned to Rocky, expecting him to react, to take charge as he had earlier, but the Conservation officer remained in the group. It was clear the loss of Wong had rattled him. Taine shouldn't be surprised. While deer shooting accidents were rare enough, colleagues gunned down by lost tribes were unlikely to be covered in the Conservation Officer's handbook. It didn't feature highly in NZDF manuals either.

"What are we supposed to do?" Rocky said. His face was sallow and long smears of Wong's blood stained the front of his trousers. "They're the ones with the weapons. They don't even speak English."

"They can't understand what we say, but we can show them," Taine said. Releasing Jules' arm, he scooped up one of the sleeping bags. The nearest warrior, the one with the flute about his neck, hissed.

"Easy." Taine raised his hands, letting the bag dangle from his fingers. The warrior stabbed at Taine's shoulder, the sharpened flint tip piercing his clothing and drawing blood.

Jules sucked in her breath. "Taine."

"It's okay."

The warrior was right to be wary. It was a common ploy to distract an enemy, diverting their attention with something banal, while you launched your attack elsewhere. These warriors might have been surprised by the force of the punt gun, but Taine's instincts told him they were well trained. He had no intention of riling them up. He zipped up the sleeping bag.

"You better not get us killed, McKenna," Loughlin said.

"Doing my best." Slowly, as if he were a tai chi master, Taine crouched and picked up a branch, threading it into the fabric. All the while, the warrior with the flute followed him with his eyes.

Read cottoned on to what Taine was building. "There's a branch over there that would make a good pole." He sidled toward the treeline, his eyes on their captors. He swung on the branch until it broke away.

The warrior bunched his shoulders and hissed, jabbing in Read's direction with his spear, but this time he kept his distance. It was more warning than threat. Letting Taine and Read know that he was prepared.

"Slowly," Taine warned. "Don't carry it like a weapon. Our man here is a little uptight."

Read handed Taine the pole. He'd already stripped it of small branches. Taine pushed it through the sleeping bag. It wasn't the sturdiest of stretchers, but Mahoe was lean. They laid the stretcher on the ground.

Nudging Loughlin, Pringle stooped to pick up another sleeping bag. "John. We need to make one of those too. To carry the other guy."

"On it. I'll grab a couple of branches." Loughlin strode towards the treeline, gesturing at the stretcher so the warriors would let him through. Taine saw him tugging at a branch. The next minute, he bolted.

Time to get out of here.

Loughlin took off, running as fast as he could down the valley. Jess had a spear through her neck, Wong was dead, killed with a fucking punt gun, and Rocky had obviously lost it if he was willing to let a slew of brutal savages herd them who knows where. The soldier boys could play at being calm, but there was no way he was going to follow along as docile as sheep in a run. Those warriors could be cannibals for all they knew!

A shout rang out behind him. It wasn't English. The savages realising he'd escaped?

Loughlin's adrenalin surged. He wasn't going to wait around to find out. Shucking off his Hi-Viz, he flung it into the bushes and sprinted on, dodging tree trunks, thrusting away the branches that tore at his clothes. Light slanted through the canopy, shafts strobing through the trunks: intense then dull, sharp then dark. His eyes watered. The canopy disappeared and he burst into the open. The glare dazzled him.

Idiot. Get back under cover.

First, he had to get across this stream. He slowed to navigate the rocks. He couldn't afford to turn an ankle.

Time slowed.

Loughlin waded through the water, cringing at the noise he was making. He held his breath, expecting to hear his pursuers at any moment. Waiting for a shaft to plunge into his neck, his back, his head...

He was still wearing his beanie! Vibrant orange, the hat was supposed to identify him to other hunters, but right now it was a beacon. A target. Loughlin whipped it off and stuffed it in his pocket. Still no zinging of spears. No more shouts. Loughlin buzzed with hope. Maybe they would let him go?

He splashed out of the stream and into the woods. The slope on this side of the valley was steeper, the going even slower. Thankfully, the bush was as thick as seaweed. He didn't look back. Better to keep climbing. Get ahead. Loughlin ran on, his legs and chest burning with exertion.

Still alive. Half way up the cliff, the gradient got even steeper, so he put his hands down and clawed his way up, hand over fist, using the tree trunks and boulders to haul his body forward. A spear thudded to the ground in front of him, the shaft trembling as it penetrated the earth.

Holy shit!

Swerving, Loughlin ploughed on, the roar of his heart loud in his ears. Okay, so they were after him. This was bad. If they caught him, they'd kill him. Sure as taxes. He had to get over the ridge, put some distance between them. He put on a burst of speed, weaving from side to side as he clambered up the slope. With a bit of luck his ducking and diving would make it harder for the bastards to pick him off.

Another spear.

From the left this time. It clattered against a boulder and fell away.

Loughlin's heart almost failed.

Too bloody close.

Suddenly, his calf shattered in pain. Twisting, Loughlin looked down. A spear to his calf. Not the meaty part, but deep enough. Loughlin took a breath and scanned the terrain below him. How far away were they? As far as a man could throw. But the trees were thick here, which meant they were closer. There was no time for cosmetic surgery. He grasped the spear and yanked, his scream shattering the quiet of the forest. Stars pricked his eyes and, for a second, he worried he'd pass out. He breathed in. Out. The dizziness cleared. Flinging the spear away, he climbed for his life, dragging himself the last few metres to the top of the ridge.

Shit.

He almost toppled. He threw out his arms. Regained his balance.

The drop was steep. At least six stories. A shingle slope down to rocks. He considered diving. The Sounds were deep. The way people talked you'd think some of them went half way to China. But they weren't deep everywhere. If he didn't leap far enough, he could strike shallow water and break his neck.

A spear whistled past him. Loughlin flinched.

Decision time!

Dropping to his bum, Loughlin scooted forward, hurling himself over the ridge, feet first, bracing himself with the heel of his boots, and clutching at roots. Half the mountain came away with him, scree, dust, and rocks racing alongside him. Two boulders the size of ovens bounced down the slope and exploded into the water. The splash echoed through the canyon, spray fanning out and falling on the rocks.

It was deep then. Dive now? No, too many rocks.

Loughlin continued his slip-slide down the slope. His pants tore. His skin burned; his arse was being grazed off. He gritted his teeth against the pain and kept skidding. He wasn't going to be an hors d'oeuvre, served up on a spike for a bunch of pale-skinned brutes. A rock hit his elbow and he bellowed in pain. Grabbing the joint with his hand, he kept sliding, twisting as he went to look back up the ridge.

The natives were watching. Why didn't they hurl their spears? He wasn't that far.

Who fucking cares?

Loughlin leapt the last few metres to the bottom of the cliff and ducked behind a shelf of rock.

The men at the top of the ridge screamed. He'd clearly pissed them off. He waited for the rain of spears that never came. Why not? Maybe they didn't want to lose their weapons. It was a smart policy, something he'd learned at Corrections. You didn't give a prisoner access to a weapon they could use against you.

What was happening up there? Loughlin peeked out quickly. Nothing. They were gone. Exhaling hard, he pushed the sweat out of his eyes. The cliff had done it. Deterred them. They'd given up. All he had to do now was swim across the inlet to the woods on the other side. It wasn't that far. Maybe a couple of hundred metres. Four lengths of a pool. The natives could try to cut him off by going around the inlet, but he was a strong swimmer; by the time they made it to the other side, he'd be long gone. He would hoof it back into town and alert the authorities. It might take him a day or two to get there – he wasn't sure exactly where he was – but if he was lucky, the others might still be alive. He felt a twinge of guilt. He wasn't proud of himself for leaving Pringle, but then he hadn't known he was going to run until the moment came. Rocky was never going to get them out of this. McKenna and Read might be up to it, but it wasn't their watch. He was their only chance. Pringle would just have to suck it up.

Loughlin tore a strip off his t-shirt and tied it around his calf, knotting the ends tight. The wound was still bleeding, but the cold water would slow it down. Wincing as the water stung the grazes on his arse and legs, Loughlin lowered himself into the dark waters of the Sounds.

～

Taine caught their movement in his peripheral vision: the three warriors who'd been sent after Loughlin. They slipped from the bush, joining the guards on either side of the stretchers as they crossed an iron sand beach.

"They're back," Herewini said. Up ahead, Herewini and Pringle were carrying the injured warrior, Herewini at the front and Pringle at the rear. The fine black sand sank underfoot, and the pair struggled to keep the stretcher balanced. Taine and Read weren't doing much better.

"Where's John?" called Barb, who was following with Jules. "Why isn't he with them?"

"He's fine. He got away," Pringle said, matter of fact. "I know John, and he'll be halfway to Invercargill by now. As soon as he gets there, he'll send someone out to rescue us."

"I hope you're right, man, but let's just say I don't think we should count on it," Herewini said, jerking his head to the left. Taine followed the movement and spied Loughlin's orange Hi-Viz tucked into the fabric at the waist of a warrior.

Pringle saw it too. "That doesn't mean anything," he insisted. "John will have tossed that away deliberately so they couldn't pick him out against the trees. He's a Corrections officer; you can trust him to know a thing or two about escapes."

"I still don't understand why they want us. We didn't do anything," said Barb.

"Everything's going to be fine," Jules reassured her. "All we need to do is to keep calm and go along with them for now. When we find out what they want, we'll give it to them and then we'll be on our way."

"You think so?"

"I do."

"I don't remember kidnap and dodging spears being on the brochure."

Taine imagined Jules' smile. "Oh, you know, we Kiwis like to deliver a little extra excitement," she said.

Tim came to. All he could feel was hurt. Every breath was agony. His chest and back were on fire, and he barely had the strength to lift his head. He let his eyes flit about and his heart sank. He'd only jumped out of the fire and into the frying pan! He was on a stretcher and they were carting him somewhere, his rescuers led at spear-point by the Merpeople. Something told him they weren't planning on taking him to a hospital. No, no, no. He needed a hospital. A hospital with an operating theatre. Real doctors...anaesthesia.

One after the other, his stretcher bearers clambered over a rotting trunk, the stretcher jolting awkwardly. Tim held his breath, the pain too much to bear. He exhaled slowly, trying desperately to breathe without moving his ribs. This was all Digby's fault. Tim wished he'd never met him, never let himself be dragged down.

Yeah, right.

If he was going to die, he may as well be honest, at least, with himself. The truth was, he'd been dragged down years ago, the urge for just one more flutter snaking into his life like a curl of cigarette smoke up a flared nostril. He'd brought this on himself.

It wasn't just him, though. Now these people were

caught up in it all. And the children. God knows where they'd be sent, what horrors were in store for them. Tim doubted they would ever see their parents again. Maybe the Mer-people would kill him for it. He could hardly blame them.

Tears came. His gambling had messed up everything. If he made it through this, if he survived, he was going to sort himself out. He'd go to counselling, Gamblers Anonymous, whatever it took. And if he didn't make it, well, dying was one way to make your debts go away. The stretcher jolted again. Tim groaned as pain carried him back into darkness.

13
___

Fiordland

Taine and Read put the stretcher down. Mahoe was out cold. Even with the stretcher, the jarring 40-minute walk through the bush had to have near killed him.

Rubbing away a cramp in his palm, Taine looked around. They were in a space the size of a school quadrangle. High above them, a canopy of tōtara and beech covered the sky, but otherwise the area had been cleared. It was as if they were standing in a cathedral.

Their captors herded them against a rock wall that bounded the space on one side, and forced them to sit down, the spears giving way to that punt gun again, now that there was space to use it.

"We should have isolated that cannon when we had the chance," Read said.

"It was better to be cautious, Matt," Taine said. "There was no way of knowing whether a firearm that ancient was capable of firing."

"I recall there were a whole lot of spears pointed at us," Pringle reminded him.

"That didn't stop McKenna, though, did it? He waltzed right past them," Read said.

"I took advantage of their confusion," Taine said.

"You could've been killed," Jules replied.

Rocky cut across their chatter. "Hey, is that a helicopter?"

Taine peered across the clearing. It definitely was a chopper and, from the looks of it, it'd been there a while, the metal hull so covered in moss and vines it was barely visible.

Jules drew in a breath. "Look."

An old man wearing a pair of shorts and a threadbare Swanndri emerged from what had once been the helicopter's cockpit. His shaggy beard streaked with white, he looked for all the world like Rip Van Winkle, just woken from twenty years of sleep. Speaking briefly to the warriors, he limped forward, dragging his left leg at the knee and stopping his advance behind the barrel of the punt gun.

"Hello." He coughed awkwardly, then started again. "It's a little late as rescues go, but I've got to say, it's nice to welcome new residents. David Summers is the name. Welcome to my little place in the Sounds."

To Taine's surprise, Rocky got to his feet. "Tom Stone, Conservation. Call me Rocky." Too far away to shake hands, Rocky put his hands in his pockets instead. "Did I just hear you speak to these guys?"

"I should hope so. I've been living amongst them for over forty years. Would've been a bit slack if I hadn't learned a word or two."

"Forty years?" Pringle said. "We release murderers sooner than that!"

"What's all this about?" Rocky demanded. "Who are these people? Why are they holding us? We're in the park on a Conservation trip, and they killed two of my staff." He waved his arm towards the stretchers. "And these two need to get to a hospital."

Summers shook his head. "Sorry, no can do. You won't be going anywhere. Not until we get the children back."

"What children?" Jules interrupted.

"The three who were stolen."

Taine stood up. "I can assure you, none of us know anything about any children," he said.

"That man knows," Summers said, pointing at Mahoe.

Mahoe had regained consciousness. His eyes went wide. "It was Digby!" he croaked, his breath shallow against the pain. "It was *his* contact. He called the men in black. They shot Digby and took the kids."

Rocky took a step forward and gripped Mahoe's arm. "You know about this? You know who took these people's children?"

"You piece of shit," Pringle hissed. "No wonder they have it in for us. I know crims who have a better moral code."

"Mahoe," Taine said quietly, "if you know anything, you need to tell us. Our safety might depend on it. Who took these people's children? Where did they go?"

"I don't know," Mahoe rasped. "Digby didn't tell me. It wasn't my idea. This thing with the kids, I mean. It was just going to be a couple of parrots, but then we saw the children in the water, so we knew."

"Knew what?" McKenna asked.

"What they could do," he whispered.

Tim drew in a breath.

His spear raised, a warrior sprinted at him, his face as hard as flint.

Weaker than a baby, he was helpless. He couldn't move. Couldn't get away. Just the effort of talking, of breathing, was excruciating.

The man hurtled toward him. It was like watching an elephant charge, everything happening in slow motion. He was in a dream, trying to run, his legs refusing to move, as if he were mired in quicksand.

The warrior twisted. He pulled his arm back...

Tim's blood ran cold. He was going to die, like that woman in the campsite. There'd be no second chance. No way for him to clean up his act now. He raised his arm across his face and prayed the spear was sharp.

McKenna pivoted. He stepped over Tim, his body in the path of the spear. "Kill him and you might never find your children," he shouted at the rampaging warrior. "Summers, tell him!" he roared.

The blackened tip of the spear kept coming.

McKenna held his ground.

The air was electric, as if a thunderstorm was about to break.

At last, Summers rattled out a hoarse translation.

The warrior slowed but didn't stop. He dropped the spear and kept coming. Tim heard a woman gasp as the warrior pulled up just centimetres from McKenna. Reaching out, he snatched at McKenna's neck, tearing something free, then he leapt back.

The whole time, McKenna hadn't so much as flinched.

Taine's skin burned where the pūrerehua had been ripped free. He grabbed at his chest, clutching at air. It wasn't like him to get attached to things, but the pūrerehua was different. He'd become accustomed to wearing it under his t-shirt, the sliver of wood warm against his heart. It was tapu. Sacred.

Already the wide-nosed warrior was spinning the pūrerehua above his head, the instrument singing as it circled in the air. If Taine stepped any closer, he was likely to get a chunk of flesh taken out of him. He might lose an eye. He stood back and waited.

Inside the spinning circle, the warrior stared out, his expression blank. His lips moved silently, as if he were praying, then his face softened and he grimaced. Suddenly, he dropped the pūrerehua as if it were a hot coal. Glaring at the instrument lying in the dirt, he kicked it back to Taine and walked away.

Rotorua township

After a bad night, Temera was in the shed, trying to get a little afternoon shut-eye in his armchair, when he heard the morepork's call. He cast around for the dark presence that had been hounding him, and, sensing nothing, gave himself over to his spirit self, stepping into the damp air of the forest.

"So where are we off to today, old friend?" he asked, jumping up on his exuberant nine-year-old legs in a lame attempt to grasp the tail feathers of the little owl.

Hooting scornfully, the morepork soared upwards to perch on the lower branches of a sturdy tōtara.

"Well, I'm ready. If we're going to go, let's do it."

The morepork ignored him. That was odd. Normally, the little scallywag raced on ahead and it was Temera's job to keep up with her. Mind you, she'd never visited him in the daytime before either. "Come on. I'm sorry, okay? I didn't mean to snatch at your feathers."

The owl twisted her head around and faced the other way.

Suddenly, Temera felt the call of the oblong pūrerehua on the leather strap about his neck. Is that what this was about? Was Taine in trouble? Temera clutched the bull-roarer in his hand. "Taine?"

Nothing.

Temera moved to a clearing, let the cord out and twirled the instrument around his head, increasing the cadence until the cord thrummed in his hand. The carved blade of the pūrerehua whistled cheerfully.

Playing the pūrerehua connected Temera to the spirit world and especially to Taine McKenna. Like most things to do with Temera's gift, the finer points of how it worked were a mystery. Just over a year ago, with no understanding of why he was doing it, Temera had chiselled the pūrerehua in his potting shed. At the same time, the NZDF soldier had been whittling his own bullroarer from a piece of matai he'd found deep in the Urewera forest. Without knowing it, both of them had adorned their instruments with the same intricate whorls, the same sweeping curves, investing their work with the same ancient magic. Perhaps Tāne, God of the forest, had had a hand in binding their spirits – their wairua – together, because now when they touched their respective pūrerehua, they were able to step into the spirit world and find one another.

Closing his eyes, Temera pictured his friend, only it wasn't Taine who appeared. Instead, the image of a pale-skinned man with a wide nose came to him.

"Who are you?" Temera demanded.

"I am Māpura." Temera felt rather than heard the words, the way you feel the hum of a refrigerator.

"Where's Taine? And why are you using his pūrerehua?"

"Pūrerehua. Ah, so you are Māori? You must be to use that term. Are you Ngāti Tama?" The warrior's eyes flashed angrily.

"I am Rawiri Temera of the Ngāi Tūhoe tribe." Temera recited his whakapapa, telling the stranger of his place in the universe, his ancestors, his mountain Te Maunga, and his connection to the land.

"I know of that place," Māpura said when Temera ended his introduction. Whakapapa was good at helping you to connect with people. It was a way of uncovering the places and people you had in common. Not this time. Temera sensed a barrier go up between them, like the sharpened spikes of a palisade around an ancient village.

Temera allowed the spinning pūrerehua to slow so it looped in big languid movements. "Why have you summoned me?" he whispered. "Is Taine safe?"

Māpura frowned. He stamped his foot, causing the pūtōrino-flute hanging at his neck to bang against the muscles of his chest. "I don't want to hurt your friend. My brother, Wai, still lives because of him. But he can't leave. No one can leave."

Temera's heart thundered. "What are you saying? That Taine's life is at risk? Where is he? Look, you can trust Taine. I know he won't say anything—"

"We cannot trust anyone. We have to kill the strangers before they kill us."

"No, look, I'm sure that's not true," Temera blurted, his young voice breaking. "No one wants to harm you."

The warrior shook his head. "What do you know? You are just a boy. You haven't lived long enough to see how the world is. It can be cruel. My people know this. We came to these shores long ago, before the Māori and the Moriori in their waka, before the white men in their tall ships with their strange clothes and their guns. This land was our home, from the soaring mountains to the grassy plateau stretching as far as a man could see, and lakes so deep you might never reach the bottom. There was plenty for every-one. We were happy to share. That was not enough for you others. You wanted it all for yourselves. Our land, our livelihood, and now even our children." Māpura's face contorted in pain. "It is not enough that strangers have stolen our past, now you want to steal away our future, too."

"Taine has nothing to do with any of that," Temera said. "I know him. You just have to explain. He'll help you."

Māpura cackled. "Do you know how often my people have heard that? They all came talking of peace. Peace is impossible. Look at what happened to the people of Rēkohu. Do you know that island?"

The warrior was speaking of an island off the bottom of the South Island. "Yes. We know it as Chatham Island now," Temera replied.

"Did you know that many seasons ago a ferocious battle took place there, leaving many of the local people dead? After that battle, their chief, Nunuku-whenua was tired of war. He wanted peace. Nunuku cried: 'From now and forever, never again let there be war as this day has seen!' That was his law. It was a good law. For twenty generations, his people lived in peace. They might still be at peace, only the Ngāti Mutunga and Ngāti Tama tribes had other ideas."

Temera let the pūrerehua slow to a stop. He pressed himself against the trunk of the tōtara, grateful for its sturdiness against his spine, and closed his eyes. "He wāhine, he whenua, e ngaro ait e tangata," he said, quoting an old proverb.

Through women and land do men die.

"Ah, so you know the story," said Māpura. "Then you will know it is a brutal and bloody tale. Nine hundred warriors paddled across the sea to kill Nunuku's people and steal the island from them. Afterwards, you could count the survivors on the fingers of a single man."

Māpura sniffed. "Nunuku's people were not our people – they were nothing to us – and so far away across the sea to the north, yet we cursed the wind that day. The victors staked the survivors out on the beach. The screams of dying souls reached us in our dreams."

"Why are you telling me this?"

"Our people are few. Perhaps we are the last of our kind.

If we are to endure, no one must know of us. You should take the chance to say goodbye to your friend."

Temera's eyes flew open. "No, wait—"

Like a dead spot in cell coverage, the connection dulled and dropped out. The pale-skinned warrior faded from view.

High up in the tōtara, the little morepork hooted sadly.

14

Seated in his armchair in the potting shed, Temera's heart pounded so hard he could've been Scott Dixon rounding the last bend at Daytona. If this kept up, his old ticker might just give out. He needed to calm down and think.

With shaking hands, Temera felt for the packet on the ledge, and placed a cigarette between his lips. Just having it there was a relief. He lit the ciggie, shook the match out, and took a deep drag. Then blew out slowly.

Taine was in danger, that much was certain, but was it happening right now, or was his vision a dream of something still to come? If it were happening now, where exactly was it happening? And what could Temera do?

Well, first thing you can do is call him. He's probably at home, watching television or something. How stupid are you going to feel then?

Only one way to find out. Leaning forward, Temera grabbed his cell phone from the workbench. It was an old one. Pania and Wayne said it officially labelled him as an old fogey. It was worse than wearing checked trousers, apparently. They said they'd take him into the mall and get it upgraded, kept going on about all these new apps that could do amazing things. Temera wasn't interested in running about the neighbourhood chasing Pokey-thingies. Phones were for making phone calls, not all that other rubbish. Still holding his cigarette, he punched speed dial and selected Taine's number.

Taine's voice was far off. "McKenna. I'm not here right now. Leave a message."

Temera pushed the red spot to end the call and dropped the phone in his lap. So, Taine was away. That didn't mean whatever was happening was happening now. Taine could be at the supermarket or something. Temera chuckled. He had a hard time imagining his friend doing anything as mundane and everyday as grocery shopping. Yet, for the first time ever, Temera's spirit-guide had come to him in the daytime. That had to be significant.

Just as Taine's telephone message was significant.

Temera sucked on his cigarette and replayed the conversation with Māpura in his mind. Temera had recited his whakapapa, but Māpura had left him in the dark about his own. Still, he'd offered Temera a few clues...a people who came to the land before the Māori. It was well known there had been others once. It was one of those hush-hush things you didn't talk about, like extra-marital sex or illegitimate kids back in the 60s. No one was denying there had already been people living in New Zealand when Temera's ancestors had arrived. Where were those people now? Did they get assimilated into other communities, or were they chased away? Someone had to know. They were people, not ghosts...

Ghosts!

A memory came to him. He'd been twelve, it was the summer holidays, and he'd been hanging round at home with his mātua. As usual, when it came to the old teacher, there was a story involved...

"A chief named Kahukura was on a journey to Te Rarawa," Mātua Rata began. He was sitting cross-legged on the concrete step of Temera's parents' state house, carving a design in a piece of matai.

"Where is Te Rarawa? Have I been there?" Temera interrupted. The concrete was warm under his legs.

"It's north of here, on the coast, and no, you haven't been there." Squinting against the sunshine, Mātua carried on with his carving. "On the way to Te Rarawa, Chief Kahukura passed by a beach littered with fish guts. They'd been left there recently because the gulls hadn't eaten them yet, and nor had they been swept away by the tide. Someone had to have been cleaning their catch during the night. But who? No one lived in the area. Kahukura decided that the fish had been caught by the Tūrehu—"

"You mean the Patu-paiarehe? The fairy people?"

"Yes, they are the same. People say they're ghosts. They say aituā, Death, hasn't carried them away in his waka yet, which is why the Tūrehu are stuck here, haunting the earth."

"Why did the chief think they were the Tūrehu?"

Mātua had laid his carving on the step. "I was getting to that," he said sternly. "It was because there were no rushes scattered on the sand. Māori know to put rushes in the bottom of our canoes to stop the smell of fish seeping into the wood. But Kahukura couldn't find any rushes. He was sure the fairy people had been there. He decided to come back to see if they would return to the beach the next night."

"They did," Temera said.

Mātua raised his eyebrows. "And how do you know that?"

Picking at the concrete with his fingernails, Temera grinned. "Because otherwise there'd be no story, would there?"

Mātua clipped him on the knee. "You think you're so clever, don't you? Well, you're right. That night, Kahukura became one of the few people to see the Tūrehu. Slipping out of the dunes, he joined them in the darkness, helping them to haul in the net of knotted rushes. When it was done, there were fish all over the beach. Kahukura couldn't believe his eyes. There were so many, one for every star in the sky, all jumping and squirming, their silvery bodies flashing in the moonlight. Up until then, our people had always used a hook and line to fish. Kahukura could see that with a net like that, no one would go hungry He decided he would take the knowledge home to his people."

"Aie, you just told me the ending, Mātua."

Mātua lifted his work to his face, blowing the wood dust out of the grooves. "Did I?" he said. "I guess I did. Off you go, then."

"But I want to hear the rest of the story."

Mātua looked at him.

"Please?"

Mātua laid the red-gold wood on his knee. "Dawn was

approaching, the sunlight a pink tinge on the horizon, and the Tūrehu were becoming agitated. 'Hurry, hurry,' they called. 'We need to work faster.'"

"Ghosts don't like sunlight, do they, Mātua?"

"No, they don't. Kahukura was determined to keep them on the beach long enough for him to learn the secret of the net. He pretended to help thread the fish to carry home, but instead he tied a flimsy slip knot that came undone under the weight of the fish. Quickly, the Tūrehu showed him how to knot the string tightly. Kahukura untied the knot, replacing it with another slip knot. Once again, the fish fell on the beach."

"He was making the Tūrehu teach him and they didn't even know it."

"He was, indeed. The Tūrehu were so busy trying to recover the fish that the morning sun caught them unawares. Kahukura was caught out, too. The sun revealed his dark skin and tattooed face. He was nothing like the Tūrehu, who were tall and slender like rata saplings and as pale as pipi shells. Seeing Kahukura, the Tūrehu fled. Kahukura was left alone on the beach. The chief gathered up the precious net and took it with him to share its knowledge with all the Māori people."

"What about the Tūrehu? Where did they go?"

Mātua shrugged.

"They have to have gone *somewhere*."

"Nobody knows. Back to their homes in the mist. No one has been able to find them."

Ghost people...
Temera blew out slowly, the stream of grey smoke

fogging the shed, and wondered...Maybe the Tūrehu weren't ghosts at all, but a people pushed into hiding. After eighty-four years on this earth, Temera had learned that the truth depended on who you were and where you were standing. Everyone wanted to cast themselves as the heroes. It was always the way. Even children's stories were like that. Like Jack and the Beanstalk. People were meant to think that Jack was the hero, coming home laden with riches to save his hardworking mother from poverty, but seen from the giant's point of view, he was nothing but a sticky-fingered thief. A blackguard. When the giant pursued him, hoping to regain his treasures, Jack had hacked at the vine connecting the two worlds and cut off the giant's retreat. Was Kahukura like Jack? Even if the chief's intentions had been noble, even if he had been resourceful and quick-thinking, wasn't he really just another thief?

Had Kahukura, and others like him, chased the Tūrehu from their home?

Temera shook his head. *Those are just stories.*

He knew better than that. Stories had meaning: there was always some truth to them, if you looked hard enough.

Could Māpura really be one of the mysterious Tūrehu? The idea was far-fetched, but far-fetched didn't mean untrue. The warrior was pale-skinned, and he'd been guarded in what he'd said. Although, he had mentioned Chatham Island, the tiny island to the south, off the coast of Christchurch. Was that where Māpura's people were hiding? Was that where Taine was now? Temera dismissed the idea. The island might be isolated, but there was still a thriving community there. There were pubs, shops, a school. Hiding a group of people on the island, and over many years, would be too difficult.

He needed to think about this. If he was being persecuted, where would he go to hide?

It was obvious. He'd find a forest. So many times throughout history, the Urewera forest had provided sanctuary for people. For outspoken Māori leaders like Te Kooti and Rua Kenana. For drug runners, pig hunters, and lost trampers. Hell, the forest was so dense, a dinosaur could traipse through there and not be noticed. The Ureweras knew how to keep secrets.

A forest to the south where a group of people could hide indefinitely? Temera crushed out his cigarette in an ashtray of amber glass.

Taine was in Fiordland.

15

The Catfish

"Before you go, sir."

For fuck's sake! "What is it now? I just gave an order to surface."

"I've picked up something on the sonar. Something approaching."

Snatching the bandeau away from his face, Meredith thrust the child at Jackson. "Wait here," he said, and stormed into the control room.

~

Fiordland

Todd revelled in the throb of the jet ski beneath him, the roar of its 300 horsepower 4-stroke engine echoing off the canyon walls and making the entire cavern thrum like a massive boom box. He glanced over his shoulder. A jet stream of white curved behind him, billowing out like the foam on a good coffee.

He'd needed this.

The wind whipped his fringe into his face. Todd inhaled a dose of salty air and tossed his head, flicking the wet strands out of his eyes as he faced forward again.

I wonder how far this channel goes.

The south was full of Sounds like these – the huge waterways carved into the land creating massive canyons, sometimes with steep walls, other times opening onto isolated beaches. This particular channel was wide, and judging by the dark teal of the water, pretty deep. He might be the only person to ever have ridden through here on a jet ski. He almost wished his girlfriend could see him right now, blasting across the blue at close to 100km/hour, but as soon as he thought it, he realised he was happier with her thirty minutes away, back at the boat. It wasn't that he didn't like Ange. He liked her well enough. Most of the time, she was okay.

Yeah, when she's asleep.

Todd revved the engine and the jet ski leapt forward in a surge of speed. He sucked in a breath, filling his lungs again. The isolation down here was dizzying. He was on a high, overdosing on solitude.

The salt water stung his eyes, and suddenly it struck Todd that he was going to have to dump his girlfriend. Things were never going to work out between them.

A bit of clear air and a stretch of water was all it took to make me realise.

The break wouldn't come from her, of course. Todd would have to do the hard yards, the way he'd made all the decisions in their relationship. It was never what he'd wanted. He wasn't a chauvinist. The silly submissive girlfriend act was all Ange's doing. It was as if she'd read one of those women's magazine articles about how to keep your man, but only taking to heart the part about letting the man make all the decisions. Todd had read one of those articles himself while he was waiting for the Warrant of Fitness on his truck, the journalist using words like 'intimidating' and 'emasculation' and 'deferring to your man'. What kind of bullshit advice was that, anyway? Sure, it'd been flattering at first: Ange letting him order her burger for her, letting Todd choose the movie they'd watch, letting him decide whether they'd have sex or not.

"What do you want to do?" he'd ask, and she'd give him that stupid little shrug.

"Not fussed," she'd say, shrugging again. "What do you want to do?"

It didn't matter what he asked, it was always the same. "So, what do you feel like eating?"

"I don't know. Anything. You choose."

"Shall we fuck, then?"

"Whatever rocks your boat, baby."

It hadn't rocked his boat. It was shite. Getting your own way all the time was shite. In the two years they'd been together, Todd had come to hate that shrug of hers. He knew exactly what people meant when they said 'the old ball and chain' because life with Ange was like dragging a dead-weight with him everywhere.

So, after lunch, he'd unhitched the jet ski and fucked off. Didn't even ask her if she wanted to come. He couldn't bear to hear her say 'if you want me to' another time, so he'd just left her there on the boat. Ange didn't know the first thing about boats, but Todd had thrown out the anchor, so he figured she was safe enough until he got back, which could be a while given that he had a full tank of gas. Of course, if she got pissed, she could always pull the anchor up, fire up the engine and head off without him.

She could definitely do that.

Except she wouldn't, would she? Because that would involve making a bloody decision.

Lost in his thoughts, Todd didn't see the swell until it almost knocked him sideways off the jet ski. He shifted his weight and sped up a little to stabilise the Sea-Doo, taking a second or two to get it under control.

That was weird. Big swell, too. A backwash from the rock wall to his left? No, the cliff was too far away for the jet ski to have created a wave that big, and backwash tended to be choppy. The swell was probably caused by freshwater currents coming downriver meeting the saltwater tide.

Todd gunned the throttle, surging forward. He'd go a few hundred metres more, to where the passage narrowed, and then turn around.

Another swell rocked the jet ski, but this time he was ready for it, adjusting his position to keep the machine stable. When the rocking stopped, he steered the machine into the middle of the channel away from the cavern walls.

Another surge, from behind now.

What?

Bracing himself, Todd surfed the jet ski down the wave. He'd been lucky not to come a cropper that time. The currents were getting trickier to manage, making him uneasy. He should turn back.

Out of instinct – he was the only person out here for miles – Todd checked the rear-view mirror before coming around. He caught sight of...something big, skimming beneath the surface and coming in fast. Todd held his breath and kept his line. Would it bump him? Fortunately, whatever it was dived deep. Todd exhaled. A whale? An inlet like this one would make a nice hidey hole for a whale to shelter, perhaps even a pod of whales. Todd shivered. As much as it would be cool to ride alongside a pod of whales, he didn't want to risk tipping the machine, or worse, stalling it, this far out from anywhere.

Time to go.

Todd was turning the jet ski when something hit him. Hard. He flew through the air like a stuntman, thrown in one direction while the jet ski went the other. Man and machine plunged into the freezing water.

Todd opened his eyes. His balls shrank.

Not a pod of harmless whales, then.

A giant squid. As the life jacket dragged him back to the surface, Todd saw it all. He'd never seen anything so colossal – just the head part was as long as a bus and that wasn't even counting the tentacles. It made the dead squid at the national museum look like a shrivelled shrimp. Through the pristine water, its eye examined Todd, cold and calculating and as big as all hell. Under that stare, Todd was paralysed.

Not far off, the jet ski was still running. Thrumming. Normally Todd wore a lanyard connecting him to the starter, so if he came off the vehicle would stop instantly, but today, in his hurry to escape Ange, he hadn't bothered with the safety line.

The creature turned its attention to the jet ski. Todd could do nothing but hold his breath as the monster gripped the vehicle between two grasping claws. Then it opened its beak and clamped down on the metal, crushing one end. The machine whined, its engine still throbbing.

Jesus.

Although he couldn't scream, Todd found the strength to move. He kicked for the surface. Thank God, the inlet was narrower here. There was a beach further up.

Too far.

It had to be the rocks. There was no way he'd make it to the beach. The fucking life jacket was getting in the way! Todd unclipped the jacket and shucked it off his shoulders. The yellow buoyancy bobbed away on the surface.

A scrape of metal sounded behind him.

He grabbed at the water, pulling himself forward. Willing himself forward.

Faster.

The throb of the jet ski stopped, dead.

No!

Todd didn't look back. He pumped his legs and churned his feet, his arms reaching out to slap at the water, dragging it behind him. His school swimming teacher jumped into his head. "Kick hard. Make the water boil, kids. Make it boil," she shouted at him from the past. Todd kicked so hard his thighs were like jelly.

Nearly there.

Heart racing, he reached the side and realised his mistake. He should have made for the beach. The rock face was too steep.

Todd felt that eye on his back. His skin, already cold,

dimpled with gooseflesh. He stole a glance backwards. The jet ski was gone. Either the creature had eaten it, or had it sunk to the bottom of the canyon. Todd couldn't tell. A tsunami raced towards him, his life jacket carried on the crest.

The monster was coming.

Close to panic, Todd reached for a handhold, but the rock was too slick. Too steep. Todd's hands fumbled, bruised, as he searched for a lifeline. Something to grasp on to.

Anything...there!

A tree root, a small miracle, growing straight of the rock. The branches were scraggly and sad, but the trunk was thick enough. Sobbing, Todd lunged from the water and grasped at the trunk. Ignoring gouges in his palms and his screaming shoulders, he hauled himself up the rock. He didn't stop climbing, didn't look around, until his feet were standing on the tree trunk, his body flattened against the wall. He clung to the rock with the pads of his fingers.

Below him, in the water, the creature was surfacing, the wave rising up the rock wall and threatening to swamp him. Todd held his breath. When the wave finally pulled back, the squid was still there, hovering, one eye turned in Todd's direction. That eye made a Dominoes mega pizza look pathetic, but it wasn't the most terrifying thing. From above, Todd could see its beak, like two circular saw heads coming together. The squid clacked them closed. The sound made Todd's teeth ache, the stab reaching behind his eyes. That beak would shred him like paper. He clung to the wall, his heart pounding.

Must not fall. Must not fall.

Todd tightened his fingers on the rock. It was okay. He was out of the water. There was no way that squid could get him up here. All he had to do was wait long enough for it to go away, then he'd head for the beach.

Except the creature didn't leave. It stabbed at the rock, its whip-like tentacle hitting the cliff face with its deadly barbed hook. Looking for him! It hammered the rock again, this time grazing Todd's boardies. Todd could hardly hold on, he was trembling so hard. If that tentacle found him, if it hooked into his flesh, there would be no escaping.

The eye stared at him, like it was calculating how much steak sauce it would need.

Hang on. An eye that big... Sure, a big creature called for a big eye, but what if it needed to be big to see in deep water? So maybe that eye wasn't so good in the bright daylight. Maybe the creature was just *guessing* where Todd was, and each attack on the rock face was helping it to build a picture of where he was hiding.

The barbed tentacle grazed the rock near Todd's head.

That was close!

The tentacle came again. Todd saw it coming and jerked his head away. Only, he moved too fast, lost his footing, and tumbled into the water.

Fuuuck!

The creature dipped its torpedo-shaped mantle towards him. Todd didn't wait. He dived, swimming for his life. Eyes darting, he searched the rock wall for somewhere to hide.

Please.

The cliff hid an overhang in the water. He ducked under

the rock. Maybe if he went far enough, he'd find an opening he could squeeze himself into and hide. Somewhere small and tight where the squid couldn't reach him.

There! A black hole. He'd squeeze in there. Wait it out. For how long? Already, his lungs were bursting. The rest of Todd's life could be measured in minutes. Seconds. A chill washed over him. He was going to die. It was just a matter of how.

He looked around. The monster was on him.

He'd rather drown than be eaten.

He turned and thrust his feet into the hole, dragging himself backwards with his hands like a hermit crab, his head skimming the ceiling of the cave and its silver lining.

Wait, there was an air pocket!

Todd couldn't believe it. A chance. He thrust his head back, his face almost kissing the ceiling, and drew in a breath. Then he pulled himself onto the shelf, pushing backwards until he couldn't go any further. He stopped, his legs cramped, folded up in the tiny space. He'd wedged himself in deep, five metres perhaps, and it was narrow here. Plus, there was air. It was stale but it would sustain him if he could keep out of reach of those grasping tentacles. Was he far enough in? The light was so dim, he could barely see the cave entrance. The shadows winked, and something faintly glowing snaked into the space.

Todd squeezed tight to the wall.

A blurred shape passed by his face. Todd turned his shoulder and ducked.

In a swirl of sand and bubbles, there was a shearing of pain. Todd's arm was gone. Shredded. The muddy water turned even darker. Cold seeped into his bones.

Todd held the socket where his arm had been, felt the blood pumping. His mind raced almost as fast. Maybe that little morsel would be enough? Those were his dreams talking. His brain was addled by too little oxygen, loss of blood, and a pain that sang like a crescendo in the tiny airspace.

Or was it him screaming?

Through the hazy swirl of water and blood, through the debris of meat and skin, a sucker came weaselling towards his face. Todd had nowhere to go. In seconds, it had plucked out his eyeball.

Todd wondered how long Ange would wait for him to return.

Something hard and unforgiving burrowed into his eye socket.

After that, Todd didn't think anything at all.

The Catfish.

"Well, where is it?" Meredith snapped.

"It was right there, sir. In the middle of the inlet, a few hundred metres back. A small signal. Just one vessel. It looked as if it was heading this way."

Meredith looked for the neon pulse that could indicate someone was on to them. There was nothing. "Well, it's not there now, is it?"

"No, sir." The sonar operator rubbed a hand across the back of his neck.

"What do you think caused it?" Meredith said. "Could it be an anomaly? A problem with the equipment?"

"Possibly. Equipment can fail, although it's more likely to be—"

"...a human error," Meredith finished.

The operator flushed. "But I was sure—"

"Be *more* sure before you interrupt me next time," Meredith snarled. He turned to leave, his heel giving a decisive squeak. "Bring us up now," he told the pilot.

16

———

Fiordland, chopper site

Taine kept one eye on the warriors as he listened to Summers' story: the crash, waking up in the mangled chopper, being cared for by the old chief and his people.

"The fellow there with the bone through his ear," Summers said, "that's the new chief. He knows a word or two of English. Yes, no, that sort of thing. Ka – he's the one holding the gun – he can say a few words, too. One or two of the children can follow basic sentences. At the beginning, they showed no interest in communicating with me. Maybe they thought if they got to know me, it'd be harder to kill me if I ever betrayed them. Over time they became less wary."

"You mean, you weren't allowed to go home?" Barb asked.

Sitting on a stump, Summers picked up a broken stick and began to fiddle with it. "I'm as much their captive as you are."

"You could have made a signal fire," Barb said. "Every boy scout knows to do that."

Summers lowered his voice. "I thought about it, believe me. Even if I'd managed to attract a plane, by the time rescuers got someone on the ground, I'd have been dead and my body…" He trailed off, intent on stripping the bark off the stick. "It bothered me the first few years, and then…" He shrugged.

"There must be someone back home waiting for you?" Jules asked.

"Not people, but yeah, there was someone. My wife, Gina." Dropping the stick, Summers pulled a battered photo out of the pocket in his shirt. He handed it to Jules. Taine glanced at it over her shoulder. It showed a pretty woman in her twenties or thirties, mouse brown hair and a wide smile. "How could I leave with my leg like this? I couldn't very well crawl out of the forest on my hands and knees, could I?" Summers insisted. "Not before they found me and dragged me back. I guess the longer I stayed here, the less I cared. I figured Gina would've moved on."

He took the photo from Jules and returned it to his pocket.

Read frowned. "But you live in the chopper, right?"

"Yup."

"I don't see any village. These people can't have been watching you all the time," Read said.

Summers paused and rubbed at his beard. "See that big gun they've got trained on you?"

Read nodded.

"It belonged to an Englishman named Somerville. A gentleman farmer. He bought the gun with him when he emigrated to New Zealand in the 1800s. I gather the People confiscated it off him after he took a shine to one of their womenfolk. They took more than just his gun: they have his diary and his clothes. Now, I ask you, what man leaves without his clothes?"

He shifted his weight to relieve his crippled leg.

"If I'd been able to walk properly, if I hadn't been lame, maybe things would've been different. Then again, if I could walk, they might have killed me outright. Who knows? All I know is they saved my life. Looked after me. I wouldn't have survived without their help. Forty years, it's been. You spend enough time with people, whatever the circumstances, they start to feel like family."

"That's true enough," Pringle said. "Even in prison, people make connections."

Summers went on. "These people can't afford for anyone to know about them. It's how they've survived all these years. Well, you've seen them. They're different. And we all know the outside world isn't very kind to people who are different."

"It doesn't change the fact that they killed my colleagues," Rocky said. "Friends of mine. And these two need a hospital."

"Wai can't go to any hospital."

"He'll die if he doesn't," Jules said.

"Then the People will make that sacrifice."

Taine's senses pinged.

On alert, the pale warriors snapped their heads up, too. There was a cry, a faint mewling. It was coming from about forty metres off, given the muffling effect of the trees. The chief signalled left and right. Several warriors slipped into the bush, leaving only four to guard them, including the pair with the punt gun.

Minutes passed. Suddenly, a little girl, a man's t-shirt bagging about her knees, burst out of the trees. She ran straight at Summers. "David!"

The old man dropped to one knee and swept the girl into his arms. "Mere!"

Panicked, the girl babbled a stream of words.

Summers' face fell. Quickly, he put the child from him, pushing her behind him as Ka and the Amazon swung the punt gun out toward the forest.

A threat coming – one that's bigger than us.

"We need to leave," Summers said, staggering backwards. "Mere didn't know what else to do. She didn't want to lead them to where the People live, so she came to me instead. There are men with guns coming. They'll be here—"

Before he finished his sentence, the promised men arrived. Like a bunch of outlaws descending on a town, they burst into the clearing. Bullets pinged off the rock wall. Those who'd grown up with television threw themselves to the ground.

The warriors did not.

One of them fell, thrown backwards in a maelstrom of noise. The child screamed. Or maybe it was Barb. Taine couldn't tell.

They had to fight back! They were like sitting ducks here.

"The barrel," Taine shouted at Read. Leaping to his feet, he ran headlong at Ka, throwing his weight at the warrior and shouldering him to the ground. A quick study, Read did the same to the warrior woman holding the barrel. It was like whipping a tablecloth out from under a pile of crockery. Now Ka and the Amazon were out of the line of fire, and Taine and Read had the punt gun. But while Taine was protected by Read's body, the young soldier was out in the open. He risked being shot at any moment.

Taine needed to shoot. One shot. He had to make it good.

The barrel on Read's shoulder, Taine aimed the gun. No need for precision. He pulled the trigger back. The hammer fell, and the gun roared, sending out a spray of shot as wide as a small shed. Bark and wood chips flew everywhere. The gun's recoil slammed against Taine's shoulder like a pick-up truck backing over him. Two of the men in black crumpled.

"Fall back," their leader screamed.

American.

Taine imagined he caught the man's gaze before they were gone, the fallen men dragged with them.

The punt gun thudded to the ground. Read charged off after the attackers. The idiot wasn't even armed. "Read!"

Goddamn. Sometimes that FNG has more courage than sense.

Taine glanced around.

Herewini was collecting the spears of the fallen warriors. He raised his eyes to Taine and shook his head, the movement almost imperceptible. They were dead, then. At least Jules was okay. Her back to Taine, she was crouched over the girl, shielding the child's body with her own. Taine wanted to stride over there and check every hair on her head, but Rocky turned to him, his face as pale as death. "I'm a Conservation officer. This – what's happening – it's beyond my expertise. You're a soldier, McKenna. What should we do?"

"Get these people somewhere safe. Hole up until I get back."

"Where are you going?"

"After the men who just attacked us," Taine said.

There was no other choice. One child was back, but there were still two missing, and the men who'd just left were involved. It was no use waiting for the authorities; by the time they turned up, those kids could be anywhere.

Nodding, Rocky put his hand in his pocket and tossed something to Taine. It was a piece of chalk. "The park's a big place. Leave a trail so you can find your way back." Rocky turned away. "Summers, McKenna's going after the other kids. In the meantime, we're going to need cover for these two on the stretchers."

Herewini handed Taine the spears. "Here. Don't go empty-handed."

Leaning in, Taine murmured in Herewini's ear. "The sat phone. It's still in the camp."

"On it."

"Be careful." Taine turned on his heel. Read was back. He put his hand out, helping the Amazon to her feet.

"Read," Taine said.

"Boss." The soldier seemed reluctant to drag his eyes away. Finally, he turned, striding across to Taine. "They left a body a few metres down the track. They took the weapons, of course. I reckon they were in a bit of a hurry because they forgot this." He handed Taine a radio and earpiece. Taine and Read both knew the radio was compromised. A smart leader would have changed the wavelength or called for radio silence by now, but there was always a chance someone didn't get the memo.

Taine clipped the radio to his belt and put in the earpiece. "Did you see what they were carrying?"

"AK47s mostly. I might have seen an M4-Carbine semi-automatic."

Taine nodded. Standard-use firearms used by almost every military in the world at some time or another. Except they weren't dealing with a military group. Militarised, but not military.

"Mercenaries," Read said. It was a statement. He took one of the spears from Taine.

"You don't have to do this," Taine said.

Read rolled his eyes. "Yeah, we should probably get going."

They plunged into the bush.

Jules sat with her back to the wall. She was in a high-ceilinged cave not far from the chopper site. Dry and well-hidden, the cave served as a kind of outdoor schoolroom according to Summers. Jules wondered what the People learned here.

Herewini was the last to arrive. He staggered into the cave, the body of one of the attackers slung over his shoulder. It dripped a trail of bloody splotches on the sandy ground. Bending his knees, Herewini dropped the corpse onto the pile already stacked against the wall. The body moaned. He was dead – the sound just gases escaping – but still Mere looked up, her face twisted in fright.

From the other side of the cave, seated near his injured comrade, Ka uttered a few words. He gave the girl a smile.

He was reassuring the child. These people might look unusual, but they weren't so different.

Herewini sat beside Jules and rested his hands on his knees. "What's going on?" he said.

Barb shushed him. "Summers is telling us what happened to the girl," she said.

"They looked at our hands," Summers translated, and the girl, Mere, raised her palm, fanning her fingers to expose the webbing. "And they wanted to see us breathe under the water. They put me in a lake with walls."

"I'm guessing she means a tank of some sort," David interjected before picking up the story again. "It was as our teacher told us. Strangers can be jealous and mean. They cut Ro, and they hurt Tau. The meanest one left me in the lake-cage for a long time, longer than I could use my water-breath. I was choking. I tried to get out. I tried..." The girl scrubbed at her eyes with the back of her hand. "It hurt Ro too much to watch, so she told them. She made the mean one take me out of there. She should have let me die. Now, the bad man knows how many of us there are. They are hunting us."

Water breath? Breathing underwater? Jules struggled to take it all in. As outlandish as it sounded, the facts lined up: the injured warrior's frilled lungs, the widespread syndactyly amongst the warriors, their lack of clothes. Even Mahoe's testimony confirmed it. Someone had tortured Mere, put her in a tank to find out what she was capable of. She was too traumatised to be lying.

Reaching out, Jules laid her hand against Mere's cheek. "What kind of monster tortures a little girl?"

"The whole thing is monstrous," Pringle said, watching

Summers move over to talk with the warriors. "Even in prison there's a code for this sort of thing. The way I'm seeing it, Mahoe and his mate – the one he claims is dead – spied the kids, saw them breathe underwater, and ka-ching: they threw over the parrots to sell the children instead."

"Only their contact – those guys in black – decided to cut out the middle men and took off with the kids," Herewini added, moving closer.

Pringle frowned. "It's not so much the children they want, but what they can *do*. Think about it: if these people have the ability to breathe for extended periods underwater, then there'll be military applications."

"Man from Atlantis," Herewini said.

"Waterworld," said Pringle.

"That film was a massive flop."

Barb put her hands on her head. "A long-lost tribe with special powers. It's so hard to believe! It's like something Michael Crichton dreamed up."

"I don't know that they're lost, just in hiding," Jules said, lowering her voice as she leaned closer to the others. "They held Summers captive to protect themselves from discovery. And they killed Jess." She swallowed, remembering. "They know there are other people, they just don't want anything to do with them," she went on. "It's possible they hid from the Moriori and from the Māori, and after that from the Europeans. These people are used to running."

Talking was good. It helped to keep her mind off what Taine and Read were doing. It was the prospect of rescuing the children that had sent Taine charging off after the armed men. He knew nothing of these people's gifts and still he'd gone, not even stopping to speak to her. "I wonder where they ran from first," she went on. "Their features look Polynesian, even with their fair colourings, and their language is unusual, a mixture of Polynesian and…I'm not sure what."

"I thought I recognised a few words when they were talking before," said Herewini. "My brother's wife is from Peru. It could just be my brain wanting to make something of what they're saying, but I think their language might have roots in South America."

"It's highly possible," Rocky said, joining the conversation. He picked up a stick and drew a rough world map in the dirt. "There's a theory that the Moriori people originated in the Middle East." He poked at the spot on his dirt map. "Whether they were escaping persecution or looking for new lands, no one knows, but the way the story goes, they made their way across Europe, sailed or walked into South America and then on to Polynesia. Eventually, they ended up here." Rocky tapped his stick on New Zealand.

"And you think these people took a similar evolutionary route?" Jules asked.

"Maybe. Or maybe their origins go even further back," Rocky said. "They could be Denisovan. It's not beyond the realm of possibility. Denisovan genes have been linked to an improved sense of smell in Papua New Guineans, and to the Tibetans' resistance to low oxygen conditions at high altitude. Why couldn't those genes also lead to an ability to breathe underwater for prolonged periods? It's not such a big step."

Jules shook her head. It wasn't just a big step; it was a massive leap. It was true that Denisovan genes were concentrated in Oceania, but could that third branch of hominins really have reached New Zealand that long ago? It was a wild theory.

Herewini obviously thought so. "Evolution takes thousands of years," he said.

"Not if there's sufficient evolutionary pressure," Rocky replied. "Happens in the wild all the time. I imagine a small population, isolated from other genetic influences, could change pretty quickly."

"That's just conjecture," Jules said.

"True. Easy enough to find out. All it needs is a few lab tests," Rocky said.

Jules' head snapped up. She glared at Rocky. "They're not lab animals. They're people! And according to your own theory, possibly the very first New Zealanders—"

"Guys," Barb's voice hitched. "Something's going on."

Something *was* going on.

While they'd been talking, the warrior with the sucking chest wound had slipped from this life into the next. His head had fallen to one side, his tongue slack.

But that wasn't what had drawn Barb's attention. Ka was crouched over Mahoe, his syndactyl-webbed fingers spread wide over the poacher's nose and mouth. Silent as death, he pushed down hard, making a seal.

Smothering him.

His eyes wide, Mahoe reached up, scratching at his neck with his fingers, trying to prise the warrior's hands away. Jules saw the webbed skin suck inwards as Mahoe strained for a breath. He kicked his feet, but in his weakened state, he couldn't do anything against the warrior's grip.

Jules pulled Mere into her arms, shielding the child's

eyes with her body. Only now she had no hands left to cover her own eyes. Her heart raced.

Somebody do something!

"Summers! What's that man doing?" Rocky demanded, scrambling to his feet. "Make him stop!"

Summers shrugged. "I think he's trying to find out where they have taken the children," he replied, his eyes sliding away.

Herewini was moving now.

Not fast enough. Mahoe's fingers twitched.

"He's suffocating him!" Jules shouted.

Mahoe tensed, then slumped, his eyes wide open in death. Herewini tackled Ka to the ground.

"Oh my God," Barb whispered.

17

Fiordland

The men in black had a head start, but they'd been more concerned with getting away than covering their tracks, so it was easy enough to follow them. Taine and Read moved swiftly, pausing occasionally to examine a trampled fern, a scuffed piece of moss, or a misplaced boot print. Taine marked their passage for the return journey. But the group in front must have realised someone was on their trail, because eventually they split up.

"Which way? This one?" Read asked, pointing to the left.

Taine nodded. It was as good as any. With a bit of luck, the group would come together again at a designated land-mark. They had to have camped somewhere.

They ran another half kilometre until the trail they'd chosen disappeared into a stream. Taine and Read followed it for a while, splashing through the creek bed, up to their knees in freezing water, but after a few hundred metres clambering over the rocks, Read stopped. "I'm not seeing any fresh prints leaving the water," he said.

Taine slowed, his eyes scanning the trees on either side of the stream. "Could be we're just too far behind," Taine replied. "Trained personnel would know to avoid the mud, and any water marks might have dried by now. Or they might not have come out of the water yet."

"It'd be easy to miss."

They gave up, doubling back to pick up one of the other trails.

They'd been following the second trail for a few minutes when Read whispered at Taine's shoulder. "Boss."

It was the pale-skinned chief and three of his warriors, the ones who had left the clearing before the attack. They were running through the bush parallel to Taine and Read. What were they up to? Herding them somewhere? The warriors closed in beside them, the chief giving Taine a quick nod.

Read raised his eyebrows. "Well, that makes a change," he said, ducking right to skirt a tree trunk. "What's that saying about the enemy of my enemy being a friend?"

...and a friend of my enemy is my enemy – joining with the warriors made them fair game for the mercenaries.

"Don't get too comfortable. Keep your eyes open," Taine said when the two of them came together again. "For all we know there could be a nice pit of sharpened spears with our name on it up ahead."

"Here's a wee pit I prepared earlier," murmured Read.

"Something like that. If what Summers says is true, and these people have been living here for decades, they'll know the terrain better than anyone."

"Maybe they realise we're on their side. If they went back

to the chopper and spoke with Summers, they'd know we're looking for the kids, too."

"Or maybe they're confident we're not likely to try anything while the rest of our group is still in the forest."

"Good point," Read said.

After another twenty minutes, the trail opened on a grassy glade, a dilapidated hut tucked to one side. The warriors fanned out, looking outwards at the forest, while the chief gestured to Taine and Read. He showed them a dark stain on the flattened grass in front of the hut.

"Whoa. That's a lot of blood," Read said, brushing the grass aside with his boot. "Looks as if someone bled out here. Or close to it, anyway."

"Some of their mercenaries had to have been hit," Taine replied. "That punt gun spewed over an arc the size of a baseball pitch. Whoever we're following probably stopped to patch themselves up before going on."

They spread out to check the area for any other signs. Taine ducked his head inside the hut. Gloomy and decrepit, it had been used recently: the dust had been disturbed. In the gap where the roof sloped away and the wall had crumbled, Taine could see Read's feet out the back of the hut.

When Taine emerged from the hut, Read called him over. "Someone went this way, look. See this tree?" Read pointed to where the bark had splintered away, leaving the pale wood exposed. "That's a new chip."

Taine frowned. "I didn't hear any automatic fire, did you?"

"Only this morning." Read's eyes widened. "You think this is where Mahoe was shot?"

"If it is, then going that way would lead us back to our camp and a pile of deer."

One of the warriors, a wide-nosed fellow, grunted at them. He shook his spear and pointed in the opposite direction.

"Looks like there's a trail over there too, boss. What do we do? Go with these guys?"

Taine nodded. "If Mahoe went this way, then it's possible the kidnappers came and left by another route. Whatever we do, we need to hurry up. We're going to lose the light soon."

They ran on, the warriors leading them through a shadowed valley, where towering silver beeches shared their breath with the majestic miro trees.

The line of warriors slowed. A plant as large as a small car was sprawled across the tiny trail, its glossy blades poking upwards.

"What's going on?" Read asked.

"It's a perching lily, an epiphyte. A big one," Taine said, picking his way around the blockade. "They grow between branches of the beech. Sometimes a high wind will dislodge them. Back in the early days, when New Zealand bush was being cleared for farmland, the forest workers would start sawing and cause these plants to fall, killing the men below." Taine peered up into the canopy. "We need to be more careful. They don't call them widow makers for nothing."

They skirted the epiphyte, emerging on the other side of the valley at a steep ridge. Once again, the party slowed, the tracker at the front conferring with his chief. Taine couldn't understand them, but it was clear it was a strategy talk. The militants' trail led off around the base of the hill. The chief and his tracker were discussing whether or not to take the higher route, over the ridge. It was a dangerous call. The further you climbed, the more the treeline gave way to rock and low-lying tussock. If the mercenaries were waiting at the top, their little group could be picked off like skittles.

Read leaned in close. "What do you reckon they're talking about?" he asked.

"Whether we'd be able to see the kidnappers from the top of the ridge," Taine said. "Since the kidnappers have wounded with them, they'd have had to take the trail around the hill. Our friends up there are thinking we can cut them off by going over, instead of around."

Sure enough, the tracker started up the ridge.

"Wow, what are you, a mind reader?" Read whispered.

"Just be ready to drop, in case our friends in black are telepathic, too."

"Sure thing, boss."

Taine wished he was telepathic. He hated second guessing what was going on. Although there was that one time...

Suddenly, Taine felt an urge to speak to Rawiri Temera.

Maybe I could?

Holding the spear in one hand, he clasped his pūrerehua in the other. The sliver of carved wood warm and familiar under his fingers. It was a long shot. Probably wouldn't work – the other times they'd spoken, he'd had to spin the little object to summon old matakite – but it was worth a go.

Still climbing, he concentrated on his friend, conjuring him in his mind: the leathery dark skin, nicotine-stained fingers and the crinkles that appeared around his eyes when he smiled. As a thin wisp of mist glided off the ridge and dropped into the valley, Taine imagined the day he first met Temera, the old man sitting on a beach chair on a pitted road heading into the Ureweras.

"Taine! I was hoping we could talk." As always, when they talked this way, Temera's voice was young and eager.

"Yes, well, I would have called sooner, but the cell coverage round here is atrocious," Taine said.

It wasn't really speech. Temera's words rumbled in Taine's mind, like the soundtrack of a walking daydream. Taine presumed the matakite perceived his words in the same way.

"You're in Fiordland," Temera said, his boy-voice matter of fact.

"You knew?" Temera's skill amazed Taine. If he hadn't met the old man, if he hadn't seen his gift at work, he probably wouldn't have believed it, even with his Māori heritage.

"A warrior, a pale-skinned man named Māpura, came to me. Issued me with a firm warning on your behalf," Temera said.

"Māpura?" Taine said aloud.

The pale warrior leading the group, the man who had charged at Mahoe, stopped in his tracks. Turning to face Taine, he tapped his chest quickly. "Māpura!" he said. He tapped a second time. "Māpura." Then he continued up the slope, picking his way through the rocks like a mountain goat.

"I think I've met him," Taine replied.

"You have?"

"Fair skin. Wide flat nose. Wears a pūtōrino on a string around his neck. Bit of a hothead."

"That's him!"

"You sound surprised?"

"No. Well, yes, actually. It's just, I thought...I thought he was a ghost – one of the Tūrehu – so I'm surprised to learn anyone has met him, not just you. The Tūrehu are rarely seen by human eyes. They're a sacred people: guardians of the forest, the coast, and the sea. Mostly, they hide away, cloaking themselves in the mountain mists. My old mātua used to say they only really showed themselves to matakite."

"Well, this guy is as real as you and me. Anyway, seeing is *your* gift, Temera, not mine. Only my mother's people are Māori. My father was Irish, remember?"

"The Irish are a fairly spiritual people as I recall. That's another thing my old mātua used to say: seeing isn't the same for all matakite. You're a seer, Taine. You're seeing me now."

"All your doing, my friend."

"Not necessarily."

"So, what are you saying? That the people I'm climbing alongside right now aren't actually real? That they exist in the spiritual realm, hovering somewhere between life and death? Forgive me if I have my doubts." If these were Tūrehu spirits, it hadn't prevented several of them from dying today.

"Is it really so far-fetched? Look at all the stuff on TV these days. It's all zombie apocalypses and paranormal investigations. Why should a spirit walking in the physical world surprise us?"

Taine grinned. "I suppose it's not the most mind-boggling thing you and I have come across since we've known each other."

"There's something else I need to tell you: I've had a vision of the ocean and of something dangerous brooding and bubbling below the surface of the waves. Something big. The image has come to me a few times now, and it's... well, if I'm honest, it's got me terrified."

Taine felt his spine tingle. Even in his boy form, Temera didn't strike Taine as someone who was easily scared. "Does it feel more or less ominous than the last time?"

"Hard to say. I get this sense of being mesmerised, carried along, as if the tide is pulling me out."

"Do you think the message is meant for me?"

Temera sighed. "I don't know. Maybe."

They were coming to the top of the ridge.

"Hang on," Taine said, letting go of the pūrerehua for a moment so he could tackle the steep section to the top. Taine hauled himself over the ridge and gazed into the Sounds below. The wind in his face made his eyes water. He blinked.

But that's...

Read got to his feet beside him. "Holy heck," he breathed, confirming that Taine wasn't seeing things. "So that's how they got here."

If they'd come via the beach, they might not have seen it, but viewed from above there was no mistaking the elongated silhouette. The waves rippled and the torpedo shape disappeared from view.

Taine put a hand to the pūrerehua at his chest. "A submarine," he whispered into the wind. "Well, I guess we know what the danger is."

18

The Catfish

Meredith stalked into his quarters and slammed the door, hard enough to make the entire craft shiver.

Talk about a fucking SNAFU!

He banged his fist on the desk so hard it stung. Not only had they lost the kid and failed to secure the additional specimens the client demanded, but two of his men had gone down in the confrontation and several more had been wounded by that ridiculous pop-gun. It was the girl's doing. The sly little bitch had run them straight into an ambush. And instead of encountering a horde of disorganised backwater natives as he'd predicted, the Mer-mutants had allies. A bunch of them. Some of those allies were quick-thinking and capable in the face of his hard-core mercenaries. When that gun had gone off like a hand grenade, Meredith had had to dive backwards into a bush to avoid being turned into Swiss cheese.

He flopped backwards onto the bed, his feet still dangling on the floor.

Who were they?

Had Digby sold the information to another party? Another potential buyer? Had that party snuck in all Henry Morgan Stanley can-I-be-of-assistance, promising to elevate the savages from their humble existence with flat screen TVs and a library card? Cosying up to the Mer-people was one approach for getting access to their unique DNA. Meredith preferred to be more forthright and take what he wanted, rather than asking permission. That's why he'd told Digby he wasn't interested in a bidding war, why he'd agreed to Digby's demands so long as the deal was exclusive. Could the shifty little bastard have gone behind his back and talked to someone else? Meredith stared at the ceiling. No, it was unlikely. There hadn't been any planes or other craft in the bay. Although there had been that blip on the sonar. There was no way of finding out for sure, not now that Digby's sorry carcass was floating somewhere on the bottom of the Sounds, a small boulder zippered into his jacket. The thought soothed him a little. Then he remembered he'd told the client he'd have the goods in hand by the morning. They would want evidence.

Meredith stood up. He straightened his jacket. *Fuck.* They'd have to go out again.

He opened the door to scream for Jackson, only to find the mercenary loitering in the passageway.

"We're going out again. Two hours. Let the men know," Meredith barked.

Jackson stiffened.

"What's the matter with you?"

"Will we be taking the kids with us?"

"No, not this time. I only took the girl last time so she could lead us to the village."

"I didn't see any village in that clearing."

"No, but it has to be somewhere close to where the girl took us, doesn't it? Per the older one, there are only forty people – make that thirty-nine now – so wherever their hidey-hole is, it'll be small."

Jackson opened his mouth to say something, then closed it again.

"The client wants us to eliminate any competition," Meredith said.

"What's that supposed to mean?"

"It means making sure we're the only supplier of the product."

Jackson's Adam's apple bobbed as he swallowed. "This is a cleaner mission? We're supposed to kill them all?"

"*Capture* them, Jackson. Capture them. What do you think I am, some kind of monster?"

"No, sir."

A muscle in Jackson's cheek twitched. Meredith hoped the man hadn't suddenly grown a conscience. Jackson was a good foot soldier. Losing him would be a nuisance. "Glad we've got that clear," Meredith said, rubbing his hand through the stubble on the back of his head. "I know my actions earlier with the girl might have seemed harsh, but I was only doing what was necessary. And it worked, didn't it? Putting her in the tank allowed us to get valuable information we might not have gained otherwise. Contrary to what you might think, I don't condone killing children."

Especially when those children are likely to be valuable.

"We were going to have to go back to that clearing, anyway. We need to collect the two men who were killed."

Jackson's head snapped up. "Yes, sir. That would be Phong" – Meredith couldn't bring the man's face to mind – "and Kilgour." Jackson's lips were tight.

So, *that* was what was bothering Jackson.

"Yes, losing Kilgour was unfortunate," Meredith conceded, not the least because collecting a body would tie up valuable manpower. "He was a good soldier."

"Yes, sir."

"We did get his weapon, though, didn't we?" Meredith asked. "His and Phong's?" The last thing Meredith needed was to face a bunch of half-naked savages armed with AK47s that he'd paid for.

"Yes. We managed to get their firearms. And Kilgour's radio. We didn't have time to get Phong's. It's why we changed the frequency, in case they were listening in."

"Yes, of course." Jackson didn't need to know the detail had slipped his mind. "Alert the men."

When Jackson had gone, Meredith leaned against the door. He put in his earpiece, changing the frequency to the one they had been using earlier, and opened the line.

"I know you're listening," he announced. "Why don't you tell me who I'm speaking to?"

"The name's McKenna." The line crackled but the voice was assured. "Who are you?"

"Someone who doesn't appreciate people interfering in his business."

The sound of the wind whistled in Meredith's earpiece and the man on the other end replied, "Business? They're children."

"Oh, they're not for me. I'm not that fond of kids."

"Put them ashore, then." There was a steel edge to the demand.

Meredith laughed. McKenna was giving *him* an order? "I don't think so. But I tell you what I'm going to do. I'm going to give you and your busybody friends a warning. Leave the area and I'll let you live." Not waiting for an answer, Meredith closed the line.

19

Fiordland

Leaving a warrior on the ridge to watch the bay, Taine's little band made their way back to the chopper, the warrior Māpura at point and Read at their six o'clock. They couldn't be sure all the mercenaries had returned to the sub. Taine was pleased he didn't have to rely on his chalk markings to retrace their steps as the dark fell. It was difficult enough to navigate the terrain even with Māpura's guidance.

When they arrived back at the chopper, the clearing was deserted. The injured and the dead had been moved, along with the bodies of the two militants. The punt gun had disappeared too.

"Rocky?" Taine called.

Pringle emerged from the gloom. "They're not far," he said, his voice low. "There's a cave these people use as a schoolroom sometimes. We've moved everyone there." He jumped, startled by the warriors who appeared from the shadows.

Taine put a hand on his shoulder. "It's okay, Karl. They've been with us for a while."

"Oh right. The cave is over here." Pringle led the way, the warriors taking over, presumably when they realised where Pringle was headed.

"How's Mahoe?" Taine asked when Pringle dropped back.

Pringle coughed. "He...died half an hour ago."

"Damn. What about the other guy? The one with the punctured lung?"

"Dead too." Pringle lifted a tree fern out of the way. Read went first, and they jogged down a small slope, turning hard left into the wide entrance of a cave.

Below the ridge and cut into the wall, the cave was tucked away out of sight. A small fire glowed at the rear where Māpura was crouched over his brother's body. Pale flickers illuminated Rocky and Barb, who stood guard at the cave's centre, their stances wide, spears trained on Ka, Summers, and the female warrior. Surrounding them, the chief and his warriors had their spears up too.

It was a Mexican stand-off.

Jules sat apart from the others. She was seated cross-legged on the dusty ground, the child asleep in her lap. She looked up at Taine, her lower lip swollen where she'd been biting it. "Did you catch them?" she asked as Taine strode into the cavern.

Taine shook his head.

"They *only* came in a submarine," Read said under his breath.

She stroked the child's hair. "Yes, Mere told us." Her

forehead crinkled. "So, they've left the Sounds. And the captured children – Ro and Tau – are they lost, then?"

"Not yet," Taine said. "Not if I can help it." He turned to the cluster of civilians and warriors in the centre of the cave. "What's going on here?"

"What's going on?" Rocky jabbed his spear at Ka. The warriors let out a collective hiss. "I'll tell you what's going on. This guy killed Mahoe, suffocated the poor bugger with his bare hands, and Summers here just watched it happen."

Summers snorted. "He deserved it. He sold the children, bundled them off like slaves."

"Mahoe said he had nothing to do with it," Rocky insisted.

"He's a liar. The kids are gone, and Mere says she was tortured."

"So you just stand by and let these people kill him?" Rocky shouted. "You've been out here in the bush for way too long, Summers. You've forgotten that civilised society has *rules*."

Regarding Rocky with disdain, Summers took a step toward the spear, his lame leg wobbling. "What about humanity, huh? What about that? The man was in pain. He was *dying*. Ka's killing him was a mercy."

"That's not true. He didn't want to die. He fought back," Barb said.

Taine banged the butt of his spear on the ground. "All of you, put your weapons down. We need to work together here."

"But they *killed* him," Rocky said. "Murdered him."

"We'll all be dead if you don't listen up. We've got a bigger problem. Read picked up a radio from one of the men who attacked us in the clearing. Their leader spoke to me."

There was silence.

Rocky and Barb lowered the spears.

Summers lifted an arm, calling the warriors to calm. "What did he want?"

Leave the area and I'll let you live.

"He's coming back. This time, he'll bring more men and they'll be better prepared. We need to get these people away from here, somewhere safe, somewhere where they won't be found."

Gesturing to the chief, Summers spoke quickly.

"Where is their village? Will it be safe?" Taine asked.

"It's not far. It's not a village. It's a cave, and it's well guarded."

"Good, tell your chief to take his people there and hide. They'll need to stay well out of sight. When the militants are ashore combing the bush for them, I'll see what I can do about sneaking onto the sub and rescuing the children."

Summer jabbered again, the chief and his warriors breaking into a heated discussion.

Jules was still cradling the sleeping child. "Taine," she said, her plea barely reaching him.

"Don't worry, Doc. I won't let him go alone," Read said.

In the end, it was the chief who turned to Taine. "No." He punched his spear in the air. "No!"

Read grabbed Summers by the shirt. "What did you say to him? Did you explain what McKenna said? They're all in danger, man. Those guys in black are coming back with their semi-automatics."

"Stand down, Matt."

"But boss—"

"Read."

Nostrils flaring, Read released the old man. He stepped back.

Summers smoothed the tatty fabric of his shirt. "The chief and his warriors will stay and fight."

"I don't think you understand," Taine insisted. "The men on the submarine plan to capture the entire tribe."

"No, it's *you* who doesn't understand, McKenna. How do you think the People have stayed hidden all these years? It's because *no one* sees them. Or if they do, they don't get to tell the tale. Why do you think I'm still here after all these years?"

"This is different. They can't win this time."

Summers gave a grim smile. "They *have* to. Do you really think the men on the submarine will go away quietly? Even if they don't find the People, they'll still know they're here. Sooner or later, they'll be back with more guns and more men, and they'll keep coming until they get what they want."

Read stepped between them. "You have *seven* warriors," he said to Summers. "There could be up to seventy soldiers on that sub."

"We can call up a few reserves."

"How many?"

"Ten."

Taine nodded. "We'll help you."

Rocky's face flushed beet. "McKenna, you can't be serious. Help them? You said yourself that they can't win."

"We're NZDF," Read said. "It's what we do: provide security for New Zealanders, and that includes from terrorism and related threats."

If the situation wasn't so serious, Taine might have smiled. Read's statement could have been lifted straight from the Defence Force website.

"Rocky, please. We need to do as Taine says," Jules pleaded.

Rocky threw his hands in the air. "Well, of course, I'd expect you to support him. He's your boyfriend, isn't he?"

"It's entirely your choice," Taine said. "I can't stop you leaving. I can't stop any of you leaving, but I hope you won't. I know they've done things we don't understand..."

Rocky snorted. "Some things! They killed Jess and Wong and murdered Mahoe."

"That doesn't mean *we* can't act with humanity," Taine replied. "Right now, we're the best chance of keeping these people from being slaughtered."

Gently, Jules put the child aside and moved to stand alongside Taine. "Please stay, Rocky," she said. "I agree these people are strange and frightening. I expect their culture is like nothing we've ever seen before, but they're still *New Zealanders*, perhaps some of the earliest people to set foot on these islands. They're at risk. With each new influx of immigrants, it's been harder and harder to survive. Think of them like the kākāpo parrot and the crested penguin. Like the kea Mahoe was poaching. Part of our natural heritage, endangered and close to extinction."

"That would make the men who attacked us like dogs and rats," Herewini said from the cave entrance. "Animals who prey on our native populations."

Rocky turned. "Herewini? I didn't see you after Mahoe died. I thought you'd done a runner like Loughlin."

"Nah." Herewini fixed his eyes on Taine's. "Just went for a leak, that's all."

"Rocky?" Jules asked.

"Okay, okay, since you put it like that. We should stay and help."

Taine looked at Barb.

"I'm staying." For once the American's voice didn't boom. She pointed to the pile of bodies and her lip curled. "If only to help put this right. One of those men is named Kilgour: he's wearing US army dog tags."

20

Fiordland

The ragtag party of warriors and civilians huddled together and held a council of war.

"We're going to need our guns back," Taine said.

Summers spoke with the chief, then pulled a face. "Yeah, about that. They don't have them anymore."

"Tell them to go get them," Read said.

Summers shook his head. "Oma threw them down a sinkhole."

Taine's jaw twitched.

"We haven't got a chance," Rocky moaned.

"We've got as good a chance as any," Taine said. "We'll just have to do the best we can with what we have. Remember, two hundred Māori took the Battle of Gate Pa against a force of seventeen hundred armed British soldiers, and all because they took advantage of their attackers' confusion in the dark."

"I'd be happier with a rifle," Rocky said morosely.

"We could drop a man down the sinkhole and get the guns back," Read suggested.

"It's pretty deep," Summers replied.

"How deep?"

"Deep enough that you can't hear anything hit the bottom."

Barb sighed. "My father bought me that Remington."

"Okay, so we've got no rifles," Taine said. "What about the punt gun?" He gestured to the cannon leaning against the cavern wall. "Any more shot for it?"

Summers screwed up his face. "The chief took all we had when he went after the children."

"We still have the gun, though," Read said.

Barb grunted. "What use is a gun without any ammo?"

"It could still be useful," Taine said. "Our opponents have seen it fire, and with lethal effects. They'll be wary of facing it again. It'll make a good deterrent, but it won't help us remove soldiers from the field."

"What if we could make some shot?" Pringle said. Taine turned to look at him. Pringle cocked his head to one side sheepishly. "One of my prison students told me how. He was a bit of a chemist – crystal meth mostly – but he knew a few other things too. Anyway, he said anyone with half a brain could make gun powder. All you need are a few ordinary ingredients."

Taine sat forward. It was a good idea, and easy enough. Plenty of old-time gun enthusiasts still made their own black powder.

"We'll need charcoal – no problem there – and sulphur," Pringle went on.

"I know where we can get sulphur," Summers piped up.

"Fiordland has a few geothermal hot spots. There's one not far from here. Positively reeks of rotten egg."

"Eau de Rotorua," Read said, smiling. The North Island town was known for its pong. "Exactly how much sulphur would we need?"

"A handful, maybe."

"A couple of the steam pools have a yellow crust on the sides," Summers said.

Pringle nodded. "Then we should be able to scrape enough off. We'd also need saltpetre. That's the common name for potassium nitrate."

Jules smiled. "Potassium nitrate has another common name," she said, and Herewini grinned. "Bird poo. Or bat poo. Either one."

Herewini cackled. "There's a crapload of that around here."

"The proportions are simple enough," Pringle said. "If we can gather the ingredients, collect stones and shells for shot, we might be able to swing it."

A gasp came from behind them, and a runner, his body glistening in sweat, rushed into the cave and barked at the warriors. Grabbing for their spears, the tribesmen leapt to their feet. One of them dragged the punt gun to the edge of the cave and stowed it out of sight under a bush.

The men from the submarine were on their way. Taine stood up and kicked sand over the coals of the fire. They were out of time.

"We'll go with the chief to draw them off while you get the girl to the village and bring those reinforcements," Taine said to Summers as he made for the front of the cave. "Regroup here in an hour."

"Can't run," Summers said.

Taine pulled up. He'd forgotten Summers was lame.

Summer waved him on. "It's okay. Mere knows the way."

Taine frowned. "There are armed men coming."

"Oma thinks fifty of them," Summers replied.

"I'll take her," Jules said.

Taine opened his mouth to protest, but Jules raised her palm. "Don't argue. The girl's already been through enough. And I'm going to need help with the bodies. We can't leave them here; dead men have DNA, too."

She was right. If the tribe was going to disappear, it meant removing all evidence of them, the bodies included. They were going to need pallbearers.

"I'll carry one," Pringle said. Herewini merely lifted his chin – Kiwi shorthand for yes. Hanging back near the rear of the cave, Rocky waved a hand.

The warriors were leaving. Summers called to the Amazon, muttered a few words to her, then turned to Taine. "Hine will go with Jules and the others," he said. "She knows the way, and she can get you those ingredients, too."

The Amazon, Hine, nodded.

"What about you? What will you do?" Taine asked while Rocky hauled one of the corpses over his shoulder.

"Don't worry about me," Summers replied. "I'll hole up in the chopper. It's hidden me well enough for forty years."

At the back of the cave, Rocky was positioning a dead man across his back.

"Jules—" Taine began.

"Go," Pringle said. "We'll look after her." He pocketed a lump of charcoal from the edge of the fire pit and bent to lift the final warrior.

Taine took Jules' hand. "Just be careful, okay? I'll find you later."

Familiar with the terrain, the remaining warriors – seven of them – moved swiftly through the forest, Taine, Read and Barb sprinting after them. They were heading back towards the inlet where they'd seen the sub; Taine recognised the fork in the trail that he and Read had taken earlier. He had to hand it to them: the tribesmen had balls if they were prepared to meet the mercenaries head on, although Taine suspected they wouldn't see it as brave at all, just surviving.

Two warriors peeled off at the fork, Ka and two others taking another route minutes later. Only the chief and Māpura remained. They kept running. Taine, Barb and Read followed them. After a few minutes, Māpura put up his hand and they slowed, crouching out of sight beneath the undergrowth.

Taine felt rather than saw the men. Dressed in black fatigues, they blended into the shadows, Taine counting maybe a dozen in this group armed with...he squinted to make out their firearms, but the light was too dim. It was light enough for their silhouettes to reveal the NVG equipment attached to their helmets. Taine swore under his breath. They needed to move. He couldn't tell what technology they were using. I^2 light intensifying devices like PVS 21s meant they could see plain as day in these light conditions. And anyone using T2 thermal on their rifles could pick out their heat signatures. Either way, it was bad. If they had one of the newer fusion technologies, it was doubly bad. There was no way to warn the chief, and even if he had been able to speak their language, Taine doubted the tribesman would comprehend the technology.

One of the mercenaries spoke into his mouthpiece.

Māpura screamed, a battle cry, both piercing and desolate. Was it only this morning that the warrior had lost his brother? The tribesman leapt away, the chief with him.

"Barb, come on!"

Taine, Read and Barb chased after the warriors, several mercenaries in pursuit. Like parkour contestants, the tribesmen used the terrain to give them speed: skipping over bushes, propelling themselves off rocks and tree trunks.

Suddenly, one of the tribesmen cut across Taine's path. Gesturing, he led the three of them off the trail. Why? Taine glanced to his right as the chief and Māpura parted, each running on either side of a clump of flax. The militants, seeing a quicker route, ran right through.

There was a shout.

Taine dived low, the ground opening before him. Four men tumbled into a pit, the sound of tearing fabric making Taine's teeth ache.

And then the true screaming began.

Taine tuned out the noise. The weapons. If he could retrieve their weapons, he might be able to even up the playing field. Using military crawl to close the distance, Taine scrambled to the side of the pit. He peeked over the edge.

Two of the mercenaries were dead, impaled on solid spikes the width of fence paling.

Shit.

He pulled back.

A bullet pinged past him.

A third man roared in anguish, pleading for someone to help him. The poor bastard had slipped between two spikes, his body passing unscathed, but not before the sharpened point had penetrated his forearm. The man couldn't get his arm high enough to free himself. He was pinned there, forced to remain standing, any movement excruciating. Taine felt a twinge of sadness for the mercenary. No pay cheque in the world could compensate for that slow and excruciating death. If he could, Taine would've jumped in and freed him; the man didn't have to die to be eliminated from the game. The problem was the dying man's comrade tucked close to the dirt wall. Wiry and lean, he'd avoided the spikes, and although he was unharmed, he couldn't crawl out of the pit without help. What he did have was the other men's rifles, and he was prepared to use them.

Keeping his body low, Taine backtracked.

"What were we saying about a pit they prepared earlier?" Read joked grimly. He pushed himself onto one knee and raised his spear to his shoulder. "I'll finish this guy off," he said.

Taine stopped him before he let the shaft fly. "No. If you miss him, he'll have your spear. It'll give him a way of crawling out."

"So, what are you saying? That we just leave him?"

"He's not going anywhere. It's not worth the risk. There are precious few of us as it is."

The chief must have realised it too because he waved a spear at Taine, signalling to him that they were about to move off. Moonlight glinted off the tip of the spear, earning him a blast from the man in the pit. Futile, since the chief was well out of the line of fire.

"His mates will come and let him out," Read said as the three of them slipped in behind the tribesmen, Taine falling in behind Barb at five.

"Maybe. At least it'll be time they'll waste not looking for us."

The moans of the dying man carried on the breeze.

Ka ran.

Two of his tribesmen were dead, shot down, including Ka's cousin, but not before the two strangers fell into the pit to perish on the sharpened spikes. It was not a fair exchange. Ka's cousin had been a good man. Now Ka was running for his life, hunted by the one who did not fall, the one who had stolen his cousin's soul.

Ka kept his feet supple, skipping and swerving through the forest, leaving only the faintest footprints in his wake. He made no sound. Even his breath was quiet. Behind him, the soldier did not bother with stealth. As bold as a sea lion, he crashed through the undergrowth. But he was younger and fitter than Ka, who was only a teacher, and he was making ground. Ka stole a glance backwards. Clad all in black, something in the soldier's face glinted in the moonlight. He was coming fast, the gun held low near his hips.

Ka shuddered and ran harder. Guns were deadly. Even the strangers were helpless against them. The big warrior they called McKenna had failed to save Māpura's brother. What could he do? What could anyone do? The gun had reached in and ripped Wai's heart from his chest. Now Wai was dead, his spirit departed on its journey home. Ka will be dead too, if the stranger catches him. Ka would be easy to kill. The soldier will barely have to raise his arm.

Legs trembling, Ka ran on, passing near the lake where the children had been taken. The lake would save him. He would slip into the water and hide in the darkness. He put on a burst of speed. It would be a close race. Ka scrambled down the hill, running through the clump of flax where yesterday he'd realised the children were in danger.

Wait!

Ka dropped to his knees. The kea. It was still in the trap. Ka flung down his spear. He opened the trap and plucked out the bird. For two days, it had been in the trap, and it was angry. It struggled in his arms, but it did not bite him, its snapping sawing beak clamped shut, bound by that strange piece of flax. Gripping the beak closed, Ka flicked the flax off with his spear. The bird flapped in his arms. Ka grasped it tighter. He peeked through flax blades.

The soldier was just paces away now. He stopped still. He had heard the bird struggling. Ka breathed slowly, trying to calm the thunder in his chest.

Wait.

The soldier lifted his gun. He approached the flax, creeping now, but it was a clumsy effort.

Ka held the bird tight, his blood surging.

Wait...

The soldier pushed the end of the gun into the flax clump, parting the blades.

Ka released the bird. It flew at the soldier.

The man threw up his gun to ward it off, but the parrot

was wild with pent-up rage. It attacked his face, yanking off the mask, and raking its claws into his skin. The man hurled the gun away and hit out with his hands. In the flurry of feathers and arms, Ka spied the loop on the man's nose; the glint of light he had seen in the darkness. The kea snapped its curved beak, like a spear, driving deep. The stranger flailed. Staggered forward. The parrot stabbed again. Wings wide, it tossed its head. Flesh tore, the sound wet as the kea plucked out the loop. Satisfied with its prize, the bird hopped to the ground and scuttled away.

For the first time, the stranger was silent. He brought his hands to his face, then pulled them away, bewildered. His nose was in tatters around a gaping hole. Blood streamed down his face. He fell to his knees just steps from Ka's hiding place.

Blinded by pain and blood, the soldier could not see him. No longer afraid, Ka got to his feet and picked up his spear. He kicked the trap into the undergrowth.

The stranger's head jerked up at the clatter, blood bubbling from the cracks where his nose had been. Desperate to get away, he scuttled backwards like a crab.

Ka lifted his spear, ready to slide it between the man's ribs, but changed his mind.

Lowering his weapon, he stepped away silently.

21

Fiordland

A fern snagged on Jules' boot. Stumbling a little, she shook her leg and kicked the branch away. Dusk had fallen while they'd been in the cave, although it was clear enough. The moon was hanging low in the sky, its pale yellow light allowing them to jog silently through the bush, Jules in front, and Hine keeping an eye out at the rear.

Like the Lost Boys of Neverland.

Mere darted through the trees, no doubt eager to be home. More than once, Jules had to reach out a hand to slow her down. She didn't want the girl to get too far ahead. As it was, burdened with the deceased tribesman, the men were struggling to keep up. To be fair, it was a wonder any of them were still on their feet. No one had had anything to eat or drink all day. Jules could murder a cheese toasty, and, unlike the men, she wasn't lugging 110kg of dead weight on her back.

Behind her, Herewini's panting was hoarse.

Jules glanced back. "You okay?" she whispered. She wondered where Taine was, if he was okay.

Herewini didn't reply, just threw her a grin - more of a grimace - a sheen on his forehead.

A chirrup sounded behind them. Mere slowed.

They were in a natural hollow, sloping downwards, probably leading to the water - Jules detected the tang of salt - but obscured by the trees and the shadows, it was hard to tell. One thing she could see was the limestone bluff flanking them on one side, its white sediment reflecting the moonlight.

"What's up?" Herewini asked.

Jules checked behind them. Hine had disappeared. "I think it was Hine, calling for a break."

"Thank God," Rocky gasped.

They laid the bodies on the trail, Rocky sucking in lungfuls of air. "Jeepers, I'm too bloody old for this," he said, straightening. He arched backwards, his hands in the small of his back, ironing out the kinks. "I wonder how far we've got to go? We should have hidden these bodies instead of lugging them all this way."

"It can't be far now," Jules said. "Much further and we'll fall off the bottom end of the country." It's true: hiding the bodies would have saved time. She hoped Hine wouldn't be too long. Taine needed the reinforcements.

Mere tugged at her hand. Jules' heart thumped as she looked around. Was someone coming? The men from the submarine? But Mere was pointing to the cliff. Hine was halfway up the chalky surface. The woman was a cat! Jules hadn't even heard her leave. The tribeswoman was carving a route across the rocky slope, webbed toes gripping the crags, her pale flanks gleaming beneath the silver moonlight. She was simply beautiful to watch: no harness, no helmet, no spikes, just fluid graceful moves as she muscled her way up the grade.

Where was she going? Jules scanned the bluff, squinting. Higher up the slope, a dark smudge revealed the entrance to a small cave.

"Please tell me that's not the way to the village," Rocky whispered. "Because if I have to carry this guy..." Several tiny shapes fluttered out of the shadows. "Ah, that's what she's up to," Rocky said. "Looking for bat shit."

As soon as he said it, Jules caught their faint clicking.

"In the bluffs?" said Herewini. "I thought bats lived in old trees: big tōtara and mataī." His eyes followed the tiny mammals as they passed overhead.

"Long-tailed bats sometimes roost in limestone crags," Rocky said. "No one's ever reported short-tailed bats living in caves. Of course, anything is possible; it's been half a century since anyone's seen one."

Pringle was moving off, heading back the way they'd come. "Hey, where are you going?" Rocky called.

Pringle's grin was wide. "To the Bat Cave."

"Damn. I always wanted to say that!" Herewini dived his hand into his pocket, offering an object to Jules. "I do have the Bat Phone, though."

Incredulous, Jules turned the phone over in her hand, but Rocky rounded on Herewini, anger shadowing his face. "What? You had the sat phone all along? I can't believe—" Rocky put both hands on his head and stepped away to calm himself. A second later, he was back. "Why the hell didn't you tell me you had it, Herewini? We could've called for help, for God's sake. We might have been able to save Mahoe. We could've been out of here by now!"

On the cliff face, Pringle and Hine looked up, alarmed.

Herewini gave them the thumbs up. "Keep your voice down, Rocky. Do you want to bring the entire mercenary force down on us? It was already too late for Mahoe – I didn't go looking for the phone until after he was dead – and anyway, I didn't want Summers to see it. I wasn't sure where his loyalties lay."

Jules nodded. Herewini had a point. She wasn't sure even Summers knew whose side he was on. It was so hard to know what to do.

"Well, just don't look at it, call someone," Rocky said.

Herewini's eyes flashed. "Call who? If I'd known, I would've called them already."

"What are you talking about? Call the police. Armed Defenders. The military. Anyone who can get a chopper in here and get us the hell out."

"Don't do it, Jules," Herewini said.

Rocky shook his head. "I don't believe this. We could all die in here. Make the call, Jules, or I'll do it myself." He took a step towards her.

Herewini pushed between them, his palms raised. "You said you'd help."

"That was before I knew you had the sat phone."

"Rocky." Stepping around Herewini, Jules laid her fingertips on Rocky's arm. "Please. We need to think about this. If I call the authorities, there'll be no going back for these people. The minute I make the call, they'll be discovered. How long do you think it will take for information to leak about their special abilities after that? It won't be one chopper that arrives. It'll be an entire fleet. There'll be scientists, academics, paparazzi, and who-knows else. Everyone will want a piece of them. Their way of life will be destroyed, every individual at risk. It's the very thing they're trying to avoid, the reason these people are prepared to put everything on the line."

"Okay, I get that, but we have to do *something*. Those militants are going to kill all of us to get what they want."

"Taine will stop them."

Rocky snorted. "I don't share your confidence."

"You don't know Taine."

He put his hands on his hips. "Okay, well, let's just say your man wins out over a team of highly trained mercenaries. Let's just imagine that scenario. What do you think will happen to us then? How long do you think we'll last? The tribesmen were prepared to kill us before. Do you think if they survive, they're just going to change their minds and let us go? Excuse me if I don't."

Rocky was right, but Herewini was right too...

"I'll call the minister," she declared.

"What minister?" Herewini looked dumbfounded.

"The Minister of Conservation. I'll call her and ask that the area be declared reserve land. We'll say it's vital for the protection of an endangered species."

Herewini shook his head. "But they're not just a *species*; they're people."

"I know that. It won't matter, so long as we can get them protected."

"I think Jules is on to something," Rocky said, suddenly

perking up. "Call it crazy, but Conservation has stronger protections for animals than Social Welfare has for people. We should ask the minister for a fifty-year embargo on entering this section of the forest. That way no one will be allowed in, there'll be no chance meetings, and they'll be safe."

"Providing we see off the mercenaries first," Herewini reminded him.

"Yes," Jules replied. "And providing Summers can convince them not to kill us."

Herewini scuffed his boot in the dirt. "You do know this is entirely fucked up."

"You got a better idea?"

"No."

Jules punched in the number.

"Good afternoon. You've reached the Houses of Parliament."

Thank heavens, they haven't left for the day.

"This is Dr Jules Asher with the Department of Conversation. I'd like to speak to the Conservation Minister, please."

"What's this in connection to, please?" The voice was unctuous.

"I'm sorry, I'm not able to say. It's confidential."

"I see," the woman replied, her tone becoming frosty. "Is the Minister expecting your call?"

"No, she isn't, but—"

"The Minister holds open hours for her constituents. Would you care to make an appointment?"

"I don't have time to make an appointment. I'm in the

field. But she'll want to hear this. It's about the imminent extinction of an important native species."

"I see," the woman repeated, her voice dripping with scepticism. "And which species would that be?"

Jules hesitated. "The thing is, she won't know the name of it. What I mean is, the species doesn't have a name yet. It's only recently been discovered."

"A recent discovery. How fabulous. When was that?"

"Um...yesterday."

She was coming across like a crackpot.

Rocky hoisted the dead cargo on his back again. Hine and Pringle were on their way down the bluff, one of Pringle's pockets smeared white.

"Dr Asher." Speaking slowly, the woman on the line drew out the work 'doctor' as if Jules had got her degree by filling in a coupon on the back of a cornflakes packet. "I'm sure you can appreciate that the minister is *extremely* busy. Every day she's inundated with calls from Greenpeace NZ, Forest and Bird, The New Zealand Sea Lion Trust. If I were to put through every call that comes to this desk, the Minister would never get anything done." She laughed. It sounded false.

"No, no, you don't understand. I'm with Conservation. I need an urgent—"

"If you have a legitimate matter to discuss with the minister, I'd be happy to put you through to appointments."

"Please—"

"Putting you through now..."

Aargh.

The phone clicked through to an automated system, and

a voice said, "The next available appointment for the Minister. Of. Conservation. Is. Thursday. At. 4pm."

Thursday. Four days away.

"Please press one for yes, two for no, or three for further options."

As Pringle and Hine leapt the last metre from the bluff onto the trail, Jules punched the phone off.

What now?

They'd gone as far as they could.

"What the hell?" Rocky said, his words echoing Jules' thoughts.

They were standing on a beach in one of the Sounds, dark waters invading the land, like fingers into a glove.

Jules crouched at the water's edge, cupping her hands to taste the water. Salty. With water washing down from the hills, she'd hoped it might be fresh.

Hine had tucked her spear into a hollow in the bluff and was wading into the water. Mere plunged in after her, scooping up a handful, her webbing acting like a paddle. She doused Jules with a spray of droplets.

"Hey!"

Mere giggled.

"I think they want us to follow them," Herewini said.

Rocky lowered the cadaver to the pebbles. "Do we trust them? They can breathe underwater, remember."

"I think this is how they've stayed hidden," Jules replied. "Summers mentioned a cave. There must be an underwater entrance."

"You don't have to go. You can stay on the beach if you like," Herewini said.

Rocky shook his head. "And miss seeing where they live? I don't think so."

Jules grinned. She knew exactly what he meant. This was their chance to see where the Tūrehu lived, possibly the only time they'd have the opportunity. A lost people with webbed fingers and the ability to breathe underwater. It was the kind of thing scientists dreamed of. They'd all go. It was worth the risk.

Water cascading down her body, Hine returned to the pebbled beach. Grasping the corpse Rocky had dropped, she dragged it into the water and ducked under the surface. Rocky, Jules, and Herewini waded in after her, Herewini towing the warrior's body.

Pringle hesitated. "Hang on. Not yet." Quickly, he shucked off his boots and unzipped his trousers.

"Whoa, no skinny dipping, man. There are ladies present." Herewini nodded at Mere and Jules. Mere giggled.

"Have to. The bat poo; it's in my pocket," Pringle explained. "We don't want it to dissolve, do we?" He hummed the theme tune from Batman.

Jules couldn't help but smile.

Herewini rolled his eyes. "Really?"

Grinning, Pringle rolled his pants around his boots and lobbed the bundle into the bush above the waterline. Then, picking up the dead man by his underarms, he stepped into the water.

"You good?" Rocky said.

"Yup, good to go."

They took a deep breath and disappeared beneath the surface.

Only Mere and Jules remained. "Right, let's do this," Jules said.

No, wait. The sat phone.

She didn't know if it was waterproof or not. Dashing back up the beach, she pulled the phone out of her pocket and buried it under a pile of pebbles. Then, leaving a large stone nearby to mark the spot, she took Mere's proffered hand, drew in a breath, and plunged into the icy water.

When her eyes adjusted, Jules caught a glimpse of Hine's pale hair trailing in the current. As she'd expected, they'd entered an underwater tunnel. Jules released her breath in a tiny stream to prevent the build-up of carbon dioxide in her blood, and wondered how far they would have to swim. The underwater landscape distracted her. It was fascinating. The watery tunnel led deep under the land, the channel bordered on either side by steep bluffs that descended into the inky depths. On one side, a huge horizontal gash appeared in the rock. Was that where the People lived? No, it was completely submerged. The People couldn't survive there. The true cave must be further on.

But Hine veered off, approaching the entrance to the elongated cavern and beckoning to Pringle and Herewini to do the same.

Jules was about to follow, when Mere grabbed her hand and held her back.

Outside the cavern, Hine had the men release the

corpses. The cadavers bobbed in the water, like animated rag dolls, slowly sinking.

What was this – some kind of burial ritual? Maybe intended to strike fear into strangers venturing into this tunnel? Most people would backpedal if they suddenly came face-to-face with a slack-faced corpse fished up from Davy Jones' locker.

The cold water turned colder. Jules' skin tingled as a shape loomed in the recesses of the cavern. Hovering at the cavern entrance was an enormous eye.

A suckered arm snaked out to probe the raft of bodies.

Oh my God.

Jules wanted to close her eyes, to not see...

Mere's touch almost made her die of fright. The child put her fingers to her lips. What was she saying? Quiet? It wasn't as if she could shout underwater.

Shaking, Jules glanced around for Hine and the men. They were gone, slipped away without her noticing.

Terror gripped her. Mere, though, was composed. 'Come,' she seemed to say with a tilt of her head.

Jules needed to hold it together. For heavens' sake, a child less than ten years old had more backbone than she did. Fighting down panic, and keeping her movements as small as she could, Jules let the child lead her away. Mere glided through the water, passing through a tiny slit in the rock above the cavern entrance.

No, not in there. It's too close. That monster came out of this cliff.

It was too late. Mere had gone. Jules was alone and running out of air, and the alternative was to go back the way she'd come...

Jules plunged through the gap. *Is that light?* Swimming upwards towards the glow, she emerged from the water on a small ledge. She gasped with relief, inhaling deeply, refilling her lungs again and again.

When her chest had stopped heaving, she said, "I saw a light—"

Mere placed her hand over Jules' mouth, urging her to keep quiet. Then, before Jules could stop her, Mere slipped into the water again, hovering in place for a moment while she waited for Jules to follow. The pause on the ledge was just for her to take on air. Her limbs still trembling with shock, Jules lowered herself into the water, following Mere as she ducked under the ledge they'd rested on only moments before.

Jules blinked. This was where the glow had come from. The ledge was the size of a football field, and the underside was a carpet of moving, waving, translucent white bioluminescence. *Squid eggs? Was this the squid's brood?* It was magical. Jules had never seen anything to rival it. Each tiny baby was a fairy light twinkling in the gloom. Line after line of fairy lights. A neighbourhood of stars. An entire world.

Enthralled, Jules swam deeper into the cavern. A year or so ago, she'd read about an egg mass as large as a car discovered floating in the waters off the coast of Turkey. At the time, Jules had thought the divers' report had been inflated, sensationalised to sell papers, or perhaps to secure a funding grant. Now she realised she'd misjudged those divers. There were so many eggs here. Millions. Treading water, she hovered for a closer look. Each translucent sac carried a single cone-shaped squid.

Mere had moved closer too; she was waving her webbed

hands over the surface of the eggs, creating a current. The eggs bobbed and danced in the swell.

Jules' eyes widened. Mere was oxygenating the eggs sacs! Nursing them.

She glanced behind her. Outside in the channel, the colossus sucked on one of the warriors, its beak crunching through the rib cage, the water turning murky with debris.

Her mind raced. Hine had fed the bodies to the monster. A symbiotic relationship? Did the leviathan guard this tunnel in return for food and services from the People? Octopuses would allow themselves to die of starvation while nursing a brood. Perhaps the People helped to stave off its demise while the babies were incubating? Was that why there were so few people? Just twenty warriors. Jules blinked. The idea was too incredible, too fanciful, and yet, strangely, it made sense.

Suddenly, Mere was there, tugging at her arm, beckoning for Jules to come away.

Out of air, still Jules didn't want to leave. Mere tugged again. She pointed towards the mouth of the cavern. The giant eye turned their way. The creature had finished its meal.

Mere's fingers curled about Jules' arm, her face a rictus of fear.

They'd stayed too long. Any mutualism between tribe and squid clearly didn't apply to friends of friends. The bioluminescence, magical just seconds ago, was suddenly garish and stark. And it was acting like a spotlight, signalling their whereabouts to the squid. Outside, in the channel, it hovered, its arms undulating gently with the wash of the tide.

Eyeing her.

Jules' heart lurched. She twisted in the water, her arms thrashing. She had to get away from the eggs. Out of the water! But first, she had to go up to the ledge for air.

Go! She waved at Mere. The child could breathe underwater. She mustn't wait.

Jules kicked for the ledge, dragged herself up with her fingertips. She didn't climb up. There was no safety there; the monster would simply slide a tentacle into the gap and skewer her off the ledge. She barely had time to take a breath before she sank again.

Mere was waiting.

No, no, no. She should have gone, saved herself. But a tiny part of her rejoiced; if there was somewhere safe in this underworld, then Mere would know the way.

Turning, Mere shot through the gap into the channel. Jules swam after her, ploughing through the water. The ceiling too low; she couldn't use crawl, so she used a breaststroke arm action and kicked as if her life depended on it.

Because her life did depend on it.

Mere pulled ahead, gliding silently through the water. Webbed fingers and toes made for speed. Jules kept her eyes on the child's feet. Wherever they were going, it had better be close, because Jules' lungs were burning. If she didn't get a breath soon, all this swimming would be for nothing.

The tunnel forked. There were several openings. She willed the girl to take the smallest entrance. Surely, the monster was too colossal to get through there. But Mere chose the larger one. Jules had to trust her. The air in her lungs was almost spent. Her head was fuzzy, like a fogged-up mirror. She imagined a curled arm reaching out of the mists and yanking her backwards... Her mind playing tricks. She swam on anyway, although she'd lost sight of Mere. She headed for where the water seemed lighter. It was as good a direction as any. The monster was close now, Jules aware of the swell building behind her; the creature so huge it pushed a wall of water ahead of it. She was running before a tsunami.

All at once, the tunnel opened into an enormous cave. Jules' head broke the surface. She dragged in a breath before it closed over her again, then she kicked out, catching the wave and coasting forward.

Her side exploded in pain. Did her rib just crack?

Worry later. *If I'm alive.*

She'd slammed into a wall, like the side of a swimming pool. Every sense screaming, Jules dragged herself onto the ledge. She was as sluggish as mud. She was breathing air, but it was small consolation if she couldn't get beyond the squid's reach. She crawled, scrabbling forward on her hands and knees. How long were its tentacles? Twenty metres? She hadn't gone far enough. Jules staggered to her feet. Stumbled. *Slippery.* Got up again.

The crack of a tentacle near her feet made her jump in fright. Curved like a sickle, it was as white as polished ivory and large enough to be the demi-god Māui's own fishhook.

Jules ran, catching a glimpse of Mere to her left. The child was up and running across a three-metre plateau, heading for a cliff.

Drawing the squid's attention away from Jules.

It was then Jules noticed the line of people standing at the top of the bluff; children, warriors, even an old woman, come out to watch them die. Part of the ritual? No, because her colleague Rocky was there too, and Herewini.

"The ladder! Take the ladder, Jules!"

Ladder? Jules saw it. Twenty metres away, it was a concoction of flax and timber. She could make it...

Jules wanted to shout to Mere, but she could barely breathe. There was nothing she could do to help the girl. Jules gripped the ladder. Lifted her foot. It took all her concentration to find the rung. The ladder swayed wildly. Four rungs up, she made the mistake of looking down. Half of the squid's mantle was out of the water, resting on the plateau. Extending its reach. Mere had made it to the bottom of the bluff.

Jules drew in a breath. Her heart clenched. There was no ladder there. The child had sacrificed herself to give her more time. All the more reason to focus on the rungs in front of her.

Above Jules, Pringle gave a woot. "Come on, Mere! Go, go!"

Cheering? Jules glanced across. Mere was climbing the cliff *without a ladder*. The girl was a real-life Spiderman, her webbed hands and feet creating a seal on the wet rock, allowing her to cling to the surface. When she reached the top, Hine was waiting to pull her to safety. Jules wanted to cheer, too, but with Mere safely out of reach, the leviathan turned its sights to other prey.

"Hurry!" Rocky screamed.

Legs wobbling like jelly, Jules climbed. Her clothes were heavy, slowing her down. She waited for that polished sickle. Another rung, then arms were grabbing her, pulling her upwards. Jules collapsed on the ledge.

"That was close," Pringle said.

On the plateau below, the squid eyed them. Then it heaved its mantle off the plateau and plunged into the water, soaking them with spray.

22

———

Fiordland

They waited a moment, listening to the forest. When it was clear, the noises still distant, they moved forward again. Suddenly, Māpura thrust his spear across Taine's path.

Taine pulled up.

Really?

But the warrior flicked his eyes to the ground ahead of them – the man had prevented him from running headlong into a second pit. As Taine nodded his thanks to the tracker, the chief crawled forward on his elbows to check the pit for survivors.

When the chieftain had given the all-clear, Taine stepped forward and glanced over the side. Two soldiers would not be re-joining the fray, but nor would the tribesmen who'd been with Ka. Shot in the back, they were lying face down on the other side of the pit. Māpura and the chief picked up the bodies and slipped into the bush.

"Where's Ka, then?" Barb said.

"Running. Drawing them away. It's the only explanation. He wouldn't have left the body here," Taine replied.

"We should drop someone down there and retrieve the weapons," Read said. Putting his spear down, he moved to the edge of the pit. "I'll go."

Shots cracked in the trees nearby.

Taine stopped Read just before he dropped into the pit. The chief and Māpura were back, urgently signalling to them to move out. "Later," he said.

The next pit was close. A bunch of mercenaries were milling around the edge. Taine, Barb, and Read crouched behind a large rock while Māpura and the chief skirted the site. Taine squinted against the gloom. The mercenaries' body language suggested that their comrades had tumbled into the pit. It can't have been pretty – one man was vomiting into the bushes. The other mercenaries were standing around the bodies of the dead tribesmen.

One of the mercenaries turned over a corpse with his toe, the action offhand.

Taine's hackles rose. The tribesman was dead; nothing was going to harm him now, yet still the mercenary's casualness annoyed Taine.

Māpura isn't going to like it either.

"How many?" Taine mouthed to Read.

Read held up his hand. Seven mercenaries. Taine nodded. It had been his count, too.

Spears whistled. Taine saw two of the seven crumple, one tumbling into the pit. Shots boomed as the remaining mercenaries peppered the area where the chief and his tracker had been just seconds before, but the quick-thinking warriors had already gone, charging off through the forest like a pair of road runners. The mercenaries shot off after them.

When the coast was clear, Taine, Read and Barb approached the pit.

"Quick, let's hide the bodies until we can come back for them," Taine said.

Taine and Read hoisted the dead tribesmen onto their backs, while Barb helped herself to the dead mercenary's NVGs, slipping them over her head.

"I'll have that, thank you very much," she said. Picking up the man's weapon – an M4 carbine – she kicked the body into the pit, grunting a little from the effort. "Not as nice as my Remington, but I guess it'll do."

"Barb," Read urged, hitching the body higher across his back. "We have to move."

At least one of them was armed. Barb should be able to defend herself. Besides, right now Taine had his hands full.

They carried the bodies far enough from the pit to make it difficult for the mercenaries to locate them, but not so far that the tribesmen wouldn't be able to find them later.

In the event that there *was* a later.

Barb showed Read where he could stow the body in the gap under a log. Read set about covering the corpse with leaf litter. Good call. The bodies were still warm; a layer of leaf litter should mask any remaining heat and prevent the mercenaries from detecting them. Laying the second corpse in a hollow, Taine was scooping up a bunch of leaves when his hands touched something. Taine pulled it out. It was a flaxen net, a large one. Whether it was meant for birds or fish, Taine wasn't sure. It was possible its owner no longer had use for it and had abandoned it, but more likely it had been stowed there deliberately. Māori typically kept their canoes stashed close to rivers and lakes where they might need them, so perhaps these people did similar things. Taine wasn't going to look a gift horse in the mouth. Leaning his spear against a tree, he snatched up the net, gesturing to Barb and Read in the gloom.

"What have you got there?" Read whispered.

"A net. It looks big enough to hold five or six men."

"You thinking Ewoks?" Read said.

"There's no time to set something like that up," Barb said, obviously familiar with the movie. "The forest is crawling with mercenaries. We're just as likely to run over it ourselves and find we're the ones hanging upside down and helpless. Maybe if we drop the net down on them from the trees?"

Taine scanned the nearby beech, searching for a low hanging branch sturdy enough to take his weight. He spied a good candidate on the edge of a small clearing. "That one looks solid enough."

"I'll take this one opposite," Read said, taking off.

Barb didn't move, waiting for Taine's instructions. He clasped her upper arm. "Barb, I'm going to need you to pick off anyone we miss. Can you do that?"

It was one thing to shoot a deer, but a person was a whole other ballgame. It was a big ask for a civilian; Taine hated to do it, but they needed her help. Barb had the skills; Taine had seen her shoot, only these were men – some of them her countrymen.

Barb nodded, her curls bobbing.

"Okay, then. You should probably find cover."

When Barb was clear, Taine twisted his torso, whirling

the net twice like a hammer thrower, before hurling one end of it into the trees. It caught in a tangle of branches and epiphytes. Taine gave it a good yank to make sure it wasn't going anywhere. It held fast. Then, using the net for footholds, Taine scrambled into the tree where he straddled the branch. Now all he had to do was free the net and toss one side to Read.

He tugged at the webbing. It was stuck. Snagged. He got his hands in, shaking the net hard to separate the tangle of flax and branches. There was a creak from a big widow maker wedged near the trunk, but the net simply tightened.

On the ground, at the edge of Taine's peripheral vision, Barb waved the rifle to attract his attention.

"Boss." Read's murmur reached him from across the clearing. "Incoming."

Taine looked over the forest, glimpsing movement where the moonlight reflected off the waxy leaves. Two separate groups were passing beneath the trees below. Two groups. Hunters and hunted?

"Wait for the second group," Taine called to Barb. "There should be five of them."

Five mercenaries. Close range. Barb was a good shot, but she wasn't familiar with the firearm or the optics. Too many for her. Across the clearing, Read realised it too. Standing on the branch, he was preparing to leap from his perch onto the passing men.

Dammit, Read. Who do you think you are? Tarzan?

Taine gave the net a last tug, but it was a wasted effort. There was no time left.

Māpura and the chief burst into the clearing, running straight past Barb, who was leaning against a tree trunk, the rifle at her shoulder. The tribesmen might not have seen her, but if the mercenaries were using thermal gear, her heat signature would announce her like an airport billboard.

Taine had to act now, or they'd all be dead.

Leaping to his feet, he glanced around, desperate for a branch to throw. If he found one long enough, if he dived from here, he might be able to bring the group crashing to the ground.

Crashing to the ground…

Crouched low to keep his balance, and his arms wide like a tightrope walker, Taine ran along the branch. Spinning, he slammed his back against the tree's massive trunk and bent his legs, his boots poised. Not yet…

The mercenaries dashed into the clearing, firing at Barb. The American returned their fire, which meant she was still alive. *Get out of there, Barb.*

Using the trunk as ballast and his body as a human crowbar, Taine shoved as hard as he could at the base of the widow maker. The huge mass shifted sideways, dirt and debris crumbling. Almost there. It wouldn't need much to tip the balance. Closing his eyes, Taine flattened his shoulder blades against the bark and heaved again. *Come on!*

The epiphyte tipped…and fell.

A shout rang out, only to be muffled by the plant mass crashing to the ground.

"Don't you fucking move," Barb said to a protruding torso. Prudent, but she needn't have bothered. The twist in his neck told Taine the man was dead.

Taine dropped inelegantly to the ground, Read arriving seconds later. They found the mercenaries, at least *parts* of them, sticking out from beneath the giant lily, the rest presumably crushed under the falling missile.

Five men killed, plus another nine in the pits, and at the cost of three tribesmen. Maybe four, since Ka was MIA. Fifty men, Oma had said, possibly more. They were running around like mad things and barely making a dent in the numbers.

"Look for the guns," Taine whispered.

Barb keeping watch, Taine and Read raced to find them, using their nails to search amongst the mass of vegetation. They found two: one was mangled, the barrel crooked at its midpoint, and the other barely visible, buried deep under the sod. They had to have a go. They needed the gun. Read used his spear as a lever so Taine could slip his fingers under the butt plate, but Taine's hands were covered in dirt and he slipped backwards. He got to his feet, rubbed his palms on his pants, and they tried again.

"Listen," Barb whispered.

Taine stopped what he was doing and strained to hear. The thrum of boots. More men were on the way. Māpura and the chief rushed into the clearing. This time, the tribesmen didn't bother with signals, the tone of their shouts warning enough. They charged straight through, collecting Read and Barb.

Taine gave the rifle a final tug. It was no use. He'd have to leave it. He grabbed the spear, still where he'd left it leaning against the tree, and got the hell out.

23

———

Fiordland

While the People were rushing about, collecting their clubs and spears and preparing for battle, Jules sat on the ground at the edge of the bluff and took in their surroundings. The underground cave was vaulted in parts, thin slivers of light dappling the rock from fissures up high in the craggy ceiling. There was a draught coming from somewhere too, natural vents that allowed the People to live here, but were too small to serve as an entrance. They had to be too small. Otherwise, why else would the People choose to swim in and out past a giant squid?

A mama squid with a very big appetite.

Emerging from a cluster of small huts at the rear of the plateau, Mere carried a gourd and a basket of food over to them. She offered dried fish, mushrooms and roots to Rocky first, then to Pringle and Herewini, and finally to Jules.

"How are you feeling?" Rocky asked Jules, as he ripped off a piece of the leathery fish with his teeth. "Ribs okay?" he said through his mouthful. "You crashed into that wall pretty hard."

"I'm okay. Nothing's broken. I'm just a bit shaken, that's all." Jules nibbled on a fern tip. Like asparagus in texture, the flavour was vaguely spicy, reminding her of radish. It was simple fare – bush food – but Jules was grateful for it, although she might've enjoyed it more if her stomach wasn't so jittery.

Taking out his mint tin, Rocky took one and offered the tin to Jules. "Last one."

"Thanks." She popped it in her mouth.

Pringle was grim. "Do you think you'll be able to swim back out?"

"Yes, I'm fine. Really. It's only a bruise." Jules cupped her hands and Mere poured fresh water into them from her gourd of bull kelp.

An older couple near one of the huts eyed them warily. It occurred to Jules they must be as terrified of her as she was of the squid.

"You know, Jules, you could stay here until this all blows over," Herewini said.

Stay here? It was a tantalising thought. Staying meant delaying her trip through a monster-filled tunnel. It would give her time to learn more about these people. Jules entertained it for less than a second. Taine and the others were still in the forest, where they were outnumbered and outgunned. Plus, two of the tribe's children were still missing. She shook her head. "I'm coming," she said.

"It looks like they're almost ready." Pringle gave her his hand and helped her up. Below them, Hine's warriors were gathering at the water's edge.

When it was her turn, Jules climbed down the ladder, Mere descending the bluff using her hands as she had before. Why hadn't the warriors done that, too? Were their larger bodies too heavy, the webbing not sufficient to hold them? There was so much Jules wanted to know about these remarkable people.

At the bottom of the ladder, Jules trembled as she considered the water. Calm and smooth, there was no sign of the beast.

The first warriors entered the water.

Jules hung back.

Mere gave her a nudge. The girl handed Jules a small bone knife and said a few words. Her face was solemn. They'd only met a few hours ago, but already the girl held a place in Jules' heart.

Crouching, Jules placed her hand on the child's shoulder. "Thank you, Mere," Jules whispered. "I promise to be careful." Kissing her on the forehead, she tucked the weapon into her belt. "We're going to find your friends and get them back."

"Jules, it's time," Rocky said.

Nodding, Jules filled her lungs and slipped into the water, her heart fluttering with fear.

Meredith's men removed the sound, digging out four dead, including two with cracked skulls and another with a broken neck. A fifth man had survived, although he was out to it, with broken ribs and a leg cranked the wrong way at the knee. He'd be a liability going forward.

Jackson picked a mangled firearm out of the pile of crap, shook the dirt off it, and used it to point to the net dangling above them. "Looks like they set this up," he said to Meredith.

Meredith grunted. He ground his boot into the turf. It'd been a mistake to split his men into smaller teams. The plan had been to come in wide of the chopper site and herd them towards the coast. The village had to be somewhere further south. Instead, the natives were picking them off in the dark. The Mer-people were canny. Finding them was like grasping at fog. "That's six dead, Jackson."

As well as these four, they'd found two others in a pit, skewered like a pair of cocktail sausages.

"Yes." Jackson fiddled with the gun. "The men are complaining about the NVGs not being effective. They're saying everything's blurred."

Meredith raised an eyebrow. "They're blaming the equipment?"

"I don't think so, sir. Are your goggles working? Can you see me?"

Meredith could see him just fine. No imaging technology worked perfectly in the bush. It wasn't the gear. He'd have to have Bones confirm it, of course, but Meredith suspected that seen through a T2 scope, Mer-people didn't give off heat signatures like regular people. He smiled. Another reason to like them: Digby's Mer-people had the potential to become super-soldiers. It made catching them harder, but it also meant he could raise the price. Maybe add a zero.

Jackson broke into Meredith's train of thought. "If it's

okay with you, boss, I'm going to send a small party back to the submarine with Peters."

Peters? Meredith realised he must be the one with the back-to-front knee.

"Should we move the bodies too?" Jackson asked.

Meredith wondered if it would be better just to push them all, Peters included, into the pit and throw a bit of dirt over it: save them a lot of time and effort. It was tempting.

"We'll get them later," he replied. "Kilgour too. Right now, I want you to round up the men. We're going to find that fucking village."

Jules, Pringle, Rocky and Herewini emerged from the water and plopped themselves on the pebble beach. Fighting for breath and firing on adrenalin and fear, they burst into nervous chatter.

"I thought I was going to die!" Pringle said.

"Tell me about it," Herewini agreed. "I knew they lived in our waters, but shit-a-brick, a squid that big? I nearly wet myself."

"Same," Pringle replied, striding up the beach to retrieve his trousers. "It wasn't so bad going in because I didn't know it was there, but coming out my heart was going for it. I don't know what I would've done if it had been there."

"Had a heart attack?"

Rocky rolled over and got to his feet. "Maybe that's why Summers didn't mention it."

"Why he lived forty years in a mangled chopper, you mean," Herewini said.

Pringle zipped up his fly. "Do you think maybe Summers wanted us dead? Because that thing came this close to killing Jules." He pinched his thumb and index together.

Too close. Jules shuddered, recalling the animal's stare.

Rocky slapped at his pants. Soaking wet, they stuck to his legs. "What happened in there – when we offered the bodies to the squid – that wasn't random. There was a ritual to it. A process. I think there's a loose mutualism between the tribe and the creature. Anyway, something went wrong. We stepped outside the ritual somehow and it set the creature off on its rampage."

"What I don't understand," Pringle said, shaking his head, "is if that's your attack dog, why do battle with the mercenaries? Why not just go wait it out in the cave until they're gone?"

Herewini cuffed him on the arm. "Hey, do *you* want to go back in there?"

Jules wrung the excess water from her shirt. "Because the leash on that attack dog is barely a single strand. And because they have to come above ground sometime." She leaned over to pull the sat phone out of the pebbles, her bruised ribs protesting, and slipped it into her pocket. "The People can't live hidden away from the sun indefinitely. They need fresh food, building materials. I think they retreated into the cave for safety. Maybe they encountered a hostile tribe, or the Haast eagle was picking them off or something. I doubt the squid was there to start with. Maybe it came later, or it returns occasionally to lay its eggs." She put her hands on her hips and sighed. "Who knows? Maybe, for them, fighting the mercenaries is about making a stand."

Hine touched Jules on the shoulder. Jules turned. The

little group of warriors was ready to move. She looked them over, seeing past the spears, the thick stone clubs and the flaxen nets, and saw the piercings. Scars. Muscles, still wet from their passage through the tunnel and lean enough that she could pick out the striations. Jules could taste the coiled energy on the air. These warriors weren't like Taine, they were too fair for that, but they reminded her of him, like a bull in that split second before the charge. She almost expected them to break into a war dance. Instead, they shifted their feet impatiently.

Oh my God. Taine! Here they were lolling around on the beach catching their breath, when they should be getting back to the cave classroom. They were almost out of time.

"Come on!"

Hine led the way, the warrior woman setting a cracking pace. After a year in an office job, Jules struggled to keep up. It didn't help that they were taking a different way back to the cave. At least, she thought they were going back to the cave. The trees seemed denser and the terrain steeper, but perhaps that was because they were heading inland. Maybe they weren't going back to the cave at all? Perhaps they were going straight to join the battle. Jules wasn't sure. There hadn't been time to make a decent plan, and any communication with the tribespeople was limited to waves and gestures. She had to trust Hine and the tribesmen to know what to do. The forest park was their home.

Gunfire hammered in the distance, the echo bouncing off the valley walls. Jules' heart jolted and she jumped off the trail into mānuka bush. The forest reverberated with the flap of birds and insects fleeing, and then, just as suddenly, everything went still.

What had happened? Had Taine been involved? Jules prayed he was safe.

Hine whispered to the men. All but one melted into the trees. Jules stepped out of the bush, and Hine led the rest of them over the ridge and down into the next valley.

"Smell that?" Herewini murmured when they were nearing the bottom of the ridge.

Jules had been so busy trying to keep her footing in the dark that she hadn't been paying attention, but now the smell of rotten eggs assaulted her.

"We're going for the sulphur," Rocky said.

Minutes later, they emerged at the base of the hill and Hine led them along the valley floor to a small hot spring, the water simmering on the edges. Just the sight of it made Jules long for a soak. "Oh God, I'd love a bath," she murmured.

"I think that 'bath' might be a little too warm," Rocky said.

"We're wasting our time. These aren't the right sort of pools," Pringle said.

"Keep looking," Rocky insisted. "Summers mentioned a yellow crust, so it must be here. And be careful. Watch where you step."

Either the moonlight was stronger or her eyes had adjusted because it was easy enough to pick out the plumes of steam. Jules played a game of join-the-dots, darting from one steaming vent to another, checking for deposits. Some of the vents were only the size of her palm, but one or two were larger.

"Over here," Herewini called to them softly. He wafted his hand in front of his face. "Yup, I reckon this one is definitely pumping out hydrogen sulphide gas. It smells like week-old socks."

Jules approached the steaming fumarole and crouched near the edge, her eyes watering. "Pringle, there are sulphur deposits on the rim here." She removed the bone knife at her belt and used it to scrape away the crumbling deposit. "What are we going to put it in?"

"Here." Rocky took a green beanie – Department of Conservation issue – from his pocket and handed it to Pringle, who began brushing the yellow powder into it.

"It gets cold out here. You might need that hat later," Jules said, angling her knife to scrape off more of the golden crystals.

"Right now, catching a cold is the least of my worries," Rocky said. "I'm more concerned about all the paperwork I'm up for."

Jules smiled. "I'm so sorry about everything. This trip—"

Rocky patted her shoulder. "None of this is your fault, Doc."

Suddenly, Hine hissed them to silence.

Something loud was coming through the trees.

Jules stood up and crept away from the vent. Whatever it was, it was big. A deer? Wild pig? Riled up, pigs could be deadly. Jules held her breath. She tightened her grip on Mere's bone knife.

A pig or a deer would be preferable to a team of armed men.

A man clad in black stumbled into view. His hands cupped to his face, he was weaving from side to side as if he were drunk. Was he injured? High on drugs? Either way, he didn't seem to notice that they were there.

They stood frozen, saying nothing.

He passed by Hine without looking up.

As he approached Jules, she realised he couldn't see. His eyes had swollen to tiny slits. Lurching sideways, his foot hit something and he stumbled, flinging his hands out in front to balance him. His face was a mess of blood.

He had no nose!

Jules gasped in shock.

"Who's there?" he croaked, full of fear. "Anyone there?" He staggered backwards.

No! Not backwards. The fumarole—

She lunged, arms outstretched, but Rocky grabbed her, holding her tight and preventing her from grasping the man's jacket.

The man lost his footing. Wind-milled his arms. Tip-tip-tipped into the gaping fumarole. It was a classic cartoon fall, his limbs flailing in mid-air before he dropped.

He wailed, but not for long.

Still, the sound might have alerted his comrades if they were close. They needed to run. Instead, they stared as the man disappeared into the steaming sinkhole. Jules' eyes filled with tears. There would be no body to find. The steam would cook the muscle off the bone like lamb shanks in broth. Even the bones would break down. It would take a few days, but the acid would do its work, removing all trace of the mercenary.

When they could no longer see him through the steam, Rocky squeezed Jules' shoulders quickly, and released her. "Let's go," he said.

24

Fiordland

When they arrived back at the schoolroom cave, it was empty.

"They're not here," Rocky said, disappointment in his voice.

Jules' heart sank. Rocky wasn't the only one who'd hoped for a miracle.

"We have to give them a chance," Rocky said. "Read thought there could be as many as seventy men on that submarine. Whatever they're up to, they'll be busy."

"Let's make the shot while we're waiting," Pringle said. "Jules, can you find me a flat rock to mix it on?"

"Will this do?" Near the entrance, the rock was too heavy for Jules to lift. She gestured to Hine's companion guarding the cave entrance to help her carry it over. By the time they'd moved it deeper into the cave, Pringle had whipped off his pants.

"All this down trou-ing is becoming an obsession," Herewini said.

"We don't want to waste any of the powder. I have to get all the bat droppings out, and I can't do it when my pants are on," Pringle replied. "Jules, here." He threw her a lump of charcoal. "If I'd known we'd be doing this here, I wouldn't have bothered to carry this around. Can you break the lump up into a powder? We don't need much. Around about the same amount as the sulphur."

Jules put the charcoal on the ground and crushed it to a fine powder with a rock, while Pringle turned his pocket inside-out, his fingers scraping every last bit of excrement from the fabric. He crumbled a couple of the bigger lumps with his fingers. When he was done, it looked as if he'd tipped a cup of flour onto a board ready to make a batch of scones. If only it smelled like baking; the salty odour pinched Jules' nostrils.

"That's the potassium nitrate sorted," Pringle said, gently brushing the powder off his fingers. "Now for the sulphur. Rocky, pass me your hat, will you?"

Using both hands, Rocky turned his hat inside-out and sprinkled the yellow grit on top of the bat poo. "There you go."

"Jules. Your turn," said Pringle, who was putting on his pants.

Jules scooped up a pile of charcoal, carrying it over to the rock while Pringle fought with his zipper. She added the black powder to the mound, then blew the dust off her hands.

"I hope you made a wish," Pringle said, sweeping the greyish mixture into Rocky's beanie with the heel of his hand.

Jules shook her head. There was too much to wish for.

"What now?" asked Herewini.

Pringle shrugged. "Now we get the gun and we load it."

Crossing the cave, the pair lifted the punt gun from its hiding place under the bush. Pringle fiddled around with it for a bit, eventually pulling out a tubular attachment from near the trigger end.

"Breech loading. The shell goes in here. I wish we had a cartridge or cardboard to make a casing. I guess we pack the powder in here with stones and shit and hope for the best."

Herewini held out a pack of cigarettes still sealed in its cellophane wrapping. "Will this do?"

Pringle smiled. "Let's give it a go." He grasped the red tab and tore away the cellophane.

Jules turned. Rocky was at the fire. Was he trying to stoke it up? Jules wasn't sure they'd be here...

Rocky dropped an ember into his mint tin and closed it up. What was he...?

She looked back at the flat rock. The sweepings were gone.

"Rocky, no!" Jules cried.

Too late. The mint tin exploded with a whump, throwing Rocky backwards and sending Pringle and Herewini diving to the ground. Jules spun on her heel. She flung her arms up over her face. Noise reverberated in the cavern. The stench of sulphur almost knocked her out. A long minute passed. A flicker of purple teased the edges of her vision.

Jules lifted her head and blinked away tears. The cave was full of white smoke. Her ears still ringing, she waved her way through the cloud to Rocky. "Are you okay?"

Did her voice always sound so hollow?

Rocky sat up gingerly. His face was chalky. "Shit." Jules could barely hear him, the blast still resonating in her head. "Sorry, I wasn't thinking properly. This whole plan seemed so hare-brained, you know? I wanted to be sure it worked. There were only the dregs of the powder left." Swaying with pain, he held one of his hands across his chest.

"Let's have a look."

Rocky winced as Jules turned his hands over. Hardly surprising. His palms were scorched black, the right one already beginning to blister, yellow liquid beading beneath the skin.

"To be honest, I wasn't sure it would work either," Pringle said, examining the cave wall where a fragment of the tin lid was embedded in the clay. "It's got a lot to do with the quality of the charcoal."

Herewini shook his head with disbelief. "It worked great. Just as well there were only traces of the dust left, or Rocky might be pushing up daisies right now."

Hine ran over, her face full of alarm. She gestured to Jules that they should leave.

"Hine's right," Jules said, getting to her feet. "We'd better get out of here. That explosion was pretty loud. They probably heard it as far away as Invercargill."

Stuffing Rocky's hat into his shirt, Pringle picked up the end of the punt gun. "Worse: the cave will have acted like an amplifier."

"Ah, shit," said Herewini, shouldering the other end. "Every mercenary in the forest is going to be on their way here."

"Rocky, we have to move. Do you think you can walk?" Jules urged.

Rocky didn't get a chance to answer. Grasping him by the armpits, Hine's warrior friend lifted him to his feet, and, draping Rocky's arm around his neck, led him out of the smoky interior, Herewini and Pringle trailing with the punt gun.

Jules glanced back. Cigarettes were strewn on the ground. Snatching them up, Jules tucked them into her bra and hurried after the others.

~

Aitken Street, Wellington

Trigger flexed his hand to get the blood moving. It was late, after six, and after all the time he'd spent at the computer today the tendons were aching, reminding him that he was down to his last hand. It was worth it. He and Michael were finally starting to get somewhere.

They'd discovered the submarine was privately-owned, its proprietors a company called NuLife Commodities. As a name, it told them nothing. Hundreds of companies went by the name NuLife – a battery company, a global medical supplier, a senior living community, even a pair of father-son wood restorers. The NuLife they were interested in gave its business description as an import-export trader. Trigger's bullshit radar had pinged. It was too banal, too *nothing*, not to be suspicious.

Why does an import-export company need a submarine?

Trigger stretched his arm to the ceiling. There were plenty of badass reasons. Drugs and weapon trafficking were offering good returns, but people were the big seller at the moment, smugglers taking their pick of desperate refugees to sell on as sex workers, fruit pickers, and diamond miners. Taking advantage of people's misery.

It was why Trigger had joined the army: to put an end to that kind of crap.

So, he'd sent Michael to check the intelligence databases, while he searched the Companies Offices of no less than four countries, trying to shake out NuLife's parent company, and, ultimately, the person or persons behind it. The whole process was a genealogy project, like one of those passages in the Bible where one thing begat another. There'd been a lot of begat-ting in Nulife's history. Whoever owned *The Catfish* wanted it well hidden.

Trigger heard Michael coming before he bounded into the room, the dance of his footsteps barely conveying his excitement.

"Sir! The submarine. *The Catfish.* I found...something."

"You know you sound like William Shatner?"

Michael grinned. "Well, remember that starship that's come boldly into our waters? It's the subject of four Interpol Special Notices: one blue, two green and a purple."

"Purple..." Trigger murmured, racking his brain for the relevant code.

"Information on modus operandi, objects, devices and concealment methods used by criminals," Michael reminded him. "I did some digging, and it seems Interpol suspect the sub was involved in a massive ivory trafficking racket brought down by their Operation Worthy II. There were 376 arrests involving 25 criminal groups, but they weren't able to pin the sub down. That was in 2015, so before our time. I've forwarded it to you."

While Trigger pulled up the file, Michael put his hands on the desk and stretched out his calves. Trigger scanned the details, reading parts of the document aloud:

"...4.5 tonnes of elephant ivory and rhino horn, thousands of other wildlife products were also seized, including 2,029 pangolin scales, 173 live tortoises...warthog teeth, big cats...python skins and impala carcasses, as well as 532 rounds of ammunition, five firearms and two home-made rifles."

He looked up. Michael had his arms folded across his body. He looked like a kid who could hear the ice-cream truck around the corner. "This is good work, son," Trigger said. "Illegal trafficking of protected species."

"Except that ring was essentially shut down," Michael said.

"So, what would a submarine suspected to have been involved in smuggling exotic species want in Fiordland?"

"Tuatara? They're exotic. Birds? Or maybe New Zealand isn't their destination. Maybe Fiordland's just somewhere to hole up on the way to somewhere else."

"Hmmm." Trigger stood up and rolled his shoulders. "I've got something, too. Let's get some coffee, shall we?"

They walked to the kitchenette on one corner of the floor. They weren't the only ones working late. Several of the outer offices were still lit up. The sink was full of dirty mugs.

Using his good arm, Trigger grabbed two mugs by their handles, holding them out for Michael, who dropped a spoonful of instant sludge into each one.

"So? What have you got?" Michael asked.

Trigger held mugs under the tap for him to fill. "A name. A director. Well, there were a lot of names, but mostly the directors were all paid representatives, trustees or company accountants, that sort of thing. The only one that wasn't is a guy by the name of Gary Cohen. There was an address – somewhere in Barber Town, Boise."

Michael lifted his cup from Trigger's fingers. "We could call," he said.

"We could, but it's after 10pm in Idaho. I'll call in the morning. In the meantime, you follow up on those Interpol notices. Try not to get too excited. Interpol deletes information when it gets past its use-by date, and Operation Worthy has been wrapped up for a while."

"Then I'll just have to be creative," Michael said. "Find out which jurisdiction posted the original information." Hyped up, he took his coffee and dashed back to his desk.

Trigger took his time returning to his office. He hadn't realised this desk stuff could be so thrilling. It was a different kind of warfare. Right now, he felt like a big cat, slinking forward on his belly in the grass, just waiting for the right moment to pounce.

They were so close. All he needed was a little more information.

~

Fiordland, chopper site

In the tail of the chopper, David squeezed his eyes tight and snuggled deeper into the bed of sleeping bags. It wasn't the first time he'd lain awake listening to the noises coming to him from the forest; the hooting of owls and the creak of the beech trees as they bent their heads together in sleep. Tonight, though, the katydids were quiet, shocked to silence by the distant roar of gunfire and the screams of dying men.

Wishing he could block out the sounds, David turned over, the new sleeping bags crinkling softly as he moved. Things had changed while he'd been off the grid; the sleeping bags were made of a fabric he'd never seen before.

There was a scrape outside in the clearing. A boot scuff?

He froze, listening. He wasn't concerned that the mercenaries would find him. The chopper was buried deep in the undergrowth, its metal chassis dulled by a layer of moss and grime. In forty years, no one other than the People had discovered it and that was only because the chief's father had heard the crash and come to investigate. McKenna and his crowd wouldn't have found it either if the current chief hadn't needed a translator. All David needed to do was to stay quiet and whoever it was would pass him by.

"Anyone there?" a voice whispered. *English.* David didn't recognise it, although he didn't think it was one of McKenna's group.

There was another scuff outside the chopper, closer this time.

David held his breath. He imagined the man holding his breath too, the pair of them listening for one another. After a while, the stumbling resumed and the intruder moved off.

Alone again, David took the battered photo of Gina out of his pocket and held it in his hand. He didn't bother to lift it to his face to examine it. It was too gloomy in there to see, the shattered windscreen replaced years ago by a line of ponga trunks. It didn't matter: he'd stared at the picture so often that every nuance of her face was etched on his mind. The way her mouth curved, the fall of her hair. Although the photo couldn't help him with her voice – he could imagine other things: her lips at his ear, the tickle of her breath against his skin – but no matter how hard he tried, her voice escaped him.

David stared at the roof of the chopper. Perhaps it was because he hadn't liked the story she'd been writing of their lives together? The plans she'd been making? Because he couldn't picture himself holding down a nine-to-five job and mowing the lawns every weekend. Because he didn't want to hear her crying.

So, instead, he'd spent forty years sleeping rough in a hollowed-out metal husk.

David closed his eyes, the warm luxury of the sleeping bags doing nothing to staunch the deep throb in his leg.

He'd let her down.

He hadn't run away, not deliberately, but he hadn't tried hard enough to get back to her either. David rubbed his calf with his free hand. It ached to the marrow. Yes, it was true, he had a bad leg. Yes, the People might've stopped him from leaving.

They were excuses.

He'd been scared. All this time, he'd wanted an extraordinary life and he'd been too scared to seize it. All this time, he'd stayed quiet and let the world pass him by.

David sat up. He pushed the sleeping bag off his legs and scrambled to the front of the chopper. Leaving the precious photo wedged between the seat and the seat back, he crept out of the chopper and into the night.

~

Fiordland

Taine gripped the spear in his right hand and sprinted through the undergrowth. As always, there was good and bad news. The bad news was, being the last to leave the widow maker, Taine hadn't seen which direction the others had gone. The good news was he'd drawn a group of mercenaries – three of them – and was leading them inland away from the others.

Except he was struggling to stay ahead.

While Taine was navigating by his wits in the moonlight, the mercenaries had NVGs and, even though he was keeping to the trees to break up the infrared scopes on their rifles, his was a moving outline and much easier to follow than a stationary one. Basically, a child could track him. They were coming in fast, the lead man perhaps only thirty paces back. He was going to have to face them soon.

Splashing through the stream, he ran parallel with the current a few metres before coming up on the bank on the same side. He plunged into the trees.

"I see him. Up to the right!"

Given their ratio, and their superior weapons, it wasn't a surprise that the mercenaries were feeling cocky, but not bothering to keep schtum was a sign of a poorly disciplined force. It improved his odds by a sliver.

Time to make a stand.

Taine dived behind a southern beech, slipping in on his bum.

His body tucked behind the tree, he glanced backwards. The pursuers were less than ten metres behind now. Slowing, the lead man gestured to the men behind him to fan to the right. The leader raised the muzzle of his M4.

With the stream to one side, they planned to box him in. If he didn't want to die tonight, Taine needed to act. Keeping his body as small a target as possible, he drew back his spear, and sighted the man's throat. He weighted the lance in his palm. Found the balance point. Imagined the pulse beating in his opponent's neck.

Go back, man. Don't make me do this. Don't make me kill you.

The man stepped forward.

Damn.

Taine threw the spear.

The man screamed. He fired wildly. Then he was gone.

What the fuck!

Where the hell was he? Taine looked left and right. He was nowhere. Leaves rustled in the canopy. Taine looked up. The man was caught in a snare, dangling upside-down by one foot, his hands clasped at his throat where Taine had grazed it with his spear. Not a fatal shot – at least not yet. The man eyed him silently, not daring to let his hands drop from the wound at his throat.

"Zac! Where are you?" someone hissed.

The man's comrades were coming. With no time to look for Zac's rifle, Taine crept away.

"He's gone," the first man said.

"Gone where?"

"How the fuck do I know? One minute he was here, and the next minute he was gone."

"He's done a runner, then."

"Probably. Coward. Meredith should cut him loose."

Meredith. Taine filed the name away for later.

"Let's just get this guy and then go find the others. He was over this direction."

Good idea. Go back to your submarine, boys.

"Canny bugger. I reckon he's in the water."

"Yeah," his companion agreed. "Trying to fool the infrared."

Waist deep in the stream, Taine dropped below the surface, his fingers feeling for a decent rock, and waited.

When he lifted his eyes, one of the mercenaries was patrolling the bank, while the other had waded in. "Let me know when you see him."

See me now? Taine lunged for the man's feet, whipping them out from under him. The mercenary sprawled backwards in the water. Taine didn't wait for him to recover, throwing his weight on top of him. Locked together, the rifle pinned between them, they tumbled in the shallows, too close for the man on the bank to risk a shot. As soon as Taine had the upper hand, he bashed the side of the man's skull. The thud was sickening, but still the man struggled. Taine bashed again. The man went limp.

Taine opened his hand and let the rock plop into the stream.

"Don't move," screamed the thug on the bank, his gun trained on Taine. "Don't you fucking move, you piece of shit."

"Okay, okay. Take it easy. I'm going to get up." Breathing heavily, Taine got slowly to his feet. He raised his hands in front of him.

Beside him, the stream gurgled about the dead man and carried on its merry way.

"Get over here." The mercenary waved the barrel of the

gun, using it like a traffic lollipop, gesturing towards the bank. It was an amateur mistake and too good an offer not to take up. Grabbing the muzzle, Taine yanked hard, unbalancing the man. Startled, the mercenary stumbled forward, the rifle slipping from his hands as he catapulted into the stream. Taine shot him before he could get to his feet, clouds of blood washing away in the darkness.

Taine rolled the dead men over and robbed them of their gear.

He should run – people were counting on him – but he allowed himself to walk the few metres back, hunting in the bushes to retrieve the mercenary's rifle, a modified M4 semi-automatic. He slung it over his shoulder with the two he'd collected from the river. A drop of blood spattered his chest. Taine looked up. Zac was still alive. Except he wasn't. Even without the nick in his carotid, he'd be dead in hours, his lungs stiffening up and the blood pooling in his brain. Zac knew it too because he turned his eyes to Taine, the whites desperate.

Taine's shot jerked the mercenary backwards. After that, he didn't move again.

25

Fiordland

Off in the distance, an explosion boomed, its echo resonating off the nearby hills. "Who fired that? Was that a Carl Johnson?" Meredith demanded.

"Not us, sir. We didn't bring any rocket launchers. Too many trees."

Meredith's eyes narrowed. Who had fired it? Did the Mer-people have more Samaritans helping them than he'd first seen? The possibility hadn't occurred to him before now. "Jackson, I'm going to take a quick recce. In the meantime, you're in charge. Keep 'em moving forward."

"Yes, sir. And if we find them? Do we capture or engage?"

Meredith paused. "The warriors are fair game, and that goes for the riff-raff helping them, but if you find the village, hold off and wait for my instructions. I want to be there when we take the women and children." The women and kids were what Meredith was after. They took up less space and were easy to manage. Men were another story. Before he'd turned to more exotic cargo, Meredith had transported men bound for mines. Sullen and dangerous, they would stare at him with naked hatred in their eyes. They would take the men if he had to, but not if they could avoid it.

He pointed to three men, pleased that there was one he could name amongst them. "You three come with me. We're going to track down that explosion."

They leapt away, the four of them running double-time through the forest, eventually descending a long slope until they were in a narrow canyon. They hugged the side of the canyon, taking cover among the rocks.

"I think the explosion came from somewhere around here," said the bearded man on point.

Meredith wasn't convinced. He was beginning to think it had been a mistake to try to pinpoint the source. In his mind, the explosion had come from further south. "Well, do you see anything? Anyone?"

"No, sir," said Oscar. The man was taller than Goliath, which was the only way Meredith had remembered his name. "I'm not picking up anything. Maybe they moved out?"

"It might not have been an explosion," the second man, a stocky fellow, said. "It could have been that rockfall over there." He pointed to a tumble of rocks on the other side of the crevasse. "Rockfalls make a racket and the noise would've bounced around in the canyon, making it a hundred times worse."

Meredith peered across the crevasse. The man had a point. Was the rockfall new? Even with his goggles, it was impossible to tell. He'd have to get closer to be sure. "Cover me," he said. Keeping low, he darted across the divide and dived into a hollow in the cliff.

Meredith crawled forward a few metres on his hands and knees, and, taking off his glove, snaked his hand up to pat the top of the rockpile. It was covered in moss and ferns.

Damn. The rockfall had probably been here a decade or more.

26

———

Fiordland

Jules had only just caught up when Hine found Summers. The old man was crouched in a thick copse of mānuka not far from the chopper site.

"Did you hear that explosion?" he said. "Over by the schoolroom."

"That was us. We had a bit of an accident making the shot for the punt gun." Herewini patted the gun, which was resting on his shoulder.

"Shhh. Not so loud," Summers said, putting a finger to his lips, and Jules realised the explosion had affected their hearing. "At least, you know it'll work."

"Yeah, about that," Pringle said, and Summers waved his hands, reminding him to keep the noise down. "I've been thinking. I'm not convinced we should fire it."

"What do you mean?" Herewini said. "We went to all the trouble of getting the stuff and mixing it up and everything. It was *your* idea."

"Yes, but now I'm not so sure. This gun is ancient.

Vintage. Every time you shoot one of these old shot guns, you stress the metal of the barrel. This gun has already been fired twice today and who-knows-how-many times in the past. So far, we've been lucky, but we have no idea if the barrel or the chamber are cracked or corroded. With the new powder, the whole thing could explode in our faces. Just a trace of it blew Rocky off his feet."

Jules looked at Rocky. His injured hand clasped in the other, the poor man was rocking like a circus elephant, his forehead clammy with sweat. They'd had no time to run his hand under cold water even if there'd been any about.

Jules gave Herewini a nudge. "Do you have any painkillers left?"

Herewini dipped his hand into his shirt pocket, pulling out a sheet of Paracetamol. He showed it to her. The foil capsules were all open. "Sorry. There were only four left. I gave them all to Mahoe."

"That's okay. I just wish we had something for Rocky..."

Tucking the empty packet back in his shirt – even now sticking to the 'pack it in, pack it out' rule – Herewini nodded at the bushes. "Pity we can't brew up. Mānuka tea is good for pain. My mum used to give it to us kids."

It was a good suggestion. Brewed into a tea, mānuka leaves and bark were well known for their analgesic qualities. But maybe they didn't have to be brewed to be effective? Pushing aside a scratchy branch, Jules tore off a strip of the papery inner bark and leaned towards Rocky. "Chew on this," she said, dropping the bark into Rocky's good hand.

"And here was me hoping for a barley sugar," he said.

"This should help with the pain."

"Better than a barley sugar, then." Rocky cupped his palm and brought the bark to his mouth.

"Right, let's dress that burn."

Taking several of the cigarettes out of her bra, Jules broke them open and put the dried tobacco in her mouth. Ignoring the taste, she chewed the dried leaf into a pulp, spitting out the built-up saliva. The whole mouthful tasted gross.

"Open your hand."

Rocky did as he was told, and Jules spat the disgusting concoction onto the wound.

"That looks like baby poo," he said.

She spat out the residue. Then, slipping her headband off her head, she looped it over his fingers. "It's like mānuka: an age-old remedy. Goes back to pre-Columbus days. Native Americans used to use a poultice of tobacco leaves to treat ulcers and burns."

Rocky looked dubious. "Does it work?"

"Probably not as well as a fresh leaf would, but with any luck it should slow the pain and stave off any infection until we can get it looked at." She wrapped the headband around his hand, twisting it several times to hold it in place. "Either that or you'll die a thousand deaths from the dreaded lurgy."

"I reckon the punt gun will be fine," Summers was saying, when she turned back.

"A fine mess," Pringle countered. His face lit up. "But we might be able to do something with the powder in Rocky's beanie. We'd need the right spot for it to work. Somewhere with a rock wall. We pack powder and rocks into a hole in the wall and touch light it. The wall means the explosion will be directed one way – ideally away from any of us. It's the same principle behind claymore land mines."

"There's a rock wall back near the chopper," Summers said. "Would that do?"

"Let's take a look," Pringle said.

Taine was sprinting back toward the chopper site, the rifles bumping at his back, when an explosion rocked through the valley.

Jesus. A hand grenade? Or the punt gun? It sounded more like a mortar shell.

He increased his pace, weaving through trees, leaping hollows. It was a trick to avoid Meredith's henchmen. They were everywhere, and talk about a lack of finesse; they were trumpeting through the undergrowth like elephants on steroids. Their leader, Meredith, had obviously given the order to tighten the noose, trying to push their quarry towards open ground. Open ground meant the chopper site. Taine could stop, take some of them out, but even with the rifles, it'd be suicide. Not the kind of odds he relished. He ran harder, putting distance between them.

At some point, Ka slipped in beside him.

Taine gave a start. Even with starlight goggles on, he hadn't seen the warrior until the last minute, the man's signature blurry and indistinct. Something to do with the People's tolerance to cold? Jules would know. Whatever the reason, being able to hide, even partially, from thermal imaging systems was a handy skill. These people had all the makings of a breed of super-soldiers. No wonder Meredith was so keen to get his hands on them.

Taine gave Ka a quick nod. The gnarly warrior was a strange one, although Taine figured he had Ka to thank for the snare back there. He'd probably saved Taine's life. It'd certainly evened up the odds. He offered the warrior a rifle, but the man shook his head. Taine didn't blame him. How many of his people had been lost to firearms over the past century? A tribesman was killed by the punt gun only this morning.

They ran on in silence.

Now that they were ahead of the mercenaries, the forest was quieter. There was only Taine's own heartbeat, and the wind whistling through the branches as it funnelled along the valley. The notes were wistful, like the sigh of a flute.

Ka nudged him. A warning?

Taine ducked behind cover. He raised the assault rifle and looked through the scope. The view was distorted: a cloud of hazy NVG green. What was that? A drift of mist? Taine wanted to reach for his pūrerehua.

All the legends said the Tūrehu were creatures of the mist...

Taine lowered the rifle. Without the scope, Taine recognised Māpura with his twisted matai flute. Taine was amazed. The Tūrehu didn't look like other people in the dark; instead they looked like drifting fog, like ghosts...

Māpura flashed a smile. The warrior was leading a cluster of his tribesmen, the chief tucked in behind his tracker. One of the tribesmen was already dead or dying, his bloodied body carried by one of his brothers. Read and Barb were squished in the middle of the group.

Taine stepped out of his hiding place, and the two

parties came together, Taine slipping into the centre along-side Read.

Read grinned. "What kept you?" he whispered.

"Ran into some old friends." Taine lifted a rifle over his head and handed it to the private.

"Yeah, Barb and I ran into traffic, too," Read said as he slipped his shoulder through the strap. "I think they might be herding us somewhere."

"It appears that way," Taine said, handed him the NVGs.

Read snapped them on. "What about the chopper site? Could we make a stand there?"

"With only four rifles?"

"Some of these guys are pretty handy with a spear."

"It'd be wiser to keep to the current game plan. Small skirmishes. Darting in, picking them off where we can. It's worked so far. There have been fewer casualties on our side..."

"Jules will be back at the chopper by now."

Taine kept running.

"I heard an explosion earlier," Read went on. "Do you reckon that was Pringle?"

"I don't know. Maybe. That whole idea was a long shot. We can't really count on it. How long have you known about the heat signatures?"

"Barb's rifle has a thermal scope. She worked it out. We figured if we stayed inside the circle, their cooler images would cloak us."

The mercenaries' gear was a mish-mash of brands and technologies. Most likely some of them were using their own equipment, supplied by their employer or looted from opponents. Taine looked over his shoulder and gave Barb the thumbs-up.

"Okay, so we stick to small skirmishes," Read said, and before Taine had a chance to respond, he charged back the way they'd come.

"Sorry Barb, gotta go. The idiot thinks he's Indiana Jones." Taine thrust the extra rifle into Barb's hands and tore off after Read.

~

"I might not have thought that out very well," Read said, when Taine caught up to him. "Did we bring any of them with us?

Taine glanced back to count the blobs behind them. "Only a couple."

"We could head for the abandoned hut," Read said. "Follow the chalk markers."

A bullet pinged off a tree nearby, sending splinters flying. An answering shot came from their left. Mercenaries? Flanking them? But why return their own fire? Unless…

"The hut's too far. Let's go this way," he said, veering left towards the gunfire.

By the time he'd located the clump of flax, the firing had ceased. Taine dropped to his belly, Read following suit, the two of them crawling thirty metres on their elbows past the lip of the pit. Still on their stomachs, they shrank behind the beech trunks as their pursuers – two men – came into view.

The mercenaries weren't fooled. They knew about the pits. Wary, they slowed to skirt about the edge.

Taine lobbed a pebble. Hitting the dirt side, it rattled to the bottom. The soldiers whirled.

The man in the pit opened fire, shooting his own comrade on the rim, who toppled forward to join him in the death trap. There was the sound of tearing flesh.

Taine clenched his teeth.

"Ah, shit. Marty. No, no, no. I didn't know it was you, mate. Oh God." The voice in the pit was Australian. Seems Meredith's men were from all over.

"Who's there?" the remaining soldier whispered.

"Brightman? That you? It's McManus. I shot Marty. Didn't mean to... He's dead. Can you get me out?"

The soldier hesitated. He looked in Taine and Read's direction. Taine could almost see the cogs whirr, the man weighing up whether to go after them alone, or to stop and help his buddy in the pit. Better odds won out, because he lay on his stomach, reaching forward into the pit. "Here, can you reach my rifle?"

Taine waited until Brightman was straining to take the weight, his comrade halfway out of the pit, before lifting Brightman by his feet, flipping both men back into the abyss.

Crouched behind a beech, Jules shifted her weight, her nerves tight.

Just get on with it.

Barb hadn't been back long, perhaps only minutes, but the expected mercenaries still hadn't appeared. They'd heard gunfire, staccato bursts that had shattered the stillness and put her on edge, but those had stopped a while ago and the forest had gone quiet again.

The silence was worse.

Suddenly, a morepork hooted in the distance. Jules' heart leapt. It was Ka. The signal. They were coming.

"About a dozen of them," Summers whispered.

"How do you know?" Rocky demanded.

Besides Jules, Summers waved his hand. "It was in the signal," he replied.

Twelve armed men. Twelve rifles to their two. She could only hope Pringle's plan would work.

In the darkness, Jules tightened her grip on Mere's little knife. Beside her, Rocky grasped a rock, his right hand too badly burned to hold a spear.

Where were they?

Perhaps remembering the punt gun, the attackers didn't rush into the clearing. Jules wasn't even aware they'd arrived until they opened fire, the forest crackling with noise, the tiny flickers from their muzzles revealing their locations. From their hiding place in the chopper, Barb and Herewini returned fire.

Spears whistled from the canopy, the air stirring in their wake.

Voices cried out as the missiles struck.

The tribesmen leapt from the branches onto the mercenaries. The canopy hiding Summers' chopper kept the moonlight out, but it couldn't hide the fact that men were dying: Jules knew it from the glint of metal and flashes of pale skin. From the rat-tat-tat of automatic fire. The anguished cries of men passing from this world to the next.

Terrorised, she was also strangely fascinated. Until now,

she hadn't known that a stone club slices flesh with a sound of tearing paper. That a skull cracks with a dull thud.

Summers' voice shook her from her stupor, shouting to the warriors over the din. The tribesmen fell back as a boot sailed into the clearing. It thumped to the ground and tumbled a few metres.

Jules held her breath as the tiny ember burned.

One second.

Two.

Please!

The flax wick disappeared. Pringle's bomb exploded. It lit up the clearing, the noise assaulting her eardrums. The rocks Pringle had crammed into the boot spewed outwards like missiles, cutting through bone and flesh. Black powder seared skin and hair. Limbs were severed. Intestines spilled. Jules ducked to avoid the debris. And smoke closed like a curtain on the scene.

The explosion over, the tribesmen vanished into the smoke to finish off the survivors.

Jules counted only six of the tribesmen, but they might have won this round.

Hine shouted something from the rear.

Summers cursed. "That's why they took so long. There's more of them come round from the back."

"How many?" Rocky demanded.

"A half dozen, maybe more. We have to use the punt gun! Jules, help me with it." The old man hobbled over to where the gun rested in the crook of a tree.

"Summers, don't," Rocky insisted. "Pringle says it's too dangerous. You'll get yourself killed."

"Okay, so I won't shoot it. Just help me point it the right

way. McKenna reckoned the sight of it might scare them a bit."

Taine *had* said that. Sliding the knife back into her belt, Jules lifted the barrel off its perch to run it around the branch, so the cannon was facing the other way. A mercenary ran out of the carnage in the clearing, and almost collided with Jules. He stumbled over the barrel of the punt gun, sending a volley of fire from his own firearm into the ground. Jules covered her eyes. Kicked-up dirt stung her legs. Her pulse pounded. She scrambled at her belt.

Hurry.

He was getting up!

Summers' spear thudded home, piercing the man's shoulder and pinning him to the ground. The man howled. Summers kicked the rifle to Rocky.

Breathing hard, Jules freed the punt gun from the mercenary's feet and set the barrel back on its perch. When she looked up, the mercenary had a handgun. Pointed at her.

There was a blast. A flash of red. Jules looked again. Left-handed, Rocky had shot the mercenary in the stomach. The man slumped, the gun still in his hand.

In the helicopter, Barb and Herewini opened fire. Hine's warning. They'd been flanked.

"Get down, Jules!" Summers screamed.

"But you said..."

"Firing in three seconds, two..."

Jules dived away.

Summers squeezed the trigger.

~

Shouts and explosions shattered the night.

Meredith dropped to his knees and covered his head with his arms. But the explosion was a way off, the sounds of a skirmish unmistakable. Meredith lifted his head as the men joined him in the hollow.

Oscar was the last to arrive, ducking his tall frame to fit into the gap. "I reckon Jackson is taking it to the natives," he muttered, gripping his rifle. The men wanted to be up there on the ridge.

"Okay, let's get up there and find out what's going on," Meredith said.

Only they couldn't climb out of the canyon – the walls were too steep – they'd have to go back the way they came.

It took them ten minutes to loop back to a point just above the rockfall. They were about to follow the shouts when Oscar motioned to Meredith. "Boss, look." He pulled back the frond of a tree fern.

Meredith descended the little bank. Tucked into the edge of the canyon was the entrance to a wide cave. Below the ridge, it had been invisible from the canyon floor. It was empty. Meredith lifted his goggles and stepped inside. He flared his nostrils, breathing deeply.

They'd been here. This cave was a place the Mer-people used. It might even be where they lived. The clearing the kid had led them to was somewhere nearby. Meredith smiled. If this was their home, perhaps they'd come back?

"Sir?"

"Wait outside. Stay out of sight."

Meredith did a tour of the cave. It'd would be worth the effort in case the Mer-people had left an artefact or two. An ancient talisman, or perhaps a forgotten gemstone. Meredith was always a starter for a bit of easy money. There was a fire pit – still vaguely warm – a flat stone, four stripped branches stacked against a wall...

A voice was coming from the entrance. A *female* voice. American.

Meredith ran to crouch behind a rocky outcropping at the rear of the cave. He pushed his body into the shadows. Just in time.

Two women – one signature clear and the other indistinct – stepped into the cave on either side of an old man. He was injured and they were supporting his weight.

Meredith snatched off his goggles. His eyes widened. A Mer-woman. She glanced about the cave uneasily as if she sensed danger. Perhaps she'd heard him remove the goggles? Meredith squeezed himself closer to the wall.

"We're nearly there. Just a few more steps," said the American.

"Don't be daft," the old man said, his voice reedy. "We both know I'm going to die wherever you lay me. I'm riddled with it." He lurched, both women reaching out to prevent him from falling.

"You're the one who's being daft, Summers. As soon as all this blows over and we can get back to camp, Rocky'll get out his sat phone and call up your Kiwi paramedics. I'm sure they have a helicopter."

She was trying to be nice. The man was dead meat. Meredith could see he had more holes in him than a fucking golf course.

The women lowered him to the ground. They tried to be gentle, but still he groaned softly. He had to be over seventy.

Were the Mer-people's saviours all like this? Decrepit old men and delusional females?

Meredith stepped out of the darkness, the Mer-woman catching his movement. She drew in her breath and stumbled backwards.

"Hine, are you okay?" the other woman asked.

The Mer-woman's eyes were on Meredith. She edged towards the cave entrance.

A second later, the American fumbled for her rifle, but, stupidly, she'd slung the weapon to the rear to support the old man.

Meredith grinned. What's that old saying, he thought. No good deed goes unpunished.

"Move again and I shoot her," he said evenly.

The American froze.

Meredith smirked. He could have killed them both three times over by now.

"Oscar, get in here."

Oscar and his comrades stepped forward, their bodies silhouetted in the cave entrance.

"Grab that woman," Meredith said, pointing to the Mer-creature. "We're taking her with us."

The old guy called out in their Mer language. It must've been a warning, because before Oscar could move, the Mer-woman leapt past him like an antelope. She might have escaped if the point man hadn't stepped sideways and tackled her, forcing her into the dust. She put up a good fight, but the ground around her was clear of any rocks and Meredith's man had thirty pounds on her. Flipping the Mer-woman over, the solider thrust his knee in the middle of her back, pinning her there. She grunted in pain.

"Leave her alone," the old guy wheezed. Like he was going to do anything about it. He was minutes away from being a zombie.

"Please. Don't do this," the American pleaded, getting to one knee.

"I told you not to move," Meredith warned.

Biting the fabric of his glove, Point-man pulled it off his hand. Then, taking a cable tie from his pocket, he bound the Mer-woman's hands together. She didn't make it easy for him, kicking and tossing and spitting out a stream of her gobbledy-gook Mer-words.

The point man pulled back on the cable, tightening it. "Hey, boss, did you see—"

Meredith cut him off. "Yes, I saw. Now, get her out of here, and duct tape her mouth, will you? We don't want her alerting her little friends."

"How can you do this?" the American said. "You can't just cart her off as if she's cattle. She's a human being. She has rights. You need to let her go." The woman's voice was grating on his nerves. Meredith was starting to dislike the sound.

"What about this one? Are we taking her too?" the last soldier asked.

"Oh God, no. She can stay," Meredith said. "Oscar will tie up the loose ends here."

Oscar gave a brisk nod. "Boss," he said, training his AK47 on the pair on the ground.

Lowering his own rifle, Meredith strode to the front of the cave. The old man followed him with his eyes. "You bastard," he croaked.

Meredith turned. *May as well stay for the finale.*

The American was shaking now, crabbing away from the muzzle. Silly bitch had finally realised that she was a loose end.

"Please. Please!" she begged. Did she know she looked like a kewpie doll with her mouth open like that?

Oscar squeezed the trigger...

The American screamed. The old man lunged, throwing himself over her body.

Meredith wanted to roll his eyes. *What a fucking hero.*

The cave thundered with noise. The old man's grizzled body jerked and bucked as round after round struck him in the back. Meredith raised his hand and Oscar ceased firing. The woman had stopped screaming.

Oscar started forward, intending to check that the pair were dead. He poked the old man with the muzzle of his AK47, and was about to flip the body over to check on the woman, when the Mer-woman ran past the cave entrance, her hands tied together.

Canny bitch had given the point man the slip.

"Leave her," Meredith barked at Oscar. The American had to be dead and his merchandise was getting away. "Come on."

Underneath Summers' body, Barb played dead. The tinny smell of blood made her want to gag. She clamped her mouth shut. It was all she could do to keep her body from shaking. Only after the footsteps were long gone did she dare to push Summer's body aside.

Covered in blood – none of it hers – she took a stick of

charcoal from the fire pit and left a message on the wall. Then she flipped the M4 to the front and crept out of the cave.

Taine and Read were almost back when they heard the second explosion. They paused for barely a second, before leaping forward again, the blast all the motivation Taine needed to dig it in. He'd left Jules...Taine sprinted into the clearing...

...and stopped.

He bit back a wave of nausea that had nothing to do with the reek of sulphur or the ghosting smoke. The chopper site looked like the killing floor of an abattoir, body parts spattered everywhere, pools of blood shining green-black in Taine's goggles. It was a scene straight out of Afghanistan.

Jules.

Taine dashed from body to body, lifting, turning, dreading what he might find.

"She's not here," Read said.

Her body wasn't here. The knowledge did nothing to stem Taine's panic.

"McKenna?"

It was Pringle. His back against the rock wall, the man was sitting on the edge of the carnage in his socks, trying on a dead man's boots. "Typical, isn't it? None of these guys is the same size as me."

Taine strode over to him. "What happened here?"

Pringle stuck out his foot, gripping the boot by its laces. "I lost my boot, and this one's too big."

Taine's jaw quivered.

Read dropped to his haunches, the rifle resting on his knees. "Pringle," he said gently. "Where is everyone? Are they all right?"

Pringle's shoulders slumped. His let his foot fall. "I told Summers not to use the punt gun. I said it was too dangerous. Stubborn old bastard wouldn't listen, would he? I tried to explain to him about corrosion, but he reckoned the gun would work just fine. Well, the gun worked fine, all right. Spewed more stones than bloody Vesuvius. Most of them went the right way, too. Except the ones that didn't. Summers must have expected it, because he twisted, but the shot found him anyway. The whole side of him looks like a game of Operation. I think he's going to die..." Releasing the laces, Pringle wiped his face in his hands.

"I don't see Summers anywhere," Read said, casting his eyes around the clearing again.

"Barb went with him down to the schoolroom cave."

"Did you see Hine?" Read demanded.

"She's helping Barb. I said I'd come when I found myself a pair of boots. It was an excuse. The truth is, I couldn't bear to watch him die..."

"What about the others?" Taine demanded.

"Herewini's okay. He took off with the chief to chase down a couple of survivors..."

An ache had settled into Taine's diaphragm. Jules was dead. She had to be. Pringle kept skirting around it, not wanting to mention her.

Taine could hardly breathe from the pain. He put his hand out and steadied himself against the wall. He shouldn't have left her.

I should've kept her with me. Kept her safe.

"...and Jules is helping Rocky down to the schoolroom."

Blood thundered again in Taine's veins.

"Rocky's in a lot of pain," Pringle went on. "He nearly blew his hand off." Pringle's shoulders rose and he cackled. "With a mint tin. Can you believe it?"

Jules was alive. It could hail bodies as long as she was okay.

Taine took a breath and crouched beside Pringle. "None of this is your fault. Greed and self-interest are the culprits here."

And someone named Meredith.

"You did your best with what you had." Taine swept his gaze around the clearing. "And from what I can see here, you succeeded. If you hadn't made the bomb, this could have been you lying here."

"Yup. You blew it out of the park," Read said. "And if it's anyone's fault, it's mine. If I hadn't charged off like a bull at a gate, Taine wouldn't have had to come after me, and we might've been back here twenty minutes ago."

Taine stood up. "We've all made mistakes tonight. Now isn't the time for a debrief – there could still be twenty mercenaries on the prowl. We need to find the others and make sure they're safe."

Pringle nodded. He yanked the laces of his boots tight. Taine took his hand and pulled him to his feet.

27

Fiordland, hidden cave

"Taine!"

Covered in blood and dirt, he looked like he was about to drop from exhaustion. Jules threw herself at him, burying her face in his chest. She'd been going out of her mind with worry.

He wrapped his arms around her. "This feels good."

It did feel good.

Smiling, she pushed him away. "That might be the sulphur fumes talking. Pretty sure I reek of it."

He grinned, but it was fleeting, and then he was all business. "How's Rocky?"

Jules lowered her voice. "In a lot of pain. He'll need antibiotics soon – his hand is probably infected. Summers is...he's dead. And Barb has gone." Jules walked him to the back of the cave and showed him Barb's message, etched in charcoal on the rock wall.

Taine read it quickly. "Matt."

Read stood up, his weapon at the ready. "Already ordered my burger to-go."

"Ten minutes."

Read took a step forward, his face pinched. "We should go sooner. The brute tortured Mere. Who knows what they might do to Hine."

Taine nodded. "If the chief and his men aren't back, we'll collect them on the way."

Jules bit her lip. They couldn't do this on their own. They needed help.

Taking out the sat phone, Jules pulled Taine to one side. "Taine, I know he isn't your favourite person, but I'm going to ask Richard to help."

Taine's jaw twitched.

"Taine—"

Taine cut her off. "You're right, Richard Foster is *not* my favourite person. If it weren't for him, Jugraj Singh wouldn't have spent these last twelve months learning to walk again, Trigger would still have an arm, and Coolie...Coolie..." He trailed off. Jules saw his fists bunch.

She stepped closer, her fingertips resting on his forearm. "Richard didn't kill Coolie, Taine. You know that," she said softly.

"Whose idea was it to capture the taniwha, then? For God's sake, he even tried to get you to go along with his hare-brained scheme."

Jules almost smiled. Hadn't Taine asked the very same thing of her only hours later? "I didn't agree to go with him, though, did I?"

"It didn't matter: he convinced de Haas to join him instead. And as soldiers we couldn't just leave them there to die of their own stupidity. They knew our mission was to protect the Task Force. It was our *duty*."

"You have to understand..." Jules turned the phone in her hands. "There's a problem with the model. For a scientist, getting published means getting funding. It's how you secure the job, how you get promoted. It allows us to shine a spotlight on our work..."

Taine was still frowning. She was making a botch of it. How could she explain so he'd understand?

She tried again. "In a sense, scientists are conditioned the same way soldiers are. Your mission is to serve the people, right? So, you're charged with protecting our borders and saving the lives of our citizens."

Taine nodded.

"Well, a scientist's mission is to serve the people too, only the way they do that is through collecting and disseminating new knowledge. Documenting new discoveries. By going after the creature, Richard thought he was doing his *scientific duty*. He was wrong and he put everyone's lives at risk, but see it from his point of view. What we uncovered in the Ureweras took scientific discovery to a whole new level. It was something special. A taonga."

"A treasure?" Taine snorted. "That *treasure* killed eighteen people. And those are only the ones we know of."

Jules chewed at her lip. "You know what I mean."

Taine sighed. "What I know is, if we hadn't been forced to double back and find him, Coolie would still be alive. For what? Foster and his scientific glory?"

"Scientific glory is exactly why I think he'll help us."

Stepping away from her, Taine inhaled deeply, his eyes

sweeping the cave's interior. He dropped his voice. "Seriously, Jules? We'd be trusting him with their lives."

"Taine, please. I have to try. It's my job to conserve New Zealand's heritage. These people *are* our heritage. I feel just as much responsibility for them as you do."

He stared at her for a moment, then gave a curt nod. "Come on. We have to go outside. The sat phone needs a clear line to the sky."

They slipped out of the cave, Jules following Taine until he found a good spot. "Try to keep your voice down," Taine said. "Just in case." He turned his back on her, his rifle pointed out towards the forest.

Jules punched in the number. She knew it by heart. She and Richard had been friends for over a decade. "Hello, Richard."

"Jules?"

"Yes, it's me. Hi."

"That's it? You don't talk to me for a year and then you ring up out of the blue to say hi? I called you. I left texts. I talked to your parents, hell, I even visited Sarah a couple of times, hoping that I'd run into you and you'd give me a chance to explain."

Jules had known about the visits. She'd recognised his car in Sarah's driveway. She'd turned her own vehicle around, calling Carol-Ann, Sarah's caregiver, to give her excuses to her friend. "I'm sorry. I wasn't ready to talk about what happened in the Ureweras, and then later it seemed best for everyone to just move on."

"So, you've moved on? And you're calling me now because you need a reference?"

"No."

"Did you split up with McKenna, then? Is that why you're calling?"

"No. Richard, please listen. I haven't got much time."

"Well, that's just dandy, isn't it?" His voice was brittle. "Jules Asher wants to talk and everyone has to down tools and listen. Too bad if I'm preparing funding applications to protect the research interests of her former colleagues. Too bad if we're in the middle of—"

"Richard, just shut it, will you?"

On the other end of the phone, Richard's breath was quiet. In. Out. In. Out. She imagined him pushing the flop of hair off his face.

"I've found something big."

"Another taniwha?" Richard's voice is infused hope.

"Bigger. At least, not size-wise, but in terms of importance—"

"Jules, what did you find?"

"You have to promise me that the information I'm about to tell you remains confidential."

There was the slightest pause. A person could be fooled into thinking it was a problem with the sat phone, but Jules knew better.

"Confidentiality, yes, of course."

Jules' turn to hesitate. If she got this wrong, she couldn't just turn the car around and drive away. People could lose their lives. Mere. Hine. *Taine.*

"We found a lost tribe, Richard. The ghost people – the Tūrehu."

"You found some bones?"

"No, we found a living community." Jules caught Richard's intake of breath. "They were here all the time, living in isolation in the bush. Well, not entirely. There have been occasional rare contacts, but essentially they've been isolated."

It occurred to her that the People's limited exposure to outsiders would make them susceptible to modern day diseases. Already, they could have put the entire colony at risk. All at once, getting Richard to agree to help became even more important.

"How many of them are there?" Richard asked.

"There were forty-three, including eight children, although we've lost some recently. The children are the reason I'm calling you. You see—"

"Jesus. I knew you could be hard, but I really had no idea that you were such a vindictive bitch. That's why you're calling, isn't it? To gloat? To tell me you're about to be New Zealand's answer to Jane Goodall?"

"I'm sorry?"

"I can't claim the giant Sphenodon, but you can claim a lost tribe? Well, you wanna know what I think, Jules? I think you can go fuck yourself."

What? "Richard? Hello?"

He'd hung up.

Taine turned to look at her, but with his goggles on, she couldn't see his eyes. She waved to let him know she wasn't done yet, then, her hands shaking, she phoned Richard again.

"What now?" he said.

"You can have it. You can name the tribe. Call them whatever you like. I'll get you the evidence you need to claim the discovery. Richard, it's possible these people are Denisovans. They have pale complexions, syndactyly of the hands and feet, their own language, their ability to breathe underwater…" She trailed off. She couldn't bring herself to mention the mutualism, Rocky's theory about the symbiotic connection between the People and the giant squid. If this backfired, the monster might be the only thing between the People and extinction.

But Richard's stunned silence told her she'd said enough.

"You're kidding me," he said eventually.

"Not at all. In fact, I couldn't be more serious."

"They can really breathe underwater?"

"The children can stay submerged for around fifteen minutes. I don't know about the adults. Possibly longer. One of them had a sucking chest wound and I was able to get a glimpse of the frilled lung tissue—"

"And you'd give me that?" Richard interrupted, clearly not concerned about who might have died. "People who can breathe underwater. I don't believe it. There has to be a catch."

She paused.

"Yes, I knew there'd be a catch. What do I have to do to claim this glittering prize then?"

"Call the minister. You know her. Get her to establish a wildlife sanctuary in southern Fiordland under the Wildlife Act."

"You want them classified as endangered *species*? But you just said they have their own language. They're sentient. You're talking about classifying them as animals."

Jules sighed. "Can you see any other way?"

"How much land?"

Jules heart leapt. Did this mean he'd help?

"As much as you can get the minister to agree to. Effective immediately. She needs to prohibit all access into the sanctuary for a period of at least fifty years, and that includes by sea. These people have to stay hidden, Richard. I'm sure I don't have to tell you why."

"Right, so let me get this straight: I name your tribe and get myself written into the history books as the person who discovered them, but unless I live past ninety, no one will know. Any accolades will be posthumous."

"Yes." Jules bit her lip. "It's the right thing to do."

He was quiet.

"Richard?"

"I'll think about it."

"What did Foster say?" Taine asked when she had punched the phone off. "Will he do it?"

Jules clasped the sat phone to her chest and shook her head. "I don't know."

"Hand me the phone," Taine said.

Aitken Street, Wellington

The phone rang. A call from the switchboard.

At this hour?

Trigger picked up. "Grierson."

"Trigger. It's me."

McKenna? That was odd. Why hadn't Taine called him on his cell?

Because no one bothers to remember numbers anymore. McKenna had contacted him through Defence because he knew the department's number. This wasn't a social call.

"I need your help with something," McKenna said, confirming it.

"Fire away."

"I'm in Fiordland with Jules." Trigger sat forward at the mention of Fiordland. "We've stumbled on something. There's a submarine—"

"We know about the submarine."

"Ah. Well, you should also know it's not friendly. A bunch of mercenaries have just come ashore. Poachers. They're armed. Up to seventy of them, judging by the size of the sub, although just recently they've taken a few casualties. I believe the leader is a guy named Meredith. An American."

Meredith...Meredith... Trigger was sure he'd seen that name. Tipping his head to one side to trap the phone against his shoulder, Trigger clicked back through the windows on his screen, searching the documents.

No, not that one. Yes, here it is: Ajax Meredith. He was Gary Cohen's stepson.

"Seems they were here to pick up some kea," Taine was saying. "An organised pick-up."

Trigger nodded. "That fits with what we know."

"Yeah, except this time, they found something else. Something more lucrative. A lost tribe."

Trigger stood up and crossed the room to the window. He leaned his stump against the black glass, his own reflection staring back at him.

"Trigger, you still there?"

"A lost tribe," Trigger echoed.

"I know. It's about as believable as our last mission, and this one's no fairy tale either. Look, I can't go into it right now, but Jules has called Richard Foster at LandCare. He's got the details."

"That moron." Trigger pressed his stump into the glass.

"Yeah. But Jules thinks he can help with getting them legal protection." McKenna spoke quickly, "The thing is, these people need help now. Any chance you can get a section down here?"

"Already standing by at Burnham. I'll put in the call, but it's going to take time."

"Thanks. Sooner would be better. And Trigger? We need to keep this behind the wire."

"Gotcha. You take care, boss."

McKenna rang off, and Trigger called up James Arnold, getting the major out of bed to send in the cavalry. When Trigger put the phone down, Michael was standing in the doorway, leaning against the doorframe.

Michael raised an eyebrow. "News?"

"Just got a tip from a source on the ground in Fiordland," Trigger said, tapping his pen on the desk.

"From Sergeant McKenna?"

"What do you know about McKenna?"

Michael shrugged. "Junior Analyst is Defence code for hacker."

Trigger glared at him.

"I checked the Passenger Name Record data for Air New Zealand. Sergeant McKenna flew to Queenstown a few days ago with his girlfriend. They hired a car and—"

Trigger cut him off. "Right, now listen up. McKenna's off limits. No mucking about in his past. If you want to know something about my friend, you ask me, okay?"

Michael rubbed the back of his neck. "Ask you. Okay. Yeah, sorry."

Trigger let the tension drain from his shoulders. "Good."

"Is McKenna in trouble?"

"He's just asked for back-up. Okay, yes, he's in trouble. So, let's do what we can at this end. McKenna says the sub's leader is a man named Ajax Meredith. He's an American citizen and Cohen's stepson. I want to know who he banks with, who he talks to, what his favourite emoji is. Give me everything you can find on him, including the last time he farted."

Michael gave a deep sigh. "You do know I've got a hot date lined up."

"No, you haven't. Junior Analyst is code for girlfriend-less."

Michael grinned. "You're right, I haven't."

"Make some coffee, Michael. Looks like we could be stuck here a bit longer."

Rotorua township

Temera tossed for a while, listening to the sound of the television down the hall, Wayne's laughter. It was hot in his room, and his head ached. He flung his covers on the floor and lay there in just the sheet...

The morepork's call was shrill. Temera woke on the beach, his spirit-self lying in the cold sand. His head pulsed and ached, its ceaseless pounding mirrored by the thump and crash of the surf. Wind whipped at his hair and made his eyes water. Temera sat up, his feet still buried in the wet sand, and wiped the grit out of his eyes.

He was here again. That didn't make sense. Taine had already seen the submarine. But the throbbing in his head told him there had to be another reason. He was supposed to see something. But what? It was late afternoon and the sky was heavy; the grey of the clouds and the grey of the sea bleeding together at the horizon.

"What am I supposed to see?" he shouted at the waves.

The little morepork cheeped.

"Yes, yes, I know. I'm supposed to work it out for myself."

Curling his toes in the sand, Temera closed his eyes and opened his mind, letting the vision reveal itself. His head ached. He breathed deep and, all at once, the dark mass was there again, surging forward with the swell of the waves. This time, the water parted and at last Temera saw what had been plaguing him: it was a taniwha, a giant wheke-squid with arms thicker than Temera's waist. It swam towards him, propelling its massive body forward in smooth ominous thrusts, an eye fixed on Temera.

He trembled as it lunged into the shallows and snaked out an arm, swiping not at him, but at Taine, who was suddenly beside him on the beach. The soldier's feet swept out from under him, the squid seized him by the ankle and lumbered backwards, dragging its catch towards the water.

Taine pulled out a spear – *a spear? From where?* – the soldier stabbing at the squid, driving the blade down hard, almost severing the limb. The creature jerked its tentacle back, yanking him beneath the waves.

No!

Temera could only watch, trembling, as man and

monster did battle, Taine's spear thrusting quick and deadly, while the taniwha's suckered tentacles snapped inwards, pulling Taine nearer and nearer to its razored beak, and all about them the sea roiled in a violent mass of foam and blood. In seconds it was over, the pair disappearing beneath the surface.

Temera held his breath, even as the waves quieted. He shivered in his pyjamas. He had to warn Taine.

They'd got it wrong: the submarine wasn't the problem.

Fiordland

Ka was sitting in the branches of a tōtara, where he had been since he gave the call of the morepork at the beginning of the battle.

Three strangers passed beneath him. The first was running hard, his breath wheezy, like wind in a blowhole. He looked back once, then ran on. He did not stop. Two more men came, this time supporting each other. With their arms clasped as they staggered through the ferns. They reminded Ka of kereru pigeons at the end of the summer after they have eaten too many juicy puriri berries. They fluttered this way and that, stumbling over things, making their journey longer. It was not the only journey they will make tonight. Ka could smell the blood on the air. These two were near death. Ka watched them pass, waiting a moment before he relayed the message to his chief using the call of the bellbird, letting the notes break a little at the end, mimicking the songbird when she is sad.

The moon had moved only a little on her path through

the sky when someone else had passed beneath him. It was the woman: Barb. Her gun raised, she was as stealthy as a rat. She crept through the undergrowth, carefully keeping out of sight. Where was she going?

Intrigued, Ka climbed down the tree and followed her.

~

At the stream, Meredith pulled the men up.

"Oscar," he said, over the babble of the water. "I want you to take the woman back to *The Catfish*." He smirked. Recapturing the Mer-woman had taken only minutes. "Bones has a condo ready for her." Meredith checked his watch. Just a few hours until dawn. "Tell the pilot we'll be leaving the minute we settle this. And Oscar?"

"Boss?"

"That woman is worth a small fortune. We've already seen how crafty she can be, so be careful. I don't want her lost or damaged."

Nodding grimly, Oscar slipped into the darkness along with the other men.

Radioing ahead to Jackson, Meredith jogged through the milky green forest, enjoying a moment's solitude. When he found the group, Jackson was debriefing a man just returned from a skirmish with the tribe.

The mercenary's jacket was ripped, and his face was smeared with blood. "I'm telling you, they had a rocket launcher!" he said.

"You're sure about that?" Jackson asked." A bunch of civilians with a rocket launcher?"

"I'm sure. Don't take my word for it. Ask the nine men

who didn't come back. They're dead, shredded to ribbons. I'm the only survivor, apart from Arnand and Siddarht over there." He dipped his head, indicating two men at the fringe of the group. Slumped on the ground, one man was cradling the other, making Meredith wonder if they were brothers. Calling them survivors was marginal. He turned his attention back to the speaker.

"Did you see the rear guard?" Jackson asked

The man shook his head. "Hardly. There wasn't much left after the natives turned their *rocket launcher* on them. It vomited shrapnel. Those who didn't fall headed for the water."

Clapping the man on the arm, Jackson dismissed him.

When he turned to Meredith, he spoke in an undertone. "I'm not liking this. I haven't called a roll yet, but we could be down twenty men."

He pursed his lips. Replacing that many men would be difficult.

Jackson fingered his rifle. "I saw the girl breathe underwater. Do you think perhaps the mutants have other...powers?"

Meredith laughed. First the man grows a conscience, and now he believes in fairies? "It's not the natives. It's McKenna and his band of Samaritans. They've done this. Get your men together, Jackson. Time to get this over with."

28

Fiordland

"There you are," Barb said.

Ka did not know these words.

Keeping his head low, he crept forward on his elbows and joined her on the crest.

Her eyes grew wide when she saw him, but after a heartbeat, she nodded, turning back to stare down the slope. Below them, the bad men had summoned the silver whale that would swallow them and carry them in its stomach. They were hurrying across the beach. Ka glimpsed the pale hair of his former student in the bunch.

Hine!

They were taking her away. So, Barb had been chasing Hine's captors. Ka wanted to kill the men, but they were too far away to reach with his spear. The shaft would fall short, and he would still be angry.

He glanced at Barb. The woman was lying with her belly flat against the rock, following one of the men with her eyes the way a tuatara watches a fly.

Only her eyes moved.

Her body was still.

She lifted the gun, setting the flat end hard against her shoulder, her elbow resting on the ground. She looked along the weapon towards their enemies.

Before you hurl a spear, you must first balance the shaft in your hand, and consider the mood of the wind. It seems using a gun was not so different. Ka thought of the two guns he had hidden in the forest earlier today.

Barb touched something on the side of the gun, and it clicked like a beetle.

She breathed evenly. Curled her finger around the tongue of the gun. Exhaled.

All at once, the lightning flashed. Thunder boomed. The gun danced with excitement.

Ka jerked his head to look at the beach. The tallest of the men had fallen to his knees. Someone ran to him – shook him – but he was dead. Even from this distance, the gun's fire had reached him. The lightning flashed again. The man's friends abandoned him, leaving him face down in the sand while they rushed to join the silver whale, dragging Hine with them.

Barb looked down the gun, but Ka knew she could not make the thunder again. She could kill Hine.

Ka's student turned her eyes to the top of the ridge, her hands behind her back. Did she see him? Ka lifted his chin to her. She was still alive. There was still hope.

Take care, my daughter. Look to the children.

A noisy canoe carried them to the whale. When Hine and the men had disappeared, Barb and Ka crawled away from the crest.

Standing up, Barb gave him a sad smile. "Just trying to tie up a loose end," she said.

Ka did not know these words either.

More gunshots rang out.

They couldn't wait any longer.

"Jules, you stay with Rocky." Taine didn't want to leave her, but this was the safest option.

Unfortunately, she had other ideas. She put her hands on her hips. "Rocky can look after himself. I'm coming with you."

Taine wanted to tear his hair out. He couldn't have eyes everywhere. How was he supposed to keep her safe?

He took her hand. "Jules. Rocky's hurt. What if Meredith comes back?"

Jules shook him off. "You don't think he's coming back," she said, matter of fact. "Because if you did, you wouldn't let me stay."

"She's got you there," Pringle said, chuckling.

Rocky got to his feet. "It doesn't matter. We're all going," he said.

Taine gave him a hard look. Rocky was her boss. He could've pulled rank. "What about your hand?"

Rocky just shrugged. "You're the one who said we need to work together."

Taine didn't have time to argue with them. He spun on his heel and strode out of the cave. "Okay, stay close. Read, watch our six o'clock."

In a valley near the chopper site, they ran into Herewini,

Māpura and the tribesmen. The sight of the warriors made Taine uneasy. There were so few of them left, although those who remained seemed larger than life, their muscled bodies gleaming in the silver moonlight.

Herewini lifted two rifles off his shoulders and handed them to Taine, who passed one to Pringle, hesitating before handing the other to Jules.

"Sit-rep," Taine demanded, forgetting Herewini wasn't a soldier.

"We saw to the stragglers," he said, unfazed. "Those were their guns. Then we collected the dead warriors and hid the bodies." He scanned the group. "Where's Hine?"

"Captured," said Read. Standing up, he faced the chopper site and raised the assault rifle to high ready.

"And Barb?" Herewini asked.

"She's here," said Read said, lowering the rifle as Barb and Ka arrived at a run.

"Hine's on the sub," Barb puffed. "Ka and I followed the men who took her from the cave. The leader wasn't with them."

"Then Meredith won't be far away," Taine said.

He spoke too soon. Bullets ricocheted, pinging off nearby trees.

Fuck.

"Take cover!" Taine shoved Jules behind a bunch of rocks and dived in after her.

Māpura pushed his chieftain to safety behind a fallen log, one of the warriors covering their passage. The tribesman lifted his arm and let his spear fly. Before the spear landed, he was blasted with gunfire, his chest pummelled. Thrown backwards, the body lay in the dirt, blood weeping from a checkerboard of wounds.

Taine leaned out, picked a target and fired. He jerked backwards as the spot he'd just been in was razed by shells. A body tumbled sideways. Shots grazed the trees. Bark flew. Branches fell. The mercenaries were hitting them with everything. At this rate, any cover would be blown to smithereens.

His back to a beech tree and being peppered from both sides, Read was struggling to get off a round. Barb was doing slightly better. The American had taken cover behind a landslide where one huge boulder was balanced on top of another, the gap in between acting like a crude tripod. It was keeping her body protected and her aim steady. She looked down the scope and fired. There was no wind to spoil the shot. The target screamed, but only once. Barb looked down the sight again.

Beside Taine, Jules poked the barrel of her rifle from behind the rock. She squeezed off a couple of rounds, before a well-aimed shot swatted the rifle out of her hands. She squealed as the weapon skittered sideways. Only a metre away, the AK47 was just out of reach. She snaked her hand towards it.

Taine grabbed her. "Leave it," he said.

"Boss!" Read shouted over the din. Taine whipped his head around. The mercenaries were creeping forward. Read was about to be pinned down.

Signalling to Read to fall back, Taine covered his retreat, emptying his magazine in a storm of noise and heat. Then he pushed Jules behind him, forcing her back the way the chief and his party had come. Rocky and Pringle joined them from where they'd been sheltering in a hollow. Rocky handed Taine his rifle. "You have more use for it than I will."

"Where does this trail lead?" Taine asked, stopping to pop off a couple more shots to allow Ka, Māpura, and the other tribesmen get clear.

"Narrows into a canyon and leads down to the beach," Pringle said. "The entrance to the People's cave is there. It's under the water." Bullets pinged above their heads.

Fuck! They were leading Meredith and his cronies right to the Tūrehu's underground sanctuary. This was exactly what they'd been trying to avoid. "This canyon. Can we hold it?"

Pringle shook his head. "Nah. Too wide. There aren't enough of us."

"Where's Batman when you need him, eh?" Herewini muttered.

Keeping to the crags, they followed the trail, Read and Barb guarding the rear.

A good marksman, Barb was making every shot count, but they would be out of rounds soon. What would they do then?

Survive first, worry about that later.

"In here." They sheltered in a crag in the limestone bluff.

"McKenna!" Read shouted, opened fire, providing them with cover. Taine herded them in, making room for Barb to slide into cover beside them. They were all on one side of the valley now, the beach just 100 metres away.

A zodiac.

There was so much gunfire that Taine hadn't heard the inflatable boat arrive. Converged around a man, shielding him as if he was the POTUS, a group of the black-clad

Stormtroopers were sprinting for the zodiac. President Meredith bugging out.

Read saw it too. "The leader. He's leaving," he said, popping off another volley.

"Let him go."

"But he's got Hine. The children. If that submarine leaves…"

Taine watched Meredith's back, and his eyes narrowed. "I know. But if the Tūrehu lose any more people, there'll be no one to bring those kids home to."

"The tribesmen have to retreat," Jules said.

"I can't go," Rocky said, holding up his injured hand.

Pringle handed him his rifle. "There's only one bullet left. I was saving it for a special occasion. Make yourself small until we get back."

"Thanks."

"We can't tell the warriors, so we'll have to show them," Herewini said. Dodging fire, he dashed into the undergrowth at the foot of the bluff.

Did people have to keep charging off? "Cover him!" Taine called.

Pringle zig-zagged over to help Herewini, Taine and Read providing covering fire.

The pair were dragging the bodies Herewini and the chief had hidden earlier. The corpses were wrapped in a flax net. It looked like a fisherman's catch, only instead of pulling the net out of the ocean, they were dragging it back in.

What on earth?

Did they think Taine and Read could hold these guys off forever? "Leave the damn bodies!" Taine shouted. "It's the living we're worried about!"

"We have to feed the guard dog," Jules said, as they hauled the net to the water.

Taine had no idea what she was talking about. Turning his attention back to the mercenaries, he raised his rifle and fired.

~

"Go!" Meredith ordered.

Men were still piling into the zodiac.

Meredith kicked them off with his boot. "Hold them off. Tell Jackson I'll send reinforcements," Meredith shouted over the parting roar of the zodiac.

He'd already decided there would be no reinforcements. Ten men had gone down in that shoot-out. Ten men in less than ten minutes. Talk about a fucking SNAFU. Everything was up the shit. It was bloody Namibia all over again. Meredith figured he'd cut his losses. McKenna and his mutants might not have a rocket launcher, but they were still more trouble than they were worth. It would be dawn in an hour. He'd just have to tell the client the price would go up.

Commodities.

Sitting low in the zodiac, he watched the battle play out on the beach. McKenna didn't know it, but Jackson only had a handful of men left. Hard men. Used to scrapping. He really should've offered them an incentive to stick it to McKenna.

Some of McKenna's group were getting into the water. So, the remaining mutants had decided to swim off into the sunset. Meredith couldn't blame them. If he could breathe underwater, it's what he'd fucking do.

Hang on.

He sat up.

It wasn't just the mutants who were getting into the water. The Samaritans were getting in, too.

Yes, he just saw two of them duck under the waves.

Why would McKenna's people do that? Unless the Mer-people lived in an underwater cave? One not too far from the surface?

Meredith's eyes narrowed as he picked out the American woman. The bitch wasn't dead. That wasn't ideal; she'd seen his face.

Well, there was still time to remedy that.

"Hurry it up," he barked at the man at the outboard. "I promised Jackson reinforcements."

When the others sank below the water, only Taine, Read and Māpura remained on the beach. They hadn't been able to get the warrior to leave. Injured, Rocky had made himself scarce. The firing ping-pong continued for a while, Taine counting five, maybe six bad guys.

Except his magazine was empty. He lifted the rifle to show Read the window. Read checked his own. He held up three fingers. They were out of rounds. The mercenaries must have suspected it. Getting bold, they flitted forward, moving in and out of cover. They weren't firing much either. Perhaps they were out of ammo, too? They were here to pick up a bunch of tribesmen with spears. They hadn't come expecting Armageddon.

"Boss." Read pointed to the water.

Had the zodiac come back? Taine hadn't heard it. He looked up, and a spike of rage hit him. *Fuck! That was all they needed.*

The submarine was on the move, coming around the headland. Was it leaving the channel? It hadn't dived yet, and Meredith still had men here. But if it dived, the children would be lost...

Time to finish this. Holding a spear in one hand, Taine stamped on the shaft, snapping it in half. He balanced the shortened weapon in his hand.

Māpura drew out his club.

He felt Read tense.

With only limited rounds, they needed to play this carefully. They couldn't afford to waste—

Suddenly, Read was off, the idiot running straight at the remaining mercenaries like a battering ram. He fired off his last three rounds. One man went down, slumping forward on the sand.

One from three wasn't bad, given Read had been moving. Only now he was out of rounds, and out of cover. Taine heard the clack as the magazine clicked empty.

Read tossed the rifle aside, just as a mercenary broke from behind a boulder. Read tackled him at the knees, putting him on the ground.

Seems he'd been right about the mercenaries being short on rounds, because, instead of firing, another man charged in, ready to slam Read with the butt of his rifle. Already on the move, Taine met the blow with a swift uppercut to the torso. The man staggered back, the head of the broken spear embedded in his kidneys.

A fourth man had leapt on Taine's back, grabbing him in a choke hold. Taine dropped his chin, and twisted right, breaking out of the hold.

By now, Read was on his feet, but the tackled man was rising too. With a flick of his boot, Taine kicked up sand, and the tackled man fell back, clutching at his eyes. Read knocked him senseless with a boot delivered to the nose. "Thanks," Read muttered.

Taine had no time to reply. The man who'd choked him was half up and running. Yanking the shortened spear out of his comrade's body, he came at Taine, but he'd forgotten Māpura. The warrior charged him from behind, slamming his club on the man's skull. He dropped, his head mashed.

Ordinarily, Taine didn't believe in hitting a man from behind, but then he didn't believe in criticising someone who'd just saved your life either. Instead, he gave Māpura a quick grin.

A shot rang out. Taine dived to the ground, taking Māpura with him. A fifth man, one they hadn't seen, dropped out of the treeline onto the sand. He'd been hit in the chest, his rifle still in his hand.

Taine rolled over. Rocky gave him a wave from the trees.

"That was close," Taine said. Careless. He should have been keeping count. "Any more we don't know about before we take our heads out of the sand?"

"I only counted five," said Read.

Taine pulled off his shirt and flung it in an arc across the sand.

When it didn't draw any fire, he stood up and put the

shirt back on. He looked toward the headland. The submarine was still in the channel. It hadn't dived yet. "Right," he said. "Let's go and get those kids."

Heading inland through the forest, Jackson heard the gunfire. Three shots, then silence. He didn't look back. Whatever the outcome of the show-down on the beach, he was done with this business. That bastard Meredith had got in the zodiac and pissed off without so much as a backward glance.

He hurdled a fallen branch. Meredith's leaving wasn't the problem. That part was fine and dandy. He was a mercenary: a gun for hire who did what he was told, no questions asked. He didn't mind cleaning up the mess, making sure there were no witnesses, but he'd expected Meredith to have his back. And that meant sending the zodiac back to pick up survivors, not fucking off and leaving them stranded.

The minute he'd seen the tower of *The Catfish* heading out of the Sounds, Jackson knew Meredith had cut them loose. Left them to die. Left *him* to die.

Well, Meredith should've thought twice, shouldn't he? Because Jackson knew enough to have him put away.

He pushed a tree fern out of his path and ploughed on.

A waft of something – a conversation – carried to him on the breeze. Jackson plunged into a bush and listened.

"Hello, anyone up there?" The voice was English.

"Shut it, will you? You're going to get us killed." Another voice; Australian this time.

"Tell it to Marty," the first man said.

"Do you have to rub it in? It was an accident. I thought he was one of those others."

"Well, we can't risk any more accidents. Meredith's going to be pissed enough after this fiasco...that is, if we ever get out of this blasted pit."

They knew Meredith. These men were from the submarine.

Emerging from the bush, Jackson crept towards the voices, keeping his eyes peeled for any movement in the nearby bushes. "Jackson here. Who's down there?" he whispered.

"Thank Jesus. It's McManus and Brightman," the Aussie said.

"We're stuck," said Brightman.

"I'm going to put my head over, just don't shoot me, okay?" Jackson craned his head over the side. In amongst the shish kebabs were two survivors. "Like a hand?"

"No, we just love it in here, don't we, Brightman?" the Aussie drawled. "All the activities. The drinks on tap. We're thinking we'll come back again next year for our holidays."

"Okay, give me a sec." Scouting around, Jackson found a fallen log. He dragged it over to the edge of the pit and hefted it in for the pair to climb up.

"What's happening?" Brightman said as he clambered over the lip. "We've heard lots of gunfire, but we haven't seen anyone in a while."

Jackson stuck out his hand and hauled McManus the last couple of metres. "They're gone."

"What do you mean, gone?" Brightman asked. "Are we pulling out, then?"

"Meredith already did. We're the only ones left."

"The fuck! He left us here?"

Jackson nodded.

"That low-life piece of shit. How are we supposed to get out of the country, then? It's a long swim to anywhere from here."

Dusting himself off, McManus shrugged. "It's fine by me. The Aussies and the Kiwis are only mortal enemies when it comes to rugby, netball or cricket. Any other time, we're the best of buddies. Open borders between the two countries. All I'll need is a ticket home."

"No one's going anywhere until we find a way out of this forest," Jackson said.

Brightman kicked the ground with his boot. "And what happens then? McManus here waltzes off into the sunset or the billabong or wherever, and meanwhile two of us are stuck here, taking the rap for Meredith's little skirmish with the natives."

"Not necessarily," Jackson replied. "I have an idea."

"I hope it's a good one," Brightman moaned.

Jackson hoped so too. He hoped the Kiwi authorities would like what he had to say about *The Catfish* and its owner.

Otherwise, they'd all be wishing they could crawl back into that pit.

Aitken Street, Wellington

Trigger took a swig of his coffee and grimaced. He peered into the cup. No wonder. Not only was it cold, but there was a scaly film of milk drifting on the top. He scrubbed his face with his hand, then lifted his arm and took a whiff. He grimaced again. He needed a shower. Sleep would be good, too. To be fair, he'd looked and smelled worse, but in the army you could blame the stink on the guy next to you.

Trigger glanced around. He was the only one left on the ninth floor. He'd sent Michael home around midnight.

"What about you?" Michael had protested.

"I'll wait until I hear back from McKenna."

"I could keep you company."

Trigger had shot him a look.

"Yeah, that didn't come out right. I'll go home." He started for the elevators.

"See you tomorrow at eight," Trigger called after him.

"But I just did four hour's overtime," he wailed.

"True. I'll see you at eight fifteen. I'm not heartless."

Michael gave a wave, the elevator doors whooshing shut behind him.

Trigger considered recommending him for a pay increase, or, better yet, a subsidised carpark. They'd just spent hours wading through the paper trail of bank transactions, army records, and company information, even pulling a couple of CITES endangered species officials away from their dinner dates. Michael had been the one to point out the discrepancy in the signatures: Meredith making free with his stepfather's identity. It wasn't bad work for a junior analyst. Trigger should write the lad a recommendation tonight, since he had the time to fill out the paperwork.

Instead, he waited for the phone to ring.

29

Fiordland

Taine, Read and Māpura swam across the Sound towards the sub. It was ridiculous. It was a sub, for Christ's sake. And full of mercenaries, too. What did they think they were going to do when they got there? Taine had no idea. At least the sub hadn't dived yet, the sail still looming out of the water.

Ahead of Taine, just beneath the surface, Māpura used his webbed hands and feet to glide smoothly through the water, easily outpacing Read and Taine's laborious crawl. Taine marvelled at the tribesman's grace. That same sleek glide was what gave subs the advantage over ships: skating unfettered beneath the waves and the weather on the surface, although being at depth created its own headaches.

Head down, he examined the sub's elongated torpedo shape, the propellers turning slowly at the rear, allowing the sub to hover over a natural shelf jutting into the sound. Taine made a mental note to keep away from those propellers. A man could be turned to mincemeat if he got caught up in those blades. Every now and again submarines would make the headlines for getting fouled up in trawlers' nets. Reports of trawlers being towed for days, of being dragged under, all hands drowning.

Taine lifted his gaze to check the distance. Halfway there. It was nearing dawn, and in the pale light, several shapes moved about the sub's tower. What was Meredith up to now? One by one, the shapes dropped off the side of the sub into the channel.

Taine tapped Read and the pair sat up, treading water, Māpura too far ahead to catch. "Some divers have just left the sub," Taine said quietly.

"Divers? To get to the beach? Why wouldn't they use the zodiac?" Read whispered.

"They aren't heading for the beach. Meredith must know about the underwater cave. He hasn't given up."

Taine and Read turned back to the cave entrance and hid in the shallows, Māpura joining them, arriving just before the mercenaries. Meredith's men were using DPV water scooters to tow them along. Taine counted four men.

Waiting for them to pass by, Taine and Read chose their targets, then took a breath and dived. Only reaching two knots, the vehicles weren't fast – more like glorified vacuum cleaners – but powered on his own steam, Taine struggled to catch up. He kicked hard, giving it everything he had, creeping forward by inches... He reached out and grabbed his target by the regulator, yanking him backwards, and forcing him to release the DPV scooter, which stalled.

The diver twisted, a dive knife in his hand. He grappled

one-handed for his regulator, trying to get it back in his mouth, while jabbing at Taine with the knife, the movement like a slow-motion parody of a fight. The diver had a tank and could afford to take his time; Taine was still operating on a single breath of air.

The other divers, now aware of the attack, were coming back to help their comrades. Taine needed another breath.

Time to finish this.

He lunged for the dive knife, but his opponent, anticipating the move, sliced by him, narrowly missing his face. Taine grasped the knife on the follow-through, and, turning in place, slit the man's BCD.

The diver backed off. Behind him, through the spewing bubbles, Taine saw the cavern, and the eye staring at him.

His blood froze.

He blinked. He wasn't seeing this. It wasn't real. He'd been too long without a breath. But when he opened his eyes, the creature's ghostly body still glowed in the gloom, suckered limbs lifting and heaving on the swell.

A kraken.

Jules' guard dog. He wanted to laugh. She had a knack for understatement. An eye that big...it had to be as large as the sub...

Unaware of the danger, the two divers were flying in fast, one brandishing his dive knife like a jouster of old. Grabbing the idle DPV, Taine thumbed the controls and thrust the wash at his opponent. The diver's knife caught in the propeller blades and was flung over to where Read was tussling with the second man. Seeing the blade, Read caught it, piercing neoprene and drawing blood.

His head starting to spin, Taine figured Read's must be too. He signalled to him to get clear, just as the colossus exploded from its lair, its beak wide, the crushing blades closing over the first man, his limbs disappearing in a vortex of white barbs. Still gnashing its beak, the creature lashed out a tentacle, sweeping the DPVs aside like a child searching for the toy in a box of cereal. It found what it was looking for. The cavern erupted in a soup of bubbles, blood and neoprene. Through the haze, Taine glimpsed Read, slipping on a dive tank.

Read, get out of there.

Taine swam further into the cave and hid behind a crag in the wall. Herewini's net – empty now – drifted past. He didn't need to ask where the bodies had gone.

He wouldn't make it back to the beach. Even if the monster didn't get him, it was too far. He'd pushed too hard. Gone too far on the oxygen he'd stored in his lungs. His vision blurred.

Damn. This wasn't how I imagined going out.

There were so many things he hadn't done yet. Jules. Their relationship. They hadn't had enough time. There were things he wanted to tell her...

His feet drifted with the current.

Jules.

Suddenly, she was there, grabbing his arm. Pulling him. She dragged him upwards, kicking hard. Weak as a kitten, Taine wanted to help her, to help himself, but he had nothing. His chest burned. His lungs were an inferno. He needed to breathe. *Take a breath, take a breath, take a breath.*

He fought the reflex. Not yet. Don't breathe yet. Wait until she turns.

I want to see her smile. One last time.

Jules didn't turn. She tugged him through a gap in the rock. Light. She shoved him upwards. He reached out, his fingers seizing something. Taine gripped the edge. He gave it everything, hauling himself upwards to the light.

Taine broke the surface and drank in the air. Gulped it in. His lungs rattled and he coughed. Gulped some more. "Squid," he gasped, when he'd filled his lungs enough to have some to spare.

"We've met," Jules said.

"Is the village far?" he wheezed.

Jules placed a hand on his cheek. He couldn't feel her warmth. "It's not so far," she said. "You can make it on a breath."

He closed his eyes, opened them again. "Jules."

"Please, Taine—"

"I can't. Read, Māpura... I have to go back."

She nodded. "I know." She kissed him quickly. "Taine, the tunnels fork. You need to use the largest one. When you want to find me." Then she was gone.

For a moment, he was lost, adrift. Every cell in his body cried out to swim after her and leave all this behind. To scream to hell with it. But he couldn't do it. There were people out there who needed his help.

Taine took several large breaths to saturate his blood. Then he dropped off the ledge and swam through the crack.

When Taine emerged, the monster was gone, but the water was heavy with debris. Taine tried not to think about what the debris was. But not all of it was unwelcome. A tank banged gently against the wall, only a metre down, two at most. Taine swam down and retrieved it. One of the straps was torn, but the tank was almost full. Taine slipped the regulator in his mouth and took a breath.

Now to find Read and Māpura.

In fact, they found him, the pair of them emerging from a narrow fissure in the tunnel wall, which Māpura must have known of. It was tight: Read had taken the BCD off to squeeze it through the gap. The dive gear back on, he held both hands apart in the classic fisherman's pose.

Yes, Read, that squid was fucking big. No exaggeration. And it's probably not far off, so, how about we get those kids, so we can get out of these Sounds?

Māpura towed them past the cavern, the tribesman gliding them out of the tunnel, Read with his hand on Māpura's shoulder, and Taine holding Read's. They were almost into the Sound when they came across the net again. Snagged on a rock near the tunnel entrance, the strands were sweeping in and out, rolling and rippling with the current.

Taine's mind raced. Trawler nets and submarine propellers. Made of flax fibres, the Tūrehu's nets were tough and flexible. And they were *designed* to catch things. The net he'd found had gotten so entangled in the branches of the beech that he hadn't been able to yank it clear. Still, what kind of force could he exert? It didn't compare. Submarines were fouled by modern polyethylene nets that were as strong as steel wire. A few flax fibres could hardly do the same.

Possibly not. But they might be enough to slow it down.

Taking a quick detour, Taine caught up the net and kicked towards the submarine.

Taine was sure Māpura saw his plan straight away, the tribesman smiling as he picked up the trailing end.

30

———

The Catfish

Between the three of them, Taine, Read and Māpura managed to drape the net over the end of the submarine. Māpura, being quicker, pulled the edges back towards the submarine's stern.

That was the idea, anyway.

In reality, it was more haphazard, having to steer clear of the blades and keep up with the sub's movement. Taine was beginning to think it wouldn't work when a propeller picked up the trailing ropes, the fibres snagging, winding and winding, until the entire weave was bound up in the screw. The machinery chewed at the fibres, trying to free itself. Taine expected the flax to snap under the engine's pressure, but the net stuck firm and a relentless grinding began.

It was time to get the children.

Māpura wanted nothing to do with getting inside the sub, so it was only Taine and Read who climbed up the rubbery side of the U-boat and dropped into the submarine.

Inside, crew were running everywhere. No one noticed

them. Made sense. Taine and Read were wearing the Catfish's own dive gear. They left the tanks near the hatch, Taine squaring his shoulders as he strode down the passageway.

"What's happening?" Taine asked one of the crewman.

"You don't know? Where have you been? In your bunk? Engineer team is short-staffed since Meredith sent everyone ashore. Some of us have been on shift for two days," the crewman said. "And now it looks as if the damn screw is caught up in something, I'll probably be on for another two." He strode off.

Read raised an eyebrow. They kept walking. Looking in doorways. Searching. Based on what Mere had said, they were looking for space large enough to hold a tank.

"Where would you keep cargo on an old submarine like this?" Read asked.

"It used to be military," Taine replied. "It didn't carry cargo; it carried weapons."

"Maybe they repurposed the torpedo bays."

They turned and went back the way they'd come. Read was right. The torpedo bay had been refitted as a crude laboratory. On one side was the tank Mere had been tortured in, and on the other, Hine and the two children were being held in individual animal cages.

Read's jaw twitched. Seeing them both, Hine stood up, her webbed fingers closing around the bars. Read put his index finger to his mouth.

His back to the door, a man in a lab coat sat at a desk. He sensed their presence because he spoke without turning. "Are the divers back? Did they catch me another one, then?"

"We did," Taine replied, grabbing him from behind in a

choke hold. The man clutched at Taine's arm. It was an easy enough hold to step out of, but his body was soft, and, although he struggled, immobilising him was child's play.

Read stepped to the desk, rifled amongst the papers, and, picking up the yellow legal pad, he read: "Water-breathing – a case study in an isolated population: a paper by Andrew F. Beynon." Ripping the sheet off the pad, Read balled it in his hand.

Taine released the choke hold slightly. Beynon opened his mouth – either to shout or to breathe – and Read stuffed the wad of paper in. They tied his hands behind his back with a cable tie Taine found on the desk and shoved him in an empty cage. Beynon heaved his shoulder against the bars, rattling them to get the attention of the crew.

"Would you prefer we stow you in the tank?" Read said. Beynon stopped his rattling and shuffled to the back of the cage.

Read opened the cage for Hine, while Taine released Ro and Tau. The boy's wrist was sprained. Or perhaps it was broken? Red and swollen, he cradled it close to his body and cringed away from Taine. The girl, Ro, clung to Hine. They were frightened. Hine spoke to them quietly, the tension easing in their faces.

It was too early to relax. They still had to get out of there.

Taine took point and they made their way towards the hatch, walking as if they were meant to be there. They were nearing the hatch when the submarine lurched. Hine clutched at the children, leaning against Read as the sub shifted on its haunches. Taine put his hand out, bracing himself against the metal hull. The propellers shrieked and groaned, like ghosts at a sideshow haunted house.

The deck rocked again. A shuddering spasm, the engines struggling. The net was tightening its grip.

Damn, those Tūrehu were master craftsmen.

The fibres were holding.

Meredith was in his cabin, waiting for the divers to report back. He was looking forward to having additional specimens to offer his client when he called them in an hour. Although, he was a realist. The divers might only be able to nab a couple. The mutants had shown they were capable of putting up a resistance. Still, Meredith wasn't greedy. Three more specimens would do it. A couple of boys and a girl to round out the sample.

At the knock, Meredith flung open the door.

He'd expected one of the divers, but it was one of the throttle men, come up from wherever it was that they did their thing. Meredith looked at him. "What?"

"We might have a problem, sir."

"What problem? I have enough problems." Did they have to come to him with every little thing?

"You might have noticed the grinding noise from the hull. The navigator says the sonar is flooded with it. Suggests we might have taken some damage. Something's affecting our hydrodynamic performance, anyway. We're only doing a knot and it's taking more RPM than it should to achieve even that speed. Plus, the planesmen are saying they're having trouble steering."

"What does that mean in English?"

"Something has caught on the shaft and fouled the screw. We think the stern planes and rudder are involved."

Meredith glowered.

The throttle man grasped the doorframe. "We're tangled in a net. If it isn't cut free, we're not going anywhere."

Meredith jumped up. For once, the squeak of his boots on metal didn't please him. "Don't just stand there. What are you, frozen or something? Send divers to clear it."

"Yes, sir."

When the throttle man had gone, Meredith paced his room. It was a short walk. This wasn't a coincidence. That bastard McKenna had to have tampered with his sub...

He would sort this out himself.

Throwing open the door, he stormed down the alley to the dive bay, where he put on his dive gear and checked the tank. He tucked a knife into his belt.

Deep in the cave, in the Tūrehu hideaway, Jules stood on the plateau with Pringle and Herewini and stared at the dark water that lapped at the little plateau beneath the ladder. The minutes were racing by and still no one had emerged from the channel, the surface ominously smooth.

Jules hugged her arms around her body and reminded herself to breathe. The uncertainty was like a fungus, eating at her from the inside, consuming everything. She was numb. Spent.

Herewini touched a hand to her shoulder. "They're going to be okay," he said. Jules shivered. Herewini's smile hadn't reached his eyes. He wasn't sure. How could anyone be sure?

All at once there was a shout, one of the tribeswomen pointing at the water. The People crowded at one end of the bluff, gesturing and shouting.

Something was bobbing on the surface.

Jules' throat tightened, and she gasped, calming a little when she saw it wasn't anyone. It wasn't *Taine*.

Dark and orange-brown, the object resembled a strange mushroom. Perhaps a sponge? Or a coral? The current swelled and whatever it was washed onto the ledge, settling at the base of the cliff. Ka climbed down the ladder and plucked it off the ledge. Water rained off it.

Scrambling back up the ladder to join the People, the warrior handed it to Jules.

Me?

Pringle and Herewini stepped closer. Jules opened her hands, water dripping down her front. It was an orange bushman's beanie. *Loughlin's* beanie. There was no longer any doubt about what had happened to the prison officer. Pringle turned away.

Letting the beanie fall from her fingers, Jules gazed down at the surface of the water. What next? What would the water give up next?

She wasn't sure she wanted to know.

31

Fiordland

The noise reached her even here, deep beneath the ledge at the entrance of the tunnel. First, it'd been the little coloured fish with their buzzing bubbling fins. Darting this way and that, their droning had been irksome. She'd eaten most of them, and the others had gone away. Now, it was the turn of the big silver fish, the one that had taken up residence beyond the headland. That fish had decided to widen its domain. Not long ago it had sidled into the middle of the canyon, where it'd been hovering, upsetting her digestion with its insistent thrum-thrum-thrumming. And if its vibrations weren't unsettling enough, its grinding and screeching were making her ache with annoyance. She slapped at the underside of the ledge, scraping her arms against the jagged surface, but even that did not soothe her. The grinding was relentless.

Insufferable.

She would have to put a stop to it.

She propelled herself out from under the ledge, turning an eye to the shallows as she glided swiftly upwards to where the fish's silhouette blurred black against the surface of the water. The fish paid her no heed. Instead, its belches and groans got louder.

She circled it, testing its defences. It didn't respond, so she lashed out with her tentacles, tearing away great chunks of its flesh. It tasted sharp, like the pinching bitter flavour of oysters crunched open and slurped from their shells. Well, she would crack the shell of this one, too. Put a stop to that racket.

The fish moaned again, the noise rising to a shriek.

Was it injured? Instinct told her it was. All the better; it would make killing it easier.

She lunged for the creature's mantle, hooking her tentacles into the brittle flesh, clasping the fish with her arms, her suckers driving deep into its hide.

The creature tried to bite her.

She clung harder, shaking it fiercely and grating it with her suckers. She scored the silver hide with her beak. Still, it would not stop its whining. It was if her mantle was about to burst. Her head pounded with pain, driving her to crunch her beak deeper and deeper.

It was weakening; she could feel it in the shuddering of its heart.

Several little spawn came to the rescue of their mother, poking her with their little barbs. Their efforts were almost endearing. She flicked them away with a swipe of an arm, stunning them. They hurtled into the depths, slipping down into the darkness where she would consume them later.

The fish screamed.

Would it never stop? She turned her attention to it once more.

32

Fiordland

No one had touched the tanks. Taine was clipping his on when Meredith appeared further down the passageway, adjusting his own dive gear. The mercenary didn't recognise Taine, but he knew the kids. He stopped, his eyes narrowing.

"Get the kids through the hatch, Read," Taine said, moving to put his body between Meredith and the Tūrehu.

Meredith was opening his mouth to shout for his crew when the submarine jolted, throwing them both to one side. Taine recovered first, pushing Hine up the ladder and climbing after her, pulling his feet out just as Meredith shot at him, the round ricocheting in the corridor.

Taine climbed, water slopping over him. Was the submarine diving? But the hatch was still open.

At the top of the sail, Taine saw why: the squid was attacking the sub, charging at the vessel and causing it to rock. Its barbs scored the metal as the tentacles whipped and slashed, the beak grinding across the surface. Almost equal in length, the squid had wrapped one end of the sub in a deadly hug and was dragging it to the sea floor. And with its propellers compromised, the sub had no way of preventing it.

Taine shoved the regulator in his mouth as the sub dropped, scrambling out of the hatch even as the water poured in. Already Māpura had taken Ro and the pair were swimming back toward the underground sanctuary. Hine, too, was in the water.

"Read, go!"

"Tau can't swim. His wrist is too injured."

"I'll take him."

But Read was already gone, plucked off the submarine by one of the gigantic suckers. Attached to the BCD, it whipped him about like an out-of-control garden hose.

Hine screamed.

"Read!"

Taine grabbed Tau and leapt away, fighting the drag of the sinking sub – falling past the ledge now – and swimming after Māpura and Ro. Where was Hine? He hoped she was ahead of them. When they were nearing the tunnel entrance, Taine glanced back, hoping to see that Read had escaped. There were plenty of people in the water behind them. Like baby spiders from a web, men were pouring from the hatch: the sub's crew, some of them with dive gear, most without. He couldn't tell if Meredith was among them. Still hugging the sub in its Cthulhu grasp, the squid snapped and swatted at the men, but it was in no rush to eat them. Taine shivered. There was no need. Sucked down with the ship, they would drown, and the squid would return to consume them at its leisure.

He had to get Tau to safety. The boy was kicking, pointing for the tunnel.

Taking a last look back for Read and Hine, Taine surged forward.

One look told Meredith that *The Catfish* was lost. Fully submerged, the sub was sinking. Somehow McKenna had harnessed a sea monster, setting the massive kraken on the sub like an attack dog. The colossal creature had buried its tentacles in the hull, gouging great chunks out of the surface as it tossed the sub from side to side.

It was ironic. All the time Meredith had been trying to get his hands on the mutants, the famous kraken, a creature as elusive as the Yeti, had been slinking about in the waters beneath the sub.

If only he'd known.

One of the creature's arms whipped out – as thick as a lamp post – sending a man barrelling past him, plummeting to the sea floor. The kraken turned a dark eye towards Meredith.

Time to go.

Patting the knife in his belt, he crammed the Glock in his pocket and thrust the regulator into his mouth. He pushed off the side of the sub, kicking hard.

Suddenly, he caught a glimpse of McKenna through the churning water. McKenna had the boy. They'd stopped to look for someone. Seconds later, the pair turned, heading for the tunnel.

Meredith dived after them.

There was still a chance to salvage something.

~

Fuck this shit.

Jared swam for the surface. There was a fucking enormous octopus hanging on the back of the sub, waving its bloody arms about. Too bad about clearing the propellers. Let someone else do it. He wasn't about to be fish food. He was getting his arse out of there.

The tank was gone – empty – Jared had let it go soon after leaving the sinking sub, but he took a suck from air in the BCD. He didn't bother to put the regulator back in. Didn't dare look to where it dangled. Just clamped his mouth shut and swam upwards, pumping his legs, and straining to scoop the water backwards. His limbs shook with effort.

Don't look back. He didn't dare, terrified of the shadows passing below him, of what might reach out to snatch at him and drag him down into the depths. He looked to the light. Look where you intend to go. Up, up, up. That's where he was going. It wasn't that far now. Ten metres and a short swim to shore. Home and dry, no suckers attached.

Jared's legs burned, he kicked so hard. Holding his breath was making it easier, helping him climb. Climbing quickly was never a good idea, but neither was getting eaten. But he couldn't feel any pain, so he kept going.

Nearly there!

He reached out, stretching his fingertips to the surface. He was going to make it. It would be morning when he got there.

Suddenly, pain blossomed in his chest.

A bubble erupted from his mouth, then blood and tissue billowing in a cloud.

He wasn't going to make it at all.

Read was descending.

Dizzy and sore, he hacked at the BCD with his knife, cutting away the straps and freeing himself from the kraken's grasp.

Now he had no air.

It didn't matter. He was already too deep. There was no going back.

Wait. Someone else's dive tank dropped past him in the gloom. Read angled his body towards it and snatched at the regulator, slipping it into his mouth and breathing evenly. He checked the dive computer and his heart fell. Only a few lungfuls. He sucked them in anyway, then let the BCD go and hovered in the water. Kicking would only speed things along.

This was as good a place as any. If this had been a proper dive, if he had a tank – a full one – he might have stopped here to decompress before ascending.

Could have, should have.

Well, he didn't have a tank, so he was stuck here...

People said drowning was a lot like sleeping. Could you trust those people? The paradox only hitting him now: if they'd survived, how could they know what it was like to drown?

Read lifted his gaze to the surface. Hine was descending towards him.

She should go back.

Read gestured to her, but she kept coming, kicking out to reach to him. He gave up trying. She looked so beautiful with her pale hair streaming out behind her like that – like a princess from Atlantis.

Hine reached him, and her brow creased. She pointed to the surface.

Read smiled. She was incredible, a real live mermaid, and yet she knew nothing about the bends. She knew nothing of the deadly bubbles that would make him jerk and kick. About perforated muscles and cracked bones. There was nothing romantic about dive tables. Nothing peaceful about the bends.

Moving closer, Hine grabbed him by the arms and tried to drag him upwards.

Read shook his head. He pointed to the mercenary, or at least what remained of him, slowly dropping past the two of them. Perhaps she understood then, because she gave up trying to make him ascend. Instead, she took him in her arms.

At least, the company was good.

It was strange, thinking these things. Read wasn't bothered about the pain; it wouldn't last long. He just didn't want her to see it. Didn't want her to watch him, doubled over in agony. It would be an ugly death.

Better if he took a breath.

Yes. That would be better. Dizzy now. Perhaps that was her fault. Those eyes.

Read smiled.

He opened his mouth to take his final breath, but Hine pressed her nose to his...

...and kissed him.

33

Fiordland

Jules kept her eyes on the water and wrung her hands. She couldn't bear this. It was killing her. Where was he? Beside her, Herewini reached out to help Māpura, who was scrambling up the ladder after a girl, who Jules assumed must be Ro, since Mere ran to hug her. So, they had managed to save the girl. But what about Hine and the boy, Tau? And where were Taine and Read?

Jules willed them to come. Tears welled. She brushed them away with the back of her hand. It couldn't end like this. It just couldn't.

Suddenly, the water lapped at the plateau below the cliff. Jules shuddered, already feeling its eye on her. It was the monster. Nothing else would make the water rise that way.

She strained to see to the back of the tunnel. Finally, she spied them. Three figures surfing in on the crest of the wave. Her throat constricted. Taine had the boy. He was alive. But where were Read and Hine? And who was the other man? Jules saw the gun in his hand.

But the squid had come too, surging in. Silvery and luminescent, the giant mantle filled the cavern with eerie light.

The tribespeople shouted, but there was nothing anyone could do, the three of them at the mercy of the wave. They were flushed forward, all of them hitting the cliff, the water draining away.

Tau was separated from the men at the other end of the plateau. There was an overhang there, and the tribesmen couldn't protect him with their spears.

Get up! Go for the ladder.

But the squid curled a sucker around the lowest rung and ripped it off the wall.

Jules gave a start. She'd used the ladder when she'd escaped it earlier today. Did the creature remember? Learned behaviour?

In the water, the squid slithered closer to Tau. It flung out a tentacle, the curled hook grating the rock dangerously close to the boy's head. Tau whimpered, grasping at his hand. Either he couldn't climb like Mere or he was too injured to make it.

They'd have to help him.

She glanced around. The flax ropes were there with the nets. Running to them, Jules threaded a rope through her belt loop and thrust one end at Herewini, carrying it around his body.

"Jules? What's going on?"

"Remember when we came in on the chopper, how I stuffed up the rappel?" He nodded. "Good. Don't drop me."

Jules turned and rappelled down the cliff, flipping upside-down near at the bottom. Reaching out, she snatched up Tau, pulling him to her with one arm. By the time she was having second thoughts, Pringle and Herewini had already hauled the two of them halfway up the cliff.

Rotorua Township

On the beach, Temera's spirit-self clutched the pūrerehua at his chest and tried to summon his friend, but if Taine was there, he wasn't answering.

Restless, the morepork flitted from the treeline to the sand and back again, urging him on with her haunting call.

What if he was too late? He had to try harder. Fingers shaking, Temera uncoiled the flaxen string tied to one end of the pūrerehua. Letting the cord dangle, he clasped the instrument in his hands, feeling the warmth of the wood and the whorls of the carving beneath his fingers.

He opened his mind. "Taine. Are you there?" The words hummed in his head. Temera concentrated on finding the soldier's spirit. It was somewhere deep in the Sounds. Somewhere near the ocean...

Temera stepped into the sea, a step closer to Taine, and closer to the danger. Freezing water surged around his legs, soaking him. Ignoring the numbing cold, Temera waded deeper into the surf and gripped the cord of the pūrerehua between his thumb and finger. He lifted his arm and twirled it, slowly at first, then faster and faster, letting out the cord until it reached its full length. Shifting his hips to make it fly. The flattened disc thrummed, the string whizzing through the air. While he spun the little instrument above the waves, Temera focused on his friend and called again.

Taine shucked off the BCD.

His back to Taine, Meredith was still getting to his feet.

Now that Tau was out of reach, the squid turned its eye to the two of them. It hovered in the water, slapping its barbs on the rocky ledge as if it was a spectator at the arena. The tribespeople threw their spears at it, doing their best to keep it at bay.

"Meredith."

The mercenary spun, his Glock pointed at Taine, but a spear whistled from above, distracting him, and the round went astray.

In the confines of the cave, the noise was deafening.

Enraged, the squid lashed out, clubbing Meredith aside with an enormous tentacle. Battling to keep his feet, the mercenary threw out his arms, letting go of the gun, which skittered across the rocky platform and into the water. The squid whipped the appendage back, its razor-sharp barbs catching Taine's side, slicing flesh, and sending him flying. His shirt was shredded. Blood welled. He fell onto the rocky ledge, nearly tumbling into the water. Taine scrambled away as the squid suckered the droplets up.

The gun gone, Meredith gripped his knife.

"Meredith. Let's just call it a day. We need to get up that cliff or we're both going to die here."

"With twenty mutants who want to kill me? I'll take my chances with the monster." He leaned forward and swiped back and forth with the knife, looking to take another slice out of Taine's torso. Taine grabbed his wrist, pulling it underhand and yanking it backwards. With his arm twisted painfully behind him, Meredith couldn't hold on to the knife. It clattered onto the rock. Taine kicked it away, the blade dropping off the ledge. As he snaked away, Meredith picked up one of the tribesmen's spears.

Taine scrabbled to get away, but couldn't get a purchase on the wet rock.

Meredith lifted the spear, just as the squid's beak came down on his back, throwing him forward and pinning him to the rock. He grunted, his eyes wide. His spear clattered to one side. Taine grasped it and staggered to his feet as the tentacles skewered Meredith from either side, gathering him up to shovel him into the kraken's maw like two chopsticks shovelling up chow mein.

In seconds, there was nothing left of the mercenary, and the squid turned its massive eye to Taine. Taine almost laughed. Here he was again, facing down a monster the size of a house armed only with a spear. Except the last time this had happened, he hadn't been alone because Temera had been with him. He wished the matakite were with him now.

The squid lunged, showering Taine with water, the beak cracking through the spear. As Taine jumped clear, the pūrerehua swung on its string, hitting him full in the chest.

It was worth a go. What did he have to lose?

Quickly taking the bullroarer from around his neck and shaking out the cord, Taine raised his arm and twirled the pūrerehua, the flaxen string whizzing through the air above his head, stepping forward as it gathered speed. The instrument keened, and Taine called upon the spirit of his friend, picturing the old man in his potting shed in Rotorua.

The squid prepared to strike again. Using its arms to anchor it to the rock, it had hauled part of its body sideways onto the ledge. Its tentacles reached for Taine, forcing him to take a step back.

Running out of room, Taine spun the pūrerehua. Temera was powerful. Taine had called on him once before, and the matakite had summoned the forest god Tāne to their aid.

"Temera!"

There was no response. Taine mustn't be concentrating hard enough. Still spinning the instrument, he thought of his friend, focussing now on Temera's boy form and the little morepork who guided him into the spirit world.

All at once, his friend's voice sounded in his head. "Taine! Thank the gods. The warning. I was wrong. It's not the submarine."

The bullroarer's thrum echoed throughout the cavern. "I know. I'm facing the squid now. Don't suppose you could send up one of your special prayers to the gods on my behalf?"

"I wish. I reckon that last time in Urewera was a fluke. The gods are like wapiti: they'd rather not fight if they can get away with tossing their antlers in a show of strength."

"So we're on our own, then."

"I think so."

The giant orb fixed Taine.

Taine drew in a breath. "Any ideas?"

"Give me a minute. I'm thinking."

"Not sure we have that long—"

The squid lunged, its giant beak snapping. Taine leapt back, dropping the bullroarer and taking a step up the wall to avoid the stinking crush of its jaws. The tribespeople screamed from the ridge. Taine imagined he could hear Jules' voice.

More spears flew from above. One of them pierced the mantle. No more than a prickle, but it stuck fast. The squid gave another swipe of its tentacle, this time taking out Taine's legs. A serrated sucker latched on to his ankle. Taine grabbed the broken spear head and stabbed at the limb.

Let go, you bastard.

He stabbed again and the sucker released him. Abandoning the broken spear, Taine crabbed backwards. His feet slipped on the rock. The squid loomed above him.

Jules screamed.

Suddenly, a flute sounded. Māpura's pūtōrino. Whispery in the trees, here in the cave the notes were pure and true. So, the Tūrehu had their own spirit-gods to call upon. For a moment, the kraken paused, mesmerised.

It was the chance Taine needed.

Jumping to his feet, he ran up the mantle of the monster. Yanking the stray spear out of its flesh, he thrust it at the eye, but his leading foot slipped sideways, and the weapon glanced away, barely grazing the creature's rubbery hide.

The squid thrashed its mantle from side-to-side, attempting to throw Taine into the water. Heart in his throat, it was all Taine could do to keep his balance. Riding the mantle like a surfboard, he raised the spear again, this time ramming it into the squid's eye. It was a clean strike. The beast bellowed and shuddered, its black eye rolling back to stare at him. Still, it rallied. Rolling and bucking, it tossed its giant head.

What would it take to kill this monster?

His palms slippery with blood, Taine clung on. Then Temera's murmur sounded in his head, a low chant at first, then becoming louder. Taine's eyes widened. The matakite was chanting a *koropatu*, an ancient ritualistic chant to kill taniwha. Taine had thought they were nothing more than ceremonial: epic poems told by storytellers to give people courage in times of darkness. He was wrong. With no gods to help them, Temera was pouring his own powerful wairua-spirit into the beast, using his own spirit to attack the squid deep at its core. A small boy was taking the battle to the beast.

The squid shuddered, and Taine seized the moment to bury the spear even further, ramming the spike deep in the animal's brain, driving it home.

The tentacles trembled.

Temera did not cease his chanting.

Taine didn't let up either, although he was almost sorry. The kraken hadn't been the worst monster here.

Even so, it refused to die. It lifted a weary arm and swatted Taine away, then, lurching to one side, it threw its massive body off the shelf.

Thrown back against the cliff, near his discarded pūrere-hua, Taine grasped it, rescuing the instrument before it spilled over the side.

The squid dropped below the surface.

Rotorua township

They had done it! Seen off a taniwha. And not for the first time. Temera couldn't wait to congratulate his friend. But first he had to get out of this freezing water. Shaking with exertion, he rolled up his pūrerehua and turned back to the beach. He waded through the surf, the waves buffeting him, his wet pyjama pants clinging to his skinny boy-legs.

Weak with relief, he didn't see the creature surge towards him, unaware until the water rose up and a tentacle whipped out of the surf to curl about his waist. He had to hand it to her: she was stealthy for her size. The air squeezed from his lungs, Temera barely had time to take a breath before she dragged him into the surf.

He tumbled on the seafloor, his legs grazing on broken shells, his head breaking through the foam, while his fingernails tried desperately to free him from the rasping suckers.

It was no use; he caught the morepork's plaintive shrill as he was pulled beneath the surface.

No, this wasn't how it worked: only his wairua lived in the spirit world. Yet somehow Temera knew this time was different. If he didn't escape, he would never wake.

Temera considered calling for Taine, but they'd already broken the connection, and what could his friend do? Watch him die?

And he would die, because what could a boy do against a taniwha?

Not just a boy, a matakite. He had to believe in his gift. The air in his lungs dwindling and the water closing silently over him, once again Temera began to chant the *koropatu*. Words resonated in his mind, a desperate prayer from a hopeless boy with no warrior's spear to drive them home. Still, words could be powerful. Perhaps the sound of them would summon the gods to slice at the heart of the creature. It was already weak; Taine's spear lodged deep in her eye, so there was a chance. Temera had nothing else. He chanted.

The squid roared. She thrashed and tightened her grip about his torso. Temera let himself drift, let the taniwha drag him through the icy water. He focused his efforts on the sound, on chanting the words.

There was no time left. He was drowning.

Temera kept chanting.

The water clouded, a strange warmth infusing Temera's body, and then suddenly, violently, the taniwha slung him through the air, ejecting him from the water and her grasp.

Temera landed heavily on the beach. He lay there a moment, grateful for the gift of breathing.

He lifted his eyes, saw the dying squid float a moment on the waves before slipping soundlessly beneath the surface. Something else moved, too, on the sand, something small and brown.

An owl.

His spirit-guide.

Temera's heart skipped a beat. He got to his knees and crawled to her. The little morepork was flopped on the sand, her feathers sodden with silt. When Temera picked her up, her body sagged. Her neck hung to one side, the yellow eye waxen and still.

The bird was dead.

The monster was defeated, but the effort of it had stolen a piece of Temera's soul.

Temera's eyes flew open. He was lying in his bed. Bathed in sweat, he turned his head to where his alarm clock glowed soft green. 4:15am.

An ambulance screeched in the distance, but otherwise, the night was silent.

Fiordland

It was mid-morning when the army turned up on the beach. By then, the tribesmen had left them, withdrawing back to the cave-sanctuary, so as not to be seen.

"Sergeant McKenna?"

Taine stood up and brushed the sand from his pants. "That's me."

"Sergeant Aaron Lemalu." The soldier held out his hand. Taine shook it.

"I'm to advise you that this region's been declared a no-go Conservation area, effective immediately. We've been asked to clear the area of any unauthorised persons."

Taine grinned. So, the Conservation Minister had come through. The ghostly Tūrehu would remain a people of legend, at least for a while.

"That would be including yourself, McKenna," Lemalu added.

This had to be Foster's doing. It was just like him to have a little dig. Taine looked at Jules, who shrugged.

"Sorry. I don't make the rules," Lemalu said.

"Boss," a soldier interrupted.

Lemalu turned. "What is it, Jones?"

"Three men. They turned up on the far end of the beach, asking to speak to whoever was in charge. Seems they have information about a submarine in these parts."

"Is that so? A submarine, aye?" He looked at Taine.

Taine smiled. "Some of my guys reported a dinosaur once."

Lemalu shook his head. "If you'll excuse me, McKenna, I'd better go and see what this is all about. In the meantime, there's a Corporal Grierson on the blower for you. He's arranging the helicopters to take your team back to Manapōuri."

Taine took the handset but didn't speak into it just yet. "Thank you. Hey, Lemalu, before you go, do you guys have a medic? One of the Conservation officers has a hand that needs looking at." Taine waited while Rocky was shown to the medic before raising the mic. "McKenna."

"You put me on hold," Trigger said, but Taine could hear the smile in his voice.

"Good to hear you, too."

"Maritime are no longer picking up any submarine."

Taine looked out over the Sound. The water barely rippled. "Sunk. Too deep to be retrieved."

"And Meredith?"

"His poaching days are over."

"We'll need a debrief when you get back. Along with any holiday snaps you might have taken."

"Thanks for lending a hand." There was a pause. "Trigger?"

"I have a chopper standing by in Manapōuri. How many are we picking up?"

"Six people."

Read tapped him on the shoulder and stepped back. Hine was standing behind him, wrapped in a towel. "Hine's coming with us," he said.

"Hang on a sec, Trigger." Taine put his hand over the mic. "Matt—"

"She's coming." Read glared at him.

Taine lowered his voice. "You realise, if she comes, she might never see her people again. And she has skills, abilities that will be hard to hide. It was the reason Meredith captured her."

"There has to be some surgery she can have. Or she'll wear gloves."

Taine had worried Read's impetuousness might get him killed one day, but he'd never imagined this; this was out of left field. "Matt—"

"Boss. I know it sounds crazy, but this is her only chance. Right now, her world is made up of a couple of dozen people crammed into a space the size of a postage stamp. She wants to be free. Branch out. See the world. Live."

"And you know all this how? Matt, you can't even speak her language."

Read's eyes flashed. "I know enough. And if she wants to live in our world, she'll learn to speak with us."

"And the tribe? What about them? They didn't let Summers go. Hell, they were willing to let their own people die to keep their secret. You really think they'll let her go?"

Read shrugged. "Māpura and the chief seem okay with it. Maybe they figure it would be good to have some allies on the outside. We both know Hine would never betray them."

Taine stared at the young soldier. Read had survived

because Hine had shared her breath with him. They had shared a hongi. Only theirs wasn't just a symbolic pressing of noses and touching of foreheads. It had been a true hongi, the way the god, Tāne, had breathed life into the soil to create the first woman, Hineahuone. It was a greeting of souls, and made them family.

Taine spoke into the radio. "Make that seven to be lifted out, Trigger."

34

Manapōuri, present day

Pumba beat her to the door. Patting her hair flat, Gina nudged the dog out of the way and opened up.

It was a couple. The young man looked like he was a swimmer. He had swimmers' shoulders; they almost blocked the doorway. The young woman hung back. Behind him on the driveway, she scuffed her sneakers in the gravel.

"Mrs Summers?" His voice was reassuring. Like a policeman's.

"Yes?"

"My name is Taine McKenna, I'm with the New Zealand Defence Force, and this is Dr Jules Asher."

A doctor. She would never have guessed. Gina would've said she was a primary school teacher.

"We'd like to speak to you about your husband."

Her husband.

Gina's knees buckled, but the man, Taine, caught her before she toppled into the gravel, gently letting her go when she'd found her footing again. Gina braced herself against the door frame anyway. They had news of David. All these years of waiting, yet Gina wasn't sure she was ready.

"Would you mind if we came inside?" Jules asked.

When they were seated in the living room, Pumba settled at her feet, Taine slipped his hand into his shirt pocket and pulled out a photograph. He held it out to her. Gina's fingers trembled as she took it. The paper was battered and creased, the edges stained yellow where the Sellotape had cracked off. Her heart in her throat, Gina turned it over:

With all my love, March 1972.

It was her own handwriting.

"You found the helicopter?" she whispered. She hardly dared to hope. If they'd found the chopper, they might have found David.

Jules nodded. "I'm with the Department of Conservation. We were on a deer culling mission when we stumbled upon it."

"It was well hidden, tucked in a valley," Taine added.

She smiled weakly. "Search and Rescue looked for weeks," she said, her eyes still on the photo. "I harassed the controller. Choat, his name was. Long since retired now, of course. He even flew over the park himself once. I think it was easier than taking my phone calls, listening to me bawling on the end of the line."

"It's unlikely they would have seen it from the air," Taine said. "Even back then. It was only by chance we found him..."

"Because the aircraft was completely overgrown," Jules said quickly.

"When they couldn't find them, there was speculation,"

Gina said. "It's a small town, and people talk. They said David had found himself another woman and taken himself off somewhere. It was true, he could be a bit of a scallywag – you know he was poaching when he and Wallace went missing? But I never believed he'd leave me deliberately. Something awful had to have happened to him. The David I knew would've crawled out of the forest on his hands and knees if he could have." She snorted. "He liked the last word."

Catching the look that passed between the couple, Gina straightened her back and gave a little cough. They'd come to deliver the news, not listen to her old lady ramblings. "Were there any...were they...?" she trailed off, unable to ask about the bodies.

Jules placed a hand on Gina's arm. Her fingers were warm. "He didn't suffer, Mrs Summers. It was a quick death."

The young man's eyes confirmed it. "Is there anyone we can call for you?" he said. "Someone who could be with you?"

Gina smoothed the photograph on her lap. She shook her head sadly. "No, thank you. I'll be fine here. There was only ever David and me."

~

Te Anau, town centre

Taine glanced to his left to where Jules was sitting in the passenger seat. The meeting with Summers' wife had made her pensive. She'd barely said a word on the drive back into town. He should have expected it. The last few days had been harrowing. Sometimes the full impact of trauma took a while to set in.

Pulling the rental into the Fiordland Conservation office, Taine cut the engine. "Have you got much to do before we head out? I said we'd pick up Read and Hine on the way back to the airport."

"Taine, I think I'm going to stay on here a few extra days and help Rocky out. His hand...it's going to be a while."

Taine nodded. Neither of them mentioned the absent staff members. "I'll have to catch this flight. I'm back on duty the day after tomorrow."

"I know," she breathed.

Taine's shoulders stiffened. He hadn't imagined it, then. The distance between them wasn't just fallout from what had happened in Fiordland. There was something else.

They got out of the car and crossed the car park to the lakeshore. Taine waited for her to talk first, to tell him what was going on. Jules said nothing. Instead, she folded her arms across her chest, her gaze fixed on the far side of the lake. Taine had faced some scary things in his life, but nothing unnerved him like her silence.

"Jules, whatever it is, just say it."

She let out a slow breath, working herself up to it, long moments passing before she turned to face him.

"Taine." Her voice was a whisper. "I don't think this is going to work."

It was as if she'd hit him dead centre with a Carl Gustave recoilless. "You're worried your mother won't like me?" he joked.

"My mum would love you," she said softly.

Would. She said would. She was leaving him. "Is it Richard?"

Smiling, she shook her head. "No, it's not him. It's not anyone else."

"I don't understand what's wrong."

She closed her eyes. When she opened them, she said, "It's because you're a soldier first, Taine. It's etched on your being. You think it's your job to save everyone."

"I don't have to—"

She placed a finger on his lips, her eyes full of tears.

"You do. And you'll do whatever it takes to protect people's lives, even if that means jeopardising your own."

"Jules, we've talked about this. Sure, it's a risk soldiers take, but we're not the only people who put our lives on the line."

"I know that. But I'm not in love with them."

He swallowed. The pain was unbearable. He'd found her and now he was losing her. Taine took her hand in his and gave it a squeeze. "Just tell me what you need me to do. If you want me to leave the army, then I'll leave."

"No." She pulled her hand free. "I can't ask you to do that. Being a soldier isn't just a job for you, it's embedded in your psyche. You're committed to it. Loyalty, comradery, sacrifice: it's what makes you, you."

"You're more important than any of that. I'll tell Arnold I'm leaving when I get back." He gritted his teeth. He could do it. Jules was worth the sacrifice.

"No." She turned away, hugging her arms about herself.

Taine pulled her back. "Jules...please...you don't have to do this. We can work it out; we just have to want it badly enough."

Lifting her hand, she stroked his cheek. The wound in his side hurt less than that tiny gesture. "Just now, when we went to see David's wife, I could see myself in her place. I was her; not today maybe, but one day, and it terrifies me. It terrifies me even more than a fifty-metre sea monster. I never want to be that alone, Taine. I couldn't bear it."

He closed his arms around her, and hugged her to him, burying his face in her hair. Moments later, she pushed him away and ran across the lawn.

Numb, Taine watched her go, the scent of her apple shampoo lingering on the air.

EPILOGUE

Aitken Street, Wellington

LYON, France – "An INTERPOL-led operation targeting criminal organizations behind the illegal trafficking of New Zealand native species has resulted in 34 arrests and the seizure of 70 endangered alpine parrots, in addition to military grade weapons and cash. Involving six countries, the operation was the result of strong cooperation between CETI parties," said David Horton, Manager of the INTERPOL Environmental Crime Programme...

"Not a word," Michael said, reading over Trigger's shoulder. "We blow open the case for them, and we don't even get a mention."

It's true, it wasn't a showy outcome. Without Meredith's promised shipment, Interpol agencies couldn't collar his client for human trafficking, but the bank transactions and phone records Trigger and Michael had uncovered meant Chinese authorities were able to conduct a surprise inspection of the client's facility, where they'd discovered the kea.

Trigger smiled. The bad guys were out of action, McKenna's tribe was safe and sound, and seventy alpine parrots had been repatriated. It wasn't perfect, but it was a good result. Sometimes, that was as much as you could hope for.

Shutting down the monitor, Trigger used his good arm to show the analyst the door. "Come on, Einstein, I'll shout you a beer."

Fiordland

The current drifts into the cavern, cool dark water sliding up the rock walls. It glistens there for a moment, then falls back gently, the movement oxygenating the endless crannies where tiny organisms cling to the rock. In and out, the current ebbs and flows, relentless and hypnotic, buffeting the brood with its life-giving caress.

Through the translucent egg sacs, the young are visible. There are thousands of them, suspended in the darkness, their creamy bodies wiggling in anticipation behind cloudy curtains. They are waiting for the right moment.

Soon.

Soon they will break away from their tethers to be ejected into the ocean current like dandelion seeds swept up on the wind. Most of them will die, eaten by passing fish before they grow large enough to fend for themselves, but one or two will survive into adulthood. Those individuals will sink deep into the ocean to live out their lives where the darkness is thick and impenetrable. And one day, perhaps, one of them will return to the cavern to spawn again.

A wave washes in, the swell rising higher up the cavern wall. At the outer edge of the brood, the first tiny sac rips open.

GLOSSARY

Māori and Local Terms

All Blacks   common name of New Zealand's national
              rugby side
barley sugar   traditional boiled candy
The Beehive affectionate name for New Zealand's
              parliament building, so-called for its
              iconic shape.
boardies   (colloq) board shorts, beachwear
down-trou   to drop one's trousers
dreaded lurgy   Brit. something highly infectious, but
              not too serious
hapu   Māori, meaning sub-tribe
hiff   (colloq) to throw, toss, hurl something,
              typically something awkward
hongi   Māori greeting, a symbolic sharing of breath
              or souls, when two people touch their noses
              and foreheads together, making them family
huia   extinct native wattlebird, indigenous

jandals	slip-on footwear, thongs or flip-flops
kākāpo	endemic nocturnal ground-dwelling parrot
karakia	prayer, song, chant, incantation, spell
kea	rare alpine parrot, indigenous to New Zealand
kōkako	endangered indigenous wattlebird
korero	surface carvings
koropatu	chant to kill a taniwha
Māori	early people of New Zealand
mataī	black pine, conifer
mātua	teacher, elder
matakite	fortune teller, seer, prophet
Māui	demi-god believed to have fished up New Zealand's North Island from the ocean, his grandmother's jawbone as his hook
Melteca™	laminate
miro	evergreen conifer endemic to New Zealand
morepork/ruru	New Zealand owl, Māori harbinger to the spirit world
Moriori	now considered an isolated subtribe of early Māori, once believed to be a separate population
Patu-paiarehe	also Tūrehu, inhabitants of New Zealand prior to the Māori, sometimes thought of as fairy or ghost people
pipi	pale shelled, bivalve shellfish
pōhutukawa	New Zealand Christmas tree, a coastal myrtle
ponga	native tree fern
pūtōrino	Māori flute carved from two branches of mataī tree
pūrerehua	bullroarer, Māori musical instrument
Rēkohu	Moriori name for Chatham Island

Schtum — to keep schtum means to keep quiet

squirrel — colloquial term for a spy

Swanndri™ — a famous New Zealand brand of felted wool outerwear

tangata whenua — the people of the land

Tangaroa — Māori god of the sea

taniwha — legendary serpent monster

taonga — treasure, not necessarily monetary

tapu — sacred (often means it should not be touched by women)

Te Reo — Māori language

tuatara — small endemic reptile of the Sphenodontia family

Tūrehu — also Patu-paiarehe, inhabitants of New Zealand prior to the Māori, sometimes considered fairy people

waka — canoe

wairua — spirit, soul

whakapapa — also Moriori, hokopapa. Genealogy more expansive than a family tree. It includes a person's links to all living things, tracing back to the origin of the universe

wheke — collective noun for octopus and squid

wapiti — elk

Acronyms

BCD   Buoyancy Control Device
DoC   Department of Conservation
                       (also Department of Corrections)
DCS   Decompression Sickness, colloquially
                       called 'the bends'
DPV   Driver Propulsion Vehicles
CITES   Convention on International Trade in
                       Endangered Species of Wild Fauna
                       and Flora
FNG   (colloq) Fucking New Guy
NVG   Night Vision Goggles, sometimes
                       called devices or NVDs
NZDF   New Zealand Defence Force
TSB   Territorial Sea Baseline

AUTHOR NOTES

The legend of Kahukura and the original of Māori nets is a popular tale told to children in New Zealand. My husband and children are descendants of Kahukura's tribe, the northern Rawara iwi. Another famous chieftain of this tribe, Atama Paparangi, was depicted by the artist Charles Goldie in 1905.

Sadly, rare species trafficking and exploitation is fact, and Operation Worthy II was a real operation, although there was no evidence a submarine was involved. An Interpol news item can be found on the Interpol website, dated December 2015.

New Zealand's much-loved kea, *Nestor notabilis*, is endangered and protected. Known to be intelligent and inquisitive, the world's only alpine parrot has a special penchant for shiny things, and their curved bills are strong enough to shred the rubber parts of cars.

Depending on the isolation techniques used, the tensile strength of flax fibres has been found to range between 1500 MPa and 1800 MPa (megaPascals), with a compressive strength of around 1200 MPa. By comparison, the tensile strength of A36 standard structural steel is 400-550MPa.

Māori culture has a rich oral tradition of histories passed on from generation to generation through story and song, only some of which have been put to paper. However, for those wishing to learn more about Māori beliefs concerning mythical and supernatural peoples, an excellent study was conducted by European explorer and historian, Elsdon Best, entitled Māori Religion and Mythology, Part 2. Mythical Denizens of the Forests and Mountains. In The Published Works of Elsdon Best. PD Hasselberg, Wellington. Further information can be found on the government site Encyclopaedia of New Zealand: www.teara.govt.nz

The history of the Moriori chieftain Nunuku and his famous declaration of peace are well documented in New Zealand historical accounts.

More information about the traditional hongi greeting and its importance to the people of New Zealand can be found on Youtube https://www.youtube.com/watch?v=39XbAjB2k-o, including a lovely description by Māori elder, Dr Rangimarie Turuki Rose Peri: https://www.youtube.com/watch?v=uwN3TcsLXsU

It's in the Bag was a game show, hosted by Selwyn Toogood, and later by John Hawkesby, which appeared on New

Zealand radio and TV from 1954 until 1990, and reprised again briefly in 1992.

The New Zealand 'Deer Wars' of the 1970s were caused by a hike in venison prices and the increasing use of helicopters for hunting, and have been the subject of numerous television documentaries, articles and books.

ACKNOWLEDGMENTS

A Nigerian proverb claims it takes a village to raise a child. The same applies to writing a book, and this one would not exist without the generous and talented help of writers Kevin Berry, Linda Dawley, Simon Fogarty, Eileen Mueller, and Alicia Ponder. I'm grateful to them for their encouragement and expertise. Thank you to my military consultants Rock Chesterman and Justin Coates for their expert advice, to my colleague Paul Mannering for giving the manuscript a final cut and polish, and to writing superstars Jonathan Maberry and Greig Beck for being on my cheer team. My special thanks to Karron Coombs, who read and provided comment on the manuscript's stand-alone readability, and to Rena Mason for the title. All my love to my family, David, Céline and Robbie, for their tolerance and understanding in the face of yet another get-your-own dinner. And finally, I'd like to dedicate this book to my dad, Morgan Thomas, a blind man who'd be pleased to see it.

ABOUT THE AUTHOR

Lee Murray is a multi-award-winning author-editor, essayist, poet, and screenwriter from Aotearoa-New Zealand, and New Zealand's Prime Minister's Award winner for Literary Achievement in Fiction. A *USA Today* Best-selling author, Shirley Jackson- and five-time Bram Stoker Awards® winner, she is an NZSA Honorary Literary Fellow, a Grimshaw Sargeson Fellow, and winner of the NZSA Laura Solomon Cuba Press Prize. Read more at www.leemurray.info

ALSO BY LEE MURRAY

Taine McKenna Novels

Into the Mist

Into the Ashes

Taine McKenna Short Stories

Into the Weeping Waters

Into the Darkness

Into the Geyserland

Into the Clouded Sky

Into the Boneyard

Taine McKenna Collected Short Stories

Into the Distant Clouds

Path of Ra series (with Dan Rabarts)

Hounds of the Underworld

Teeth of the Wolf

Blood of the Sun

Other Collections

Grotesque: Monster Stories

Penny Divers and Other Stories

Poetry

Fox Spirit on a Distant Cloud